Praise for *The Young Survivors*

'*The Young Survivors* is a haunting account of the atomisation of a Jewish family during the Holocaust. Told from the perspective of the three children who survived, in a manner so intimate it gives the impression of reading their personal diaries, we witness the slow loss of innocence as they each come to an age when they are able to understand what has happened to their lost relatives. It is a devastating story of twins separated, of grandparents, parents and cousins, entire families, disappeared – a story that had to be told.'

Elizabeth Fremantle

'A story that will make you weep, wonder and remember.'

Tatiana de Rosnay, author of *Sarah's Key*

'*The Young Survivors* is a poignant and gripping debut. Set against the darkest days of WWII, the novel reminds us that the bonds of family and the power of love can never be extinguished.'

Alyson Richman, bestselling author of *The Lost Wife*

'A heartbreaking yet uplifting story of loss and love told through the eyes of children... gripping and deeply moving.'

James MacManus, author of *Midnight in Berlin*

'I loved reading *The Young Survivors*. I was desperate to know what happened to all of the characters.'

Nick Stafford, playwright and writer

'Passionate, thoughtful and deeply important. *The Young Survivors* is essential reading.'

Robert Rinder

'A hugely impressive debut. A gripping and traumatic account of childhoods lost in war-time France amid the barbaric destruction of European Jewry.'

Michael Newman,
CEO of The Association of Jewish Refugees

'Debra Barnes has written a novel that is arrestingly sincere, full of touching moments and informed by careful research. The beating heart of *The Young Survivors* is the author's emotional connection to her characters, which is unmistakably based on longstanding and deep engagement with her own family's past. Throughout the book, readers are offered rich and detailed insights into the grave peril and struggle for survival that Jews faced in Vichy and Nazi-occupied France, which is still not a widely-understood aspect of the Holocaust. We therefore have many reasons to be proud to add Debra's skilful re-imagining of her family's inspiring and moving story of survival to our Library's collections.'

Dr Toby Simpson,
Director of The Wiener Holocaust Library

DEBRA BARNES

The Young Survivors

Waterford City and County
Libraries

WATERFORD CITY AND COUNTY
WITHDRAWN
LIBRARIES

DUCKWORTH

This edition published in 2020 by Duckworth,
an imprint of Duckworth Books Ltd
1 Golden Court, Richmond TW9 1EU, United Kingdom
www.duckworthbooks.com

Copyright © Debra Barnes 2020

The right of Debra Barnes to be identified as the author
of this Work has been asserted by her in accordance
with the Copyright, Designs & Patents Act 1988.

All rights reserved. No part of this publication
may be reproduced, stored in a retrieval system, or
transmitted, in any form or by any means, without
the prior permission in writing of the publisher.

This book is a work of fiction. Names, characters,
businesses, organisations, places and events other than
those clearly in the public domain, are either the product
of the author's imagination or are used fictitiously.
Any resemblance to actual persons, living or dead,
events or locales is entirely coincidental.

ISBN: 9780715653555

Printed in Great Britain by Clays Ltd

For my mother – Paulette Barnes: 1938 – 2010

'Come on, Georgette. Come outside and play with me.'

'Is that you, Henriette?'

'Yes, of course it is, silly. Are you coming to play now?'

'I've been waiting for so long.'

Juan-les-Pins
June 2006

I checked my watch for the umpteenth time. Jacqueline was due any minute. The ceiling fan had an irritating click which wasn't helping to quell the churning fear in my stomach.

The sound of children's laughter came from outside. Through the window, I caught a brief glimpse of them playing in the garden, which made me flinch and look away. Instead I looked in the mirror – the woman I saw there was very different from the six-year-old girl with the shaved head who Jacqueline had last seen and assumed dead.

I sat and thought about my life, and the lives that had been lost. I thought of the awful choices Jacqueline and my brother Pierre had been forced to make at such a young age. How can someone choose between saving his mother and his infant sisters, or between saving themselves and saving the children they are looking after?

I jumped as the telephone on the bedside table sprang to life. Alan answered it, exhausting most of his French in one short conversation.

'*Oui? D'accord. Merci.*'

He put the phone down and, turning to me, said, 'She's downstairs, my love.'

My heart was racing as we left the room. I took a sip of water on the way out; my mouth was completely dry. The journey down one flight of stairs to the hotel lobby seemed unbearably long, as though I was travelling back through the years, back towards the horrors of the past. I felt faint and clung to Alan for support.

For so many years I had survived by blotting out the terrifying memories. My family had learnt not to talk of those years in front of me and were scared what it might do to me if I had to confront the nightmares. And how many times had I nearly cancelled this trip?

In the end my desire to see my beloved Jacqueline had triumphed, but I had been in a state of constant anxiety since I made that decision. What would she look like? Would we even be able to talk? I had buried my knowledge of French along with the memories and Jacqueline's English was, in her own words, 'very small'.

I had so many questions to ask, so many memory blanks – but I didn't know if I could even talk about the ugly past.

As I walked through the hotel lobby, the slight figure of Jacqueline Goldstein approached me and we embraced for the first time since 1944. I was weirdly surprised by the tiny, fragile old lady she had become. The last time we had seen each other, the seventeen-year-old Jacqueline had towered over me. She had been like a mother to me and my sister all those years ago. I was overwhelmed as she stood with her arms open waiting for me. We held one another close, and I wept as I remembered the innocence of our last moments together.

Samuel

Metz
April 1938

'Come on, slowcoach!' Claude shouted back to me as we ran onto the bridge over the Moselle river. I was breathing heavily and sweating under my jacket. My brother had been excitedly counting the days until his sixth birthday – only three more to go, as he had reminded me more than once that day. But even though I was three years older than him, I struggled to keep up. I'd just recovered from yet another chest infection – the coal dust which blew into town from the nearby mines made the air foul.

The women in our family all doted on Claude. 'Oh, what a handsome boy,' they would say as they pinched his cheeks and ruffled his thick dark hair. Our grandmother Bubbe even said so, and she was *blind*. She might not have been so adoring had she known about the boyish pranks Claude and I played on her.

'Let's put pepper in Bubbe's tea!' said Claude, one rainy afternoon when we were stuck indoors.

'Let's move Bubbe's slippers so she can't find them!' was my suggestion on another day.

'Let's pull ugly faces in front of Bubbe's face. At least that's something you can beat me at!'

This was our favourite trick. When we pulled the ugliest face was the moment her eyesight was miraculously restored, at least it seemed that way because she always seemed to know when we were doing it. When Maman found out we would get told off, although she almost always ended the scolding by winking at us.

Claude looked up to me and followed me wherever I went, which was fine because he was fun to be around and he was my best pal. Also, I remembered how upset I was when my older brother Pierre suddenly told me he didn't have time to play 'childish games' with me anymore, and I didn't want to cause the same hurt. Poor Claude, he didn't seem to realise this was his last day of being the youngest and cutest member of the family.

We were wearing our weekend clothes: white shirt, white shorts held up with a black leather belt, white knee-length socks and white shoes. It was asking for trouble living in such a filthy town. The huge cathedral and buildings in the centre of Metz were black from soot, so we would get our white clothes dirty if we accidentally rubbed along a grubby wall. But our family was in the clothing business, and Papa always said wouldn't it be a fine thing if the clothing merchant's own kids looked scruffy.

Even though we were always well dressed, the bully boys called us dirty Jews. Anyone could see they were a lot scruffier than us. Too often they waited for me, in groups of three or four, to come out of school alone. I would run home through narrow, cobblestoned streets, the sound of their feet close behind. They usually gave up after a few blocks, throwing

10

stones at me before turning back for their next victim and leaving me to catch my breath.

It was Shabbat and we'd been sent to have lunch with our uncle and aunt. Maman had gone into the hospital even before the pains started. Papa was with her. I hadn't been allowed to give her a kiss because of my illness – the last thing she needed was to catch an infection. No one could get their arms around her huge belly in any case. She rarely complained, but she did say how uncomfortable it was to carry around two babies. She said it sometimes felt like they were fighting, but she knew they would be best friends once they were born.

We were all nervous, despite the doctors telling us everything seemed fine. Maman was thirty-seven, which was ancient when it came to having one baby, never mind twins! Pierre and I remembered how happy our parents had been when our brother Phillipe was born. I would sit in the kitchen and watch him in his crib, I was so happy to have a baby brother. Only a few short days later he and the crib disappeared. Our parents' joy turned to sadness and our home filled with relatives and neighbours – some we knew well, others we'd never met – but everyone brought us food. They comforted Maman and told Pierre and I in whispered voices that we needed to be quiet around the house. Papa told us Phillipe was in Heaven now. I was terrified the same thing might happen again this time.

Lunch at Uncle Isaac's home that day was a real feast. Aunt Dora needed to use up the chametz from her kitchen; Pesach was only a couple of days away and any food which was not 'kosher for Pesach' had to go. No one could afford to throw food away, so it all had to be eaten. I was delighted

11

to help out. I knew that soon I wouldn't get to eat bread for eight days – dry matzah was always a poor substitute, and it gave me a stomach ache.

Before we ate we made the Shabbat blessings. Aunt Dora used her best tablecloth, as she was going to give it a really good wash before Pesach, and the silver candlesticks were still out after being used the evening before, so it felt almost like a celebration. Uncle Isaac was Maman's brother, but he was twenty years older than her, so his five children were much older than me and my brothers. They were all there that day, crammed around the dining table in their modest apartment, even my cousins Simone and Louise who were both married with children of their own.

'Well, boys, how is school?' asked our uncle.

'Terrible!' said Pierre.

'The teachers hit me with a ruler because I want to write with my left hand. And the German kids try to beat us up,' I said.

'Sometimes I wonder why they bothered building the Maginot Line,' said Uncle Isaac. 'It's supposed to keep the Germans out, but Metz is half full of them anyway. We came here from the shtetls of Poland to escape persecution, but now we're in danger of being persecuted here too. It's been nearly twenty years since the Treaty of Versailles: can't they go home now?'

'Best not to grumble about it,' said Aunt Dora. 'That Line paid for the food on our table.'

Uncle was a contract painter and had spent the last few years painting and repainting some of the five hundred buildings along the German border which made up the Maginot Line. I'd learnt at school that it had been the idea of military hero Marshall Pétain, to replace the crude trenches of the great war. Everyone knew someone whose father, uncle or grandfather had died in the last war and no defence was considered too much. The Line had been under construction since 1930, which suited Uncle fine, as it kept him in a steady job while so many others were out of work. With not enough work, money or food around these days, people were nervous. Some of them blamed the Jews, which was why we got bullied at school.

After lunch, Pierre went to the hospital. I was disappointed he wouldn't let me go with him; he said he would be quicker without me but promised to come back as soon as there was news. It wasn't long before he returned to tell us that two baby girls had safely arrived.

'Mazel tov! How wonderful!' said Aunt Dora. 'How is Maman?'

'She is exhausted!'

'Two daughters. Baruch Hashem,' said Bubbe. 'Please God they are healthy, and may He bless them, so they can grow up to be good Jewish wives.' She began to quietly chant prayers of thanks.

'Mame!' said Uncle Isaac. 'Give the poor girls a chance. They've only just been born and already you're marrying them off!'

'Can we go and see Maman now?' pleaded Claude.

'Yes, Papa says you and Samuel should come back with me,' said Pierre. We grabbed our jackets and hurried off over the bridge towards the hospital.

I'd been to the hospital before when I had a particularly bad chest infection, so it usually filled me with dread, but this time I was excited.

I was so relieved to see Maman lying in her hospital bed with my new sisters in her arms. Papa sat next to her, looking adoringly at the two new members of our family. When Claude spotted Maman he rushed straight over.

'Careful, my darling,' she said, as he was on the verge of jumping into her bed in his hurry to give her a hug. 'Mind the babies!'

'You see, boys,' said Papa, grinning, 'God was listening to my prayers this time. "Enough boys", I said to him. "Please, God, bring me a daughter." And what happens? He brings me two beautiful girls!'

The moment I saw the girls I fell instantly in love with them. They were tiny and very alike, but there was something in their faces which made them ever so slightly different. I couldn't say what it was, certainly not their almond-shaped eyes which were just like Maman's and mine as well. Maman gazed adoringly down at the little bundles in her arms.

'Hello, girls. Aren't you lucky little ones? You'll never be alone because you will always have each other. I'm lucky too; I have my beautiful boys and now I can watch my darling daughters, Henriette and Georgette, grow up into lovely young women.' She bent down to give each one a mother's kiss on their forehead. It was the first time I heard their names. *I'll always be there for you, Henriette and Georgette*, I thought to myself.

Pierre

We left Maman resting in the hospital with the twins and walked home with Papa. My steps were wide and straight, like my father's, while Samuel and Claude ran about from side to side, jumping over cobblestones and hiding from each other in doorways. When I was much younger I used to enjoy playing with Samuel, but now I had no interest in joining in with my brother's silly games; I was practically thirteen and ready to take on my responsibility as the eldest brother of baby girls. Word had already spread around the neighbourhood and people were congratulating Papa in the street. As we walked past our synagogue, members of the congregation came out to greet us.

'Mazel tov!'

'Such a blessing! Such nachas!'

I never understood how everyone knew everyone else's business almost before it had happened. When we reached our apartment building, Maman's good friend Madame Hausner came running over with a dozen cloth diapers.

'You'll need plenty of these with twins!' she said.

Papa brimmed with pride as he thanked everyone for their presents and good wishes.

Once back in our apartment, Papa made the final preparations for the new arrivals. There was only one bedroom which my parents would now share with my sisters; the crib we had all used was placed there ready for when they came home. My brothers and I slept in the living room. When Zayde died and Bubbe came to live with us, her bed was put in an alcove in the living room, with a curtain pulled across. Much of our family life revolved around eating, which we did in the dining room.

****

From the moment Henriette and Georgette were born, I understood that, as the eldest, it was my job to protect them. Papa wasn't going to be around much. He worked as a merchant and he'd be off on the road again within days, his car filled with clothes he bought in Paris and sold all over France. We were one of few families in our neighbourhood to own a car, which Papa had worked hard to pay for.

Even in my earliest memories, Papa travelled all over the country, sometimes staying away for weeks at a time. When he was in the north-east he would come home at night, but I was usually asleep by the time he returned, and he would leave again early the next morning. When I was a bit older, I would pinch myself in bed to try to stay awake so I could spend a few moments alone with him, but I rarely managed it.

Some mornings, when I woke, I got the feeling Papa had come to watch me sleep after coming home late at night. I imagined him sitting on my bed whispering to me, but soon realised it had been Maman. I knew the man's job was to bring money in, and the woman's job was to look after the children and the home. Soon would be my bar mitzvah when I became a man and took on the responsibility of looking after the family while Papa was away.

Papa worked hard, but Maman was also always busy. Cooking, cleaning, looking after the little ones, shopping, scrubbing and caring for her own mother. Just doing the laundry was a huge task. Maman would boil the dirty clothes and bedding at home, then carry it in pails down to le lavoir on the banks of the Moselle river. When I was younger, before Samuel was born, I would go with her. While she struggled down the stairs with the heavy, wet clothes Maman would say how lucky she was that our apartment was so near le lavoir. There would always be neighbours and friends there and the housewives would rinse their laundry together in the river, then help each other wring it out before carrying it all home to hang up to dry in the attic, where each apartment in the building had a washing line.

Maman took care of washing us too. Every Friday morning, she would take us to the public baths, a fifteen-minute walk from our home. She would scrub us clean and only when we were done would she take a bath herself.

She was also an excellent cook and made delicious Polish-style dishes like chicken noodle soup, gefilte fish, challah and crumb cakes. Maman never rested, never complained and always had a warm smile and hug for us and a cheerful song on her lips. She was wonderful. One day I will meet a girl as lovely as my mother.

****

Occasionally, when Papa was home in the evening, Maman would put down the scrubbing brush and put on her best clothes. She would sit at her dressing table with the three-fold vanity mirror, brush her hair, put on some of her favourite lipstick and her pearl drop earrings, and they would go dancing. On those rare times when Papa took a day off, we went to the movies or out for a cake or ice cream. I particularly remember one of those days. I was six and Samuel just two. We went to a pâtisserie. Maman told us about her eldest sister Cloe, who had moved to England from Poland in 1905 as a young bride. Cloe wrote regularly and Maman would read the letters to Bubbe. Aunt Cloe must have spoken good English after twenty-six years in England, but she wrote to her family in Yiddish. My parents were both really smart; they knew French, Yiddish, Polish, German and Russian, but they didn't speak any English.

'Did you know that you have three cousins in England?'

'No, Maman. Can I go and play with them?'

'Well, it's quite far away and actually your cousins are the same age as me.'

'How come?'

'Cloe is twenty-two years older than me, so she is like a mother to me and her children are like my cousins, but really they are my nieces and nephews!' Maman and Papa laughed at how complicated her explanation sounded. Samuel had already given up trying to understand what was being said and was asking for another piece of cake, but I was fascinated.

'So, can I play with the children of my cousins instead?'

'Well no, because your cousins don't have any children. That is what your Aunt Cloe wrote in her letter. Her children – your cousins…'

'Oh, don't start that again for goodness sake, or we'll be here all day!' said Papa with a smile.

'Ha, yes you could be right! Cloe has written she would very much like to be a grandmother, but so far none of her children have had any babies of their own. She has one son and two daughters, all happily married for a few years now but still no grandchildren!'

I lost interest in what Maman was saying by this point, but Papa was looking at her curiously.

'All this talk of babies, are you trying to tell me something?'

'What do you mean? Oh! No, no! Don't worry, darling, nothing like that… yet!' And they both laughed again. I had no idea what they were talking about, but I enjoyed seeing them so happy together.

'I was thinking of Cloe because in another letter she wrote that in London they have afternoon tea at a place called the Lyons Corner House as a special treat, just like us coming to the pâtisserie. She said they have dainty sandwiches and slices of cake, served with a cup of tea by a waitress wearing a white apron and lace hat. It sounds so lovely that I remember every word. It would be wonderful if we could go to visit her one day in London and have afternoon tea with them.'

'Well, maybe we will one day,' said Papa. 'It's not that far away. We travelled further from Poland to here after all.'

'That's true. Even if we never get to London then our children will go one day, please God.'

'Let's not forget that would be more likely if we had more children.'

'What is your hurry?' asked Maman with a giggle.

'Well, my love, you're not getting any younger!' He loved to tease her about the fact that she was a year older than him.

'Hey! Show some respect for your elders please!' she said, and they laughed.

I couldn't remember a happier time in my life as we sat in the pâtisserie laughing and joking around. My only regret was that Papa was home so little, and life couldn't always be this way.

****

As I grew up, I thought more about my uncles, aunts and cousins in England and America. My Aunt Alisa had moved to America a few years ago. She was a couple of years older than Maman and had married in Metz to a Polish man called Abraham. He had family who had gone to New York and wrote to him of their lives in the Bronx and the opportunities available for Jews there. They were living in a tiny apartment in a tenement building, but other Jews were putting on hit musical shows and building business empires. Alisa and Abraham didn't take much convincing and left France as quickly as they could, in a hurry to start their new lives. Once they were settled, they wrote to my parents and told them to come to America too, but Papa was building up a good business and didn't want to leave his hard work behind and have to start over.

I wished we could go to America. I was the only member of the family to have French citizenship, which had been arranged by my school, but I would have happily given it up. I went to a Jewish school, where boys and girls were taught in separate classrooms, although this didn't bother me as I had little interest in girls. Papa said that wouldn't last long, but I didn't understand what he meant. There were also classes of non-Jewish children. You might think these goyim, being the minority in a Jewish school, would try to get along with the other kids or at least just ignore us. But no, they were mostly bullies, Jew-haters who would call us names, throw stones at us in the playground and start fights. I wasn't afraid of them, but I looked out for my brothers; I taught them not to get caught on their own and to hurry home from school if they wanted to avoid a beating.

I had little interest in studying; my only passion was football. On Sunday mornings I played for a team in the Jewish league and the rest of the time in the street with the other Jewish kids. I taught my brothers too, although Samuel wasn't allowed when he was wheezing. We always needed to keep an eye out for the anti-Semitic kids in the neighbourhood whose favourite sport was ruining our football games. Now I had two sisters to look out for too. I hoped that when they grew up they would be free to play in the streets without having to look out for the Jew-haters.

Pierre

Metz

January 1939

It was a Monday. My brothers had gone to school as usual, but I'd stayed home and Papa hadn't gone to work. Neither of us wanted to miss the speech Hitler was due to make at the Reichstag. This was the first time I would be allowed to listen with my parents. Papa turned on the radio some time before the speech was due to start, to warm up the tubes.

I thought about the day electricity was first connected to our apartment, which I could never forget because it made Maman smile so much she said her cheeks hurt. Sometimes Maman sewed in the evening after her busy day, but mostly she sat in her favourite armchair reading – she had a whole bookcase full of books about things I didn't understand. We would sit on the rug by her feet and read comics bought with our allowance. *Bibi Fricotin*, *Mickey Mouse* and *Superman* were our favourites. The electric light made all this easier, especially in winter when the days were short. When Papa returned home late from work, he could just turn the light switch on rather than fumbling around to find a match for the gas lamps.

Shortly after we got electricity, Papa struggled home with a large wooden box with 'Deutsche Philips-Ges' written on the side.

'Quick, Rosa, get a mat for the sideboard so I can put this down. It's heavy.' He knew the polished wooden sideboard was one of Maman's most treasured possessions. It had been a wedding present and housed the best china, glassware and silver candlesticks. Whatever was in that heavy box, it wasn't worth scratching the furniture.

'What is it?'

'I have bought us a radio,' he said proudly. 'Now you boys can listen to the Olympic Games this summer!'

'Really, Papa?' Samuel squealed with delight.

We stood around eagerly as Papa set up the radio. He plugged it in to the electricity supply and it crackled into life. As he started to move the dial, we heard a faint voice through the static.

'What are they saying?'

Papa continued to turn the dial slowly. The voice from the radio was getting clearer.

'…behind every murder…'

Maman fidgeted nervously with her dust cloth. Papa moved the dial slightly to the right.

'…incited to crime…'

Then, suddenly, as clear as anything came a voice screaming into our home:

'…the hate-filled power of our Jewish foe!'

'That is enough, Albert!' said Maman, pulling the cable from the electricity supply.

'Who was that, Maman?' asked Samuel.

I had a good idea of who it was: Hitler. Our teacher had told us of his victory in the German elections. All the kids in school spoke about him; a madman who hated Jews. Sometimes I felt frightened that we lived so close to Germany, although I would never admit it to my brothers.

'No one for you to concern yourselves with, my darlings,' said Maman, pulling Samuel and Claude close.

'Yes, yes. We don't want to listen to that,' said Papa. 'I'll get a list of radio stations and programmes tomorrow so we can choose what we want to listen to, and avoid the other dreck.'

Papa did as he promised and that summer of 1936 we listened to Jesse Owens win four gold medals at the Berlin Olympic Games.

'Hitler must be furious!' said Papa with delight.

****

The radio soon became worth its weight in gold. I enjoyed the music channel Maman liked to put on, singing along to the popular songs and sometimes dancing around the living room. She looked like a film star! Maman listened to the plays broadcast during the day and discussed them with other housewives when out shopping. Sometimes I went with her and overheard the gossip. It was as if they were talking about people from the neighbourhood and not characters from a radio soap opera.

'Did you hear what happened to Marie?' one would ask.

'Her husband really is a terrible rat!' another would hiss, and everyone would shake their heads in agreement. The housewives arranged their days around their favourite radio plays. The markets would be empty when the most popular programmes were broadcast, and suddenly fill up straight afterwards so the ladies could discuss that day's episode.

There were programmes for children at weekends and during the school holidays. Maman and Papa would listen to news broadcasts. 'For goodness sake, what idiots we have running the country!' Papa would shout furiously at the radio set. Half of Metz spoke German and I had a pretty good understanding of the language – it helped that it had similarities with Yiddish, which we sometimes spoke at home. We picked up German stations on our radio, and it was difficult to avoid tuning in to Hitler's speeches.

****

The speech that I stayed home from school to listen to in January 1939 will be etched in my memory for the rest of my life. I had celebrated my bar mitzvah the previous summer. Rabbi Epstein had tutored me to read from the Torah in synagogue. My parents had rented an empty apartment in our building, hired tables and chairs and a caterer, and organised a celebratory party. Our family and friends came, but best of all was the Kodak camera I was gifted, which made me the envy of my brothers.

'You are now a man,' said Papa. 'Old enough to listen to the ranting of the Nazi mashugana.'

I wasn't sure if I trembled from excitement or fear. I agreed with my father that it was important to try to understand our enemy and I was reassured that we were in France and not Germany – although we were close enough! The radio had warmed up and Maman had put the twins down for a

25

nap and joined Papa and I in the dining room. I was proud to be the only one of my brothers old enough to share this moment with our parents. Hitler was celebrating his sixth anniversary of coming to power by making a speech at the Nazi Reichstag and Papa knew it would be an important one.

Europe will not have peace until the Jewish question has been disposed of. The world has sufficient capacity for settlement, but we must finally break away from the notion that a certain percentage of the Jewish people are intended, by our dear God, to be the parasitic beneficiary of the body, and of the productive work, of other peoples. Jewry must adapt itself to respectable constructive work, as other peoples do, or it will sooner or later succumb to a crisis of unimaginable proportions. If the international finance-Jewry inside and outside Europe should succeed in plunging the nations into a world war yet again, then the outcome will not be the victory of Jewry, but rather the annihilation of the Jewish race in Europe!

Papa held Maman's hand, as though it would protect her from the horror coming from the radio. I was confused. I could understand the words in German, but they made no sense to me at all. Was Hitler really saying the Jewish people were not productive? He clearly had no idea how hard my parents worked. That evil man with his stupid moustache, what reason could he have to hate the Jews so much? His speech went on and on, his voice sounding more terrifying as it progressed.

'Shall we turn it off now?' asked Papa, after we had endured an hour of listening to Hitler.

'No, leave it on,' said Maman. 'It's important.'

'Yes, you're right. We need to know what is coming so we can be ready to defend ourselves.'

'How will we do that, Papa?' I asked.

'I have no idea,' he replied.

****

It was clear that war was coming. The message from the French authorities in leaflets and on posters all over town left us in no doubt:

> *Every means of defence will be put into action to stop enemy aircraft. However, some may get through. If nothing holds you back, as soon as the threat arrives, LEAVE! LEAVE with your family. DO NOT WAIT. LEAVE!*

The threat from aircrafts wasn't the only thing to worry about; Metz was only fifty kilometres from the German border. War was inevitable, although most believed France would defeat Germany, just like they had in the Great War. I hoped they were right.

Samuel

Condé-Northern
Summer 1939

It was the last day of term before the summer holidays. I wasn't feeling well. I started to walk home after class; my friends had gone to play football, but I just felt like going to sleep.

'You! Jew-boy! Where you going? Home to Mummy?'

A group of boys from my year came up behind me, looking for a way to celebrate the end of term. I ignored them and carried on walking.

'We're talking to you, Jew-boy. Are you deaf… or are your ears dirty? I heard Jews are dirty.' One of them grabbed my ear and swung me round to face him.

'Let me look in your filthy ears,' he said, pulling hard.

'Get off me!' I tried to shout but I started wheezing and it came out as a strange noise.

'Aww, listen to him. He can't speak either. He's deaf and dumb!' someone said, and they all joined in, taunting me with cries of 'Dummy'.

When they hit me on my head, I put my arms up to protect myself. I didn't have the strength to run home. How was I going to get out of this one?

'Get off him!' a familiar voice shouted.

I looked up and saw Pierre and some of his classmates running towards us. The bullies were no match for my brother and his friends, and they ran off leaving me to recover my breath.

I could see concern in Pierre's eyes when he reached me. He put a protective arm around my shoulder and said, 'Let's go home.'

****

It turned out I had a bad chest infection. The coal dust in Metz made breathing difficult so my parents sent me to stay on a farm which took in young convalescents, in Condé-Northern, midway between Metz and the border with Germany. As Maman packed my suitcase I saw she was crying.

'What's wrong?' I asked.

'I'm going to miss you very much,' she said.

'I can stay if you like?'

'No, Son, you need to get better. It's best for you to go but, please, just be careful.'

'Careful of what? Of the farm animals?' I joked.

'Of everything. If you want to get me an urgent message you must telephone Monsieur Wolff. I've written his telephone number on a piece of paper and packed it with your things.'

The only person with a telephone on our street was Monsieur Wolff, the kosher butcher who was happy to deliver messages to his frequent customers along with some chicken livers or a piece of brisket.

The thought of leaving my family was upsetting. What would little Claude do without me to follow around? The word around town was that there was going to be war with Germany. Everyone seemed on edge, including Maman. When it came to saying our goodbyes, a lump formed in my throat. Maman held me tight and her voice trembled as she spoke, 'I love you, Samuel. Get well and come home soon,' she whispered in my ear before letting me go.

I had my own bedroom in the farmhouse – it felt strange to not share, and to sleep in a proper bedroom rather than in the living room. Still it was all very basic; there were no paintings on the walls like we had at home, and no shelves crammed full of books and trinkets. Neither was there electricity or running water. The farmer and his wife were simple country folk.

When I first arrived at the beginning of the summer, I was quite unwell. By mid-August I felt stronger and could help with light chores. The clean country air smelt good, although maybe not when mucking out the barns! The farmer and his wife had no children, so I went with the daughter from the next farm, Giselle, to take the sheep and goats to graze. There was a sign in one of the fields: 'Joan of Arc used to tend the sheep and goats in this field as a child.' *Well*, I thought, *if it was good enough for Joan of Arc, then I really shouldn't complain*. I missed my family but I enjoyed those summer days, at least until I heard a rumbling like storm clouds in the distance.

I asked the farmer about the noise. He said it was the German army training their soldiers behind the Maginot Line. As the days passed, the gunfire and shelling became more frequent and closer. I was frightened and wanted to go home. It was time to get a message to my parents. I went to the post office and made the call.

'Hello, Monsieur Wolff. It's Samuel Laskowski.'

'Hello, Samuel. How are you doing, Son? I heard you got away from this filthy town for a while.'

'Yes, and I'm feeling better now, thank you. Could you please get a message to my parents and ask them to come and pick me up?' I hesitated, then added: 'It's very important.' I'd already decided I wasn't going to mention the gunfire because I didn't want my dear mother to panic, but on the other hand I did want them to come as soon as possible.

'I understand. I'll tell them.'

'Could you go today please, Monsieur Wolff?'

'You know, Samuel, I also have a lot of orders to deliver as well as messages. If I can get there today, then I will do so. Goodbye, Son.'

****

Where were they? It was two days since I telephoned Monsieur Wolff and still no sign of my parents. Had he forgotten to give them the message, or was he punishing me for asking him to hurry? There had been a fair amount of gunfire that morning, but it stopped around midday. I was standing in front of the farmhouse wondering if I should go back to the post office and call again, when I heard a car approach. Maman smiled and waved to me from the passenger seat as Papa drove in and parked. She looked tired, but then she did have my baby sisters to look after. I was eager to see them again, but I guessed they had been left at home, probably with Aunt Dora or cousin Simone. Maman rushed over to kiss and hug me.

'Samuel, my darling boy. How are you? We missed you so much!'

Papa came over. 'Hello, Son. You're looking well,' he said with a smile, slapping me gently on the back.

Suddenly there was a round of gunfire in the distance. Maman jumped in fright. 'Was that…?' she asked, as another round sounded. The front door to the farmhouse opened.

'Hello, Monsieur and Madame Laskowski. Please, come in,' invited the farmer's wife. Maman practically pushed me inside as the clamour continued.

'Why didn't you tell us about this?' Maman demanded.

'We assumed you knew, Madame,' replied the farmer's wife, matter-of-factly. 'This has been going on for some time although I admit it is more frequent now. What can we do? We can't leave our farm.'

'Perhaps not, Madame,' said my mother, 'but that doesn't mean our son has to stay. Samuel, pack your bag! You're coming home immediately.'

Papa hadn't said a word, but Maman didn't wait for his approval. 'Albert, please pay these people for their hospitality and let's go.'

I didn't have to be told twice. I got in the car. Maman sat on the back seat with me and held me close the whole drive back.

****

Just two weeks after I returned from Condé-Northern, Britain and France declared war on Germany.

Pierre

Many Jews lived in our neighbourhood, but still I looked over my shoulder when I walked about. If I was with my siblings, I would clutch a stone, ready to defend them from attack. Walking home one day, I heard music as I approached the courtyard of our apartment building. My fists clenched when I saw a minstrel strumming his guitar and singing, 'I will beat you to death, you Jew, you Jew.' Usually this space would be full of families enjoying the warm afternoon but the minstrel was alone. No doubt he had scared everyone back to their apartments; I could make out my neighbours watching from behind twitching curtains. Nearly half the families who lived around that courtyard were Jewish, yet no one did anything. I'm sure Papa would have reacted, but he was rarely home. I was furious, but stopped myself from attacking him there and then – he was larger than the school-kids I usually confronted. I decided I would get some of the other guys involved and plan my revenge for another time. When the minstrel came around again, Maman had heard about my plan to run him out of our neighbourhood.

'Pierre, promise me you won't do anything. I don't want to draw attention to our family, and I'm concerned about repercussions.'

'But, Maman, have you heard what he sings?'

'No, Son, I choose not to. I'm too busy looking after the twins and Bubbe to listen to such rubbish, thank God.'

Bubbe was showing the first signs of senility and hadn't left the apartment in many months. She only went outside now to use the WC out the back, and even that was only occasionally. She was a large lady which made it more difficult for her to move, so Maman had gotten used to giving her a chamber pot to do her business. More work for poor Maman. While Papa was away it was my responsibility to protect my family, but I didn't want to burden my mother with more worries, so I agreed not to act against the repulsive minstrel.

The little Jew-haters at school started to sing those songs too. When summer arrived and I was old enough to leave school, I worried for my brothers without me there to look out for them. I was to enrol in trade school where I could try my hand at carpentry or bookmaking. And then, just as term was due to start at the beginning of September, war broke out and classes were postponed until further notice. Papa volunteered to join the French army, but was refused on the grounds that he had to provide for five children. I wished I was old enough to go in his place to fight the Nazis that threatened my family.

****

The line leading to the depot went all the way down the street and around the corner: hundreds of people waiting

34

for their turn to collect gas masks for their families. There had been no bombing yet, but the mood was uneasy. I was thrilled when Papa asked for my help carrying the masks for our family. *Let it take the whole day*, I thought, as it meant I would have Papa to myself for once.

'They said the trade school would reopen once the war is over. When do you think that will be, Papa?'

'From what I've read in the newspapers, we are expecting to win pretty quickly, so hopefully your classes won't be delayed too long.'

'I hope so,' I said eagerly.

'So do I, Son. So do I,' said Papa, with a look of strained optimism.

When we reached the head of the queue, Papa handed over the family book where our birth dates were recorded, as well as the Polish birth certificates of himself, Maman and Bubbe.

'Let's see. You need masks for three adults, four children and two infants,' said the clerk after checking the paperwork.

Papa flinched. 'No, just three children.'

'Pardon? Ah yes, I see. Sorry,' he muttered, checking the book again and noticing the handwritten cross marked against Phillipe's name. He gave us a ticket for each mask needed and told us to join the next queue.

The gas mask for an infant was a hood which went entirely over their head. Henriette and Georgette screamed and kicked and made a terrible fuss when we tried to put theirs on, but they calmed down when they could once again see each other through the glass visors. They seemed to take comfort in knowing they were together and even started smiling and giggling. I suggested we put the hoods on the girls a couple of times each week so they got used to them in case we needed to put them on in a hurry – they would need to move a damn sight quicker than they had on that first attempt.

Everyone tried on their masks. We walked around the room like monsters. I pretended I was doing it to amuse my brothers but, really, I couldn't wait to have a go! The contraptions were pretty uncomfortable and the rubber smell was awful, so we didn't keep them on for long.

Meanwhile, Maman reasoned with Bubbe. 'Mame, you need to learn how to put on yours.'

'NO!'

'And if there is an air raid and no one is here to help you?'

'Then I will die. I am a blind old woman. No one will miss me!'

'Mame! How can you say that?'

Bubbe had made up her mind. She didn't want anything to do with the gas mask. Maman walked away in defeat, but I decided to have a go.

'Bubbe, it's Pierre.'

'I know who you are. Did you get me my sweets?'

Bubbe had a sweet tooth. She would send us out to buy her sweets, which she ate all day long. We daren't refuse her even though her teeth were rotten from eating so much sugar. When she needed more supplies, she would rummage around in the many pockets of her skirt to find some centimes. Bubbe carried all her money and treasured possessions in her skirts, along with her bonbon stash.

'Yes, I already gave it to you, Bubbe. You know Papa and I queued for hours to get the gas masks.'

'Well you needn't have bothered to get one for me.'

'But you are the head of the family, absolutely you need one.'

'Bah!' Clearly flattery was not going to work.

'I'm going to leave the gas mask here on the right-hand side of your chair. It has a handle so it will be easy to take with you to bed.'

'I won't use it,' she said, but as I went to walk away I saw her reach down and touch the gas mask before quickly snatching her hand back to rest in her lap.

Success! I thought.

****

For the first months of war, the only fighting going on in France was in the school playgrounds and on street corners. The reports on the radio and in the newspapers spoke of battles in Poland and I was relieved we no longer had family there. We were told the politicians were busy negotiating and, no doubt, the armies were planning their attacks. Biplanes flew overhead and we heard the German army on manoeuvres across the nearby border, but there was little else to this war so far. Many expected it to end before it had even begun.

When it didn't end, my parents decided to take the advice of the municipal government for all families with young children to evacuate away from the German border. I was delighted Claude and Samuel wouldn't be returning to school where the bullying was getting worse as the war marched forward. Papa rented a house in a town called Behonne, some one hundred kilometres from Metz in the direction of Paris. We were to leave as soon as possible.

We had the great advantage of owning a car, but once we were all in, there wouldn't be much room for anything else. Papa decided he would return to pick up the belongings that we couldn't take with us. All we would carry on our first journey west were clothes and essential household items. Maman went into action. Suitcases and boxes were packed ready. Furniture was polished and then covered with blankets and carpets, to help protect them from whatever was coming. Finally, floors were swept and scrubbed.

'Rosa, what are you doing that for when we are leaving?' asked Papa.

'I don't want to come back to a dirty home,' she replied.

Finally, Maman was satisfied. She rinsed out her dishcloths and left them to dry in the kitchen, then walked through the apartment for one last look.

'Alright, everyone, time to go,' she said. 'Come, Mame.' She went to help Bubbe out of her chair.

'I'm too old, Rosa. Go without me. My husband is buried here, I won't leave him.'

'Don't be silly, Mame. We're not going without you. You are coming with us.'

'NO!'

Uncle Isaac and Aunt Dora came to reason with Bubbe. They were also evacuating to Behonne. There were eight of them including the three children who still lived with them, our cousins, Gabriel, Anna and Simone, along with Simone's husband, Leon, and their two children. Everyone was ready to go, except for my grandmother.

'*Elle est têtu comme une âne!*' everyone agreed. 'She is as stubborn as a mule!'

'And as blind as a bat!' I heard Samuel whisper to Claude, which set them off giggling.

Maman and Uncle Isaac argued with Bubbe for hours while we loaded the car and said goodbye to our friends and neighbours. Most of them were also preparing to leave for other villages.

'What will you eat? How will you look after yourself? What happens if you need help and there is no one here?' But nothing was going to persuade her to leave. Papa and Uncle Isaac tried to lift her up and carry her out against her will but she wailed, screamed and flailed her arms and legs and so they gave up, defeated. Finally, a compromise was reached. Papa would continue to drive around, running his business. He would call in as often as possible to check on Bubbe and Maman would prepare food for him to bring.

****

Leaving Metz was bittersweet. I was happy to leave the Jew-haters and the minstrel behind and my brothers felt the same. Only our baby sisters were oblivious to what they were escaping. On the other hand, I had no idea what would be waiting for us in Behonne, although it felt good to be moving away from Germany.

The journey was a nightmare. Maman cried much of the way, upset about abandoning Bubbe, and Papa worried for his business and whether he could continue providing for us. The roads were jammed with people leaving their homes in the east to travel to safety in the west. There were refugees from Holland and Belgium, and the French army were also trying to get through. It was chaos.

Cars, weighed down with entire families and their belongings, made slow progress on the congested roads. Through the windows people appeared grey and frightened. When we saw someone we knew on our way out of town we merely nodded to each other; this was no time for chit-chat. Some who didn't have their own cars travelled on buses, others used a horse and cart for their journey, and a few walked along the side of the road. Everyone carried as much as they could manage, not knowing what they would find at their destination or when they would return home.

My parents' spirits were tested even more once we arrived at Behonne. The house we had rented was completely empty. Maman's shoulders slumped and she sighed as she realised the task ahead. Then she straightened, rolled up her sleeves and set to sweeping the floors with the broom we had brought with us. Papa and I drove to a lumberyard for pine boards and tools to make bed-frames for us all. We got straw from the stables to put on top of the timber frames and that was what we slept on, except for the twins who slept in the drawers of a dresser we found in the yard.

We had only been in Behonne for a week when Papa returned after spending the day working in the Metz area and brought Bubbe back with him. The solitude and the ever-closer sounds of gunfire and shelling from Germany had proved too much for her and she finally agreed to join us. Maman jumped for joy when she saw her mother get out of the car. We had all secretly missed Bubbe's eccentric ways. It had been quiet without her constant crying and singing.

Without knowing how long we would be staying at this new home, we settled into our routines. Samuel and Claude were enrolled in the local school and said the teachers and children were very nice and kind to them. Papa continued to work, and Maman cooked, cleaned and looked after us all. Henriette and Georgette were good little girls, but they were walking now and we needed to keep an eye on them. Thank goodness they were often happy just sitting, talking gobble-dygook to each other. It was fun watching them together – they appeared to have the most interesting conversations which only they understood. Maman made cakes, but as there was no oven I was sent to find a baker to cook them. When they were ready I asked how much I owed for use of the oven and was told, 'No charge, Son, just tell your mother to give me the recipe for her butter crumb cake!'

I was the only one who wasn't busy. There was no trade school nearby for me and Papa refused to take me on the road with him, saying he needed all the space in the car to carry his merchandise and that I should stay behind to look after the family. I was happy with this plan; it made me feel use-ful, but it hardly filled my days as Maman insisted on doing almost everything herself. So, while everyone else got on with their lives, I explored our new surroundings. There was an airfield nearby and I found a spot hidden between some trees as a good viewpoint. People were saying how quickly we were going to mobilise the troops, thrash the Germans and get this war over and won. But when I peered through the trees, I saw the men at the airfield had no uniforms, and no weapons except for old rifles left over from the last war. The aircrafts were even worse – old-fashioned biplanes that wouldn't stand a chance against the sleek German aircrafts we saw flying overhead. There was no barracks; the men went home every night to sleep. I couldn't believe it. How could they defend us if this was the state of our military? I decided not to tell anyone in the family what I had seen; I couldn't imagine what good it would do to worry them.

****

Just months after arriving in Behonne, a letter arrived from the authorities informing us we were to be relocated to Poitiers. This was followed by a visit from the gendarme.

'Can you tell me when you will be leaving?' Papa was asked.

'My family will travel in a few days, but I have decided to stay for the time being. Poitiers is too far for me to visit my customers and I need to support my family.'

'Monsieur, that will not be possible. The relocation order is exactly that, an order. It is for your own safety.'

'I appreciate that, Monsieur, but I'm sure you can appreciate my need to protect the livelihood of my loved ones.'

'Albert, I think it best if you do as the authorities ask,' reasoned Maman.

'But, darling, how will we live?'

'Monsieur Laskowski, I'm told you will receive a stipend as acknowledgement of having to leave your business behind.'

'Bah! Refugee money!' said Papa. 'It would be better for our country if that money was used for the war effort.'

'Albert! I don't think we should be ungrateful for money which will allow us all to stay together,' said Maman, and with that the discussion ended. Papa would come with us. There was a house available in a small village called Sarry. I was not encouraged by what I remembered from my Jewish History studies at school. There had been no Jewish community in Poitiers for the past six hundred years, since it was expelled by Philip the Fair. I remembered we laughed at his name – he seemed anything but fair.

Maman was upset, having spent much effort on making a home for us in Behonne, but happy to learn we would be reunited with old friends and neighbours from Metz. We also heard Rabbi Epstein, who had tutored me for my bar mitzvah, was now living in Poitiers.

We packed the car up once more. This time there would only be one journey as we had just enough fuel to get us to our new destination and little chance of getting more for a civilian vehicle. There would be no return to the east for the time being, so we took as much as we could fit in and on top of the car and were forced to leave the rest behind. After ourselves, top priority was given to the radio set as it would be our main source of information. Papa promised Maman he would come back at the first opportunity to collect the possessions we were leaving and, as expected, Maman left everything neatly packed and labelled, as well as mopping the floors of what had been our home for such a short time.

We were on the road again, this journey even more difficult than the last, not only because we had Bubbe with us this time but also because we were going much further – six hundred kilometres south-west. But no one complained. We kept our spirits up by singing and playing word games. We took it in turns to tell stories. Samuel and Claude did impressions of their school teachers and made us all laugh. Bubbe chanted prayers and stared at her hands to see if she could see her fingers, something she did often which we all thought strange.

Our journey was hampered by the late December weather. The roads were less busy than when we left Metz, but our progress slowed by having to drive around the abandoned cars we passed along the way. Some had broken down, while many had run out of fuel, forcing the owners to leave their belongings and continue their journey on foot. In different circumstances people might have been tempted to rifle through the cars to see if there was anything worth taking, but everyone on the road was already carrying as much as possible and the only thing that would be of any great value at the time was food, jewellery and money, not the furniture and clothing which was left. People continued their journeys and left the pickings for the locals.

****

We didn't know the area we were being sent to and so we were pleasantly surprised when we eventually arrived. Sarry was a tiny village a few kilometres outside Poitiers: a line of around thirty houses on either side of the Route Nationale 10, the main highway from Paris to Bordeaux. There was a primary school, a railway station and little else. It took a while to find our new home as it was one of few houses which were not on the main road. It was set apart from the rest of the village and could only be reached by turning down a dirt track. Maybe living in a remote house might not be such a bad thing, almost hidden from anyone who might want to find us. We were at war and I was learning that we should plan for the worst.

Apart from the day my twin sisters were born, this was the only time I heard my father thank God. During the last part of our journey he kept an eye on the fuel gauge. It was unreliable at the best of times and had showed empty since

44

Châtellerault, some forty kilometres away. Had it not lasted, we would have had no choice but to walk, carrying our belongings with us. If there is a God he was looking down on us that day and it wasn't until we turned into the gravel driveway that the engine began to splutter and then cut out. Papa coasted the car into the barn next to the house.

We shared the house with Uncle Isaac and his family who travelled by train – sixteen of us in total. It was an old farmhouse without running water or electricity, built on two floors, each split into two rooms: a bedroom and a kitchen which also had a couple of beds. Kitchen furniture was limited to a table and chairs, a dresser, which thankfully contained some crockery and cooking utensils, and there was also a chest of drawers in the bedroom. Our cousins took the downstairs which had a fireplace in the kitchen, while we went upstairs where there was a wood-burning stove. My parents, Samuel and my sisters shared the bedroom while Bubbe, Claude and I slept in the kitchen. At night we heard the rats running around above us in the attic. It was basic, but more comfortable than what we had in Behonne, and we were grateful to the French authorities for providing for us.

****

Papa had bought two bicycles and we rode side by side down the gravel path away from our new home and towards the Route Nationale 10. It was early morning and we were on our way to work, having both found jobs almost immediately in a nearby foundry making casings for aerial bombs. I was happy to go to work, especially doing something to help the war effort. After what I saw at the airfield near Behonne,

I knew France would need all the aerial bombs we could make.

This was my first paid job. It was hot, hard work, but Papa would have gone stir crazy if he had been idle for more than a couple of days. The salary wasn't much, but any extra money coming in was put to good use, giving it all to Maman to manage the home. More valuable to me was the time I got to spend with my father: cycling to the factory; sharing our packed lunch; and then coming back home together in the afternoon, chatting about our day. It seemed crazy that it took a war to make me feel so… contented. I had never been happier than during those first months in Sarry. My brothers were also happy: when we first arrived at the house they couldn't believe what they found.

Samuel

Sarry
January 1940
After two terrible days crammed in the car, Claude and I couldn't believe our luck. This was going to be so much more fun than living in an apartment in Metz! There was a barn, and space around the house. There were fields too, and we could hear a stream nearby. I couldn't wait to explore, but the first thing I had to do on that cold day was find some milk for my sisters.

Back in Metz I bought the milk from the grocer and would hope the Jew-haters didn't steal my money before I got to the store. But, driving through the village, we hadn't seen a grocery store.

'Go and find the dairy farmer,' said Maman, as she handed me a can and some coins. 'And be careful of the traffic on that busy road!'

I walked up the path and turned into the main road. At first there was no one around, but then I saw an old man walking towards me. 'Excuse me, sir. Do you know where I can get some milk for my young sisters?'

He looked confused, as if he didn't know what I was saying. I couldn't understand what the problem was, so I repeated the question slowly. He said something which I didn't understand but I smiled and went in the direction he pointed. I found the farmhouse and knocked. The farmer's wife opened the door. I showed her the can and explained that my mother had sent me for milk.

'The cow is in the barn at the back.'

'What do I do?'

'You look like a smart boy. You'll figure it out,' she said, grinning at me and holding out her hand for the coins. Then she shut the door.

I went round the back of the house. In the barn there was a cow tied up and a milk churn behind her. *Great*! I thought. *I fill up my can from the milk in the churn.* I walked around the cow, giving her a wide berth, and prised the lid off the churn. It was empty. Next to it was a bucket and a three-legged stool. I had hoped it was going to be easier than this. I had never milked a cow before, but I had seen people do it when I stayed on the farm in Condé-Northern. I knew what to do, I just didn't know the technique. How difficult could it be?

I grabbed the stool and my can and sat down at the back end of the cow. I took off my woollen gloves, wrapped my fingers around one of her udders and closed my eyes. I summoned up the courage to pull gently downwards towards the milk can in my other hand. Nothing! The cow was still and silent. She wasn't giving me any clues. I looked around for someone who might help but I was alone. There was no one to show me what to do, but no one to laugh at me either. I tried again a few more times, changing the position of my fingers and squeezing rather than pulling and eventually managed to get some milk. I was giddy with success although I soon realised it was such a small dribble I must still be doing something wrong.

I put down the can and took the bucket from next to the churn. I placed it between my legs and wrapped each hand around one udder. I remembered the farmer in Condé-Northern milking the cow with two hands, pulling one and then the other. I tried to copy what I had seen, and it worked. After a while, the bucket was half full. I poured it into the milk can and took it home to Maman. The farmer's wife was right – I had figured it out!

****

Papa and Pierre found work soon after we arrived in Sarry. Maman was busy as usual, doing the household chores and looking after Georgette and Henriette, while Bubbe would sit downstairs with Aunt Dora, leaving Claude and me free to explore our new home.

'Sam?'

'What?'

'What's that?'

'What's what?'

'That, in the ceiling.'

'I don't know. It looks like a door.'

'Where does it go?'

'To the attic, I suppose.'

'What do you think is up there?'

'Rats!'

'There might be a dead body!'

'If there was a dead body then blood would be dripping through the ceiling.'

'Oh yeah. Maybe a pit of snakes?'

'Then we would hear them hissing.'

'That's true. Maybe pirate treasure?'

'Maybe.'

'If it is pirate treasure, we could give the jewels to Maman. That would make her so happy.'

'Yes.'

'So?'

'So, what?'

'So, shall we go up and see what's there?'

'OK, but we'll need a ladder.'

'There's one in the barn.'

Claude and I brought the ladder in from the barn, struggling between us and giggling as we almost knocked each other out. It made us think of the Charlie Chaplin movies we saw at the picture house in Metz, which made us laugh even more. We set it against the kitchen wall and climbed up into the attic. When we opened the door we heard the rats scurrying away to the far corners. *Let's hope they stay there*, I thought to myself. It was dark except for a few shafts of light coming in through the gaps in the roof.

'We were right. Look over there, a treasure chest!' shouted Claude.

We scrambled over to the wooden chest in the corner and dragged it over to the light. Luckily it wasn't locked because I think Claude would have exploded if he'd had to wait a moment longer. Inside the chest we discovered something better than either of us could have imagined, better even than pirate treasure: a gun and two dusty old military uniforms complete with white trousers, waistcoats and navy-blue jackets with red tassels on the shoulders.

We somehow brought the chest down from the attic and showed the others what we had found. Papa told us the uniforms were from the Napoleonic war, over one hundred years old, and must have belonged to whoever lived in the house back then. He made sure the gun was safe, which it was because it had no ammunition and was rusty, and Maman checked the uniforms for fleas, then took them outside to beat the dust out. Then they were ours to use as playthings.

Claude and I spent the rest of the day dressed up and marching around the house, taking turns to hold the gun. So far, our new home was turning out to be splendid!

There was plenty of fun to be had outdoors too, but first we needed to take care of our chores. As there was no running water in the house, it was my job to make sure the water barrels were kept at least three-quarters full. Carrying two empty buckets down the path to the nearby stream for the first time, I tripped over a tree root I hadn't spotted, too busy looking around for good branches to come back and climb later with Claude. When I got to the stream I thought, *Wow, this will make a great place for swimming in the summer*. But now it was freezing cold and I wanted to get back to the house as soon as possible. It was difficult to walk quickly with the heavy buckets of water, but I went as fast as I could, thinking ahead to games of hide-and-seek and looking for places where Claude wouldn't find me. It had rained the night before and the path was slippery. I hadn't learnt my lesson on the way there and I stumbled over roots and rocks on the way back. When I got to the house most of the water I collected at the spring had spilt out. I poured the remainder into the barrel but it hardly lifted the water level at all. Everyone in the family thought that was funny, and I loved to make them laugh so I didn't mind too much, but after that first journey I took more care walking with the full buckets. Over time the trips got easier as I got stronger. The air in the Poitiers region seemed to agree with me; my chest stayed clear of any infection.

Claude and I joined the local school. I was happy to see a few Jewish children from Metz, who had also come to live in the village. School was a short walk from our new home up the steep hill of the Nationale 10. There was just one classroom, and the teacher, Madame Noyer, lived at the school. We made new friends: Claude with the youngest kid there, Louis Klein (everyone called him Little Louis), and me with a boy around my age, Ernst Rubin. I was pleased that Claude had his own pals now, although he would always be my best friend. Madame Noyer, who was kind and patient, gave us lessons in the local dialect, Poitevin, so we could go home and teach our parents, to help them fit in with the locals. I soon realised that was why I couldn't understand the man I asked about the dairy farm the day we arrived in the village.

****

In spring the cherry tree in front of our house blossomed with pale pink flowers. Claude and I picked some from the lower branches and Maman, having left her vases back in Metz, arranged them in an old jam jar on the kitchen table. There was a bench under the sweet-smelling tree where Bubbe sat happily all day long. Maman and Aunt Dora liked to sit there too and the twins played in the shade, their fair skin protected from the sun by the blossoming branches.

Sometimes a neighbour, Madame Klein, would come to sit and chat with Maman and bring her two boys, Little Louis and Victor.

Papa and Pierre were still working at the foundry. The hours weren't as long as Papa had been used to as a travelling merchant. Moving to Sarry hadn't been our choice, and the house wasn't as comfortable as our apartment in Metz, but the first months living there were happy times. I wasn't sick, I wasn't bullied at school, Claude and I had lots of places to explore, and Papa was at home much of the time. Life was good.

In his new spare time Papa got involved with village life. The first thing he did for the community was to arrange for the electricity company to bring the supply to Sarry. We were used to electric light and listening to the radio and we were excited to get these back into our lives. I couldn't wait to listen to my favourite programmes again, but Papa said the radio was particularly important as it was our way of finding out how the war was progressing and what was happening outside of the village. Not everyone had a radio and my parents welcomed our neighbours to come and listen to ours. Soon the other Jewish refugees in Sarry considered my father their leader. He didn't seem to mind this unelected role; he enjoyed organising and telling people what to do!

****

It was the last lesson of the week and I looked forward to playing football with my friends after class. It was only going to be a quick game as we had to get home to do our chores;

I would need to fetch water so Maman could prepare the Shabbat dinner.

I can't remember what Madame Noyer was saying. I had given up trying to concentrate and was daydreaming while waiting for the bell to ring. I noticed more traffic than usual that day along the main road in front of the school building, but I hadn't thought much about it until a gendarme came into the classroom. Something was going on; Sarry was too small for a police force. I hadn't seen any policemen since we arrived, and here was one now right in front of me.

'Good afternoon, boys and girls.'

We stood up. 'Good afternoon, Monsieur.'

'You may sit down. I am here to tell you that the German army has invaded France today.'

A gasp went around the room and some of the girls burst out crying. We all had questions. 'What does that mean?' 'What will happen to us?' 'What should we do now?'

The gendarme called for silence and continued: 'We don't know what will happen, but you should go home directly after school and be with your families. Tell your parents as they might not know yet.' Then he left as abruptly as he had arrived, no doubt to pass the news on to others.

A boy put his hand up. 'Madame?'

The colour had drained from Madame Noyer's pretty face. 'No questions please, children. I don't know anything more than what we just heard. We will finish school a little early today. Class dismissed and make sure you take your gas masks with you. Please be careful if you need to cross the road to get home, there has been a lot of traffic today.'

'Does that mean no school on Monday?' asked one of the boys.

'No, it does not. I will see everyone here as usual on Monday,' came the reply, to groans from the class. 'Go home safely and may God look after us all.'

When Claude and I arrived home we were happy to see Papa and Pierre were already safely back from work. The factory had also sent everyone home early. They were both sitting in front of the radio with Uncle Isaac and my older cousins.

'What news, Papa?' I asked.

'There are reports of German troops in France and some air battles, but nothing around here, thank goodness. We need to remain alert and make sure we do nothing wrong and we should have no problems, don't you think, Isaac?'

'Yes, of course. They won't want anything from us. We'll be fine,' agreed Uncle.

The weekend was quiet. Maman asked that I stay near the house. On Monday, Claude and I went back to school as usual. The day passed without incident to the disappointment of some of the children.

As we came out of school at the end of the day, one boy shouted excitedly, 'Look!' and pointed up the road. A line of French soldiers marched down the Nationale 10. They looked worn out. A little way past our school they were ordered to stop and took it in turns to dig at the side of the road. They only had a couple of spades which they passed from one soldier to the next. After a while they had dug a trench and set up their machine guns.

Madame Noyer told the smaller children like Claude and Little Louis to go back into the school building but Ernst and I and some of the others stayed outside and settled down to watch the action, peering over the top of the thick stone school wall. We whispered between us, wondering what would happen next. Were the Germans coming? Should we run home, or wait? One of the boys told us to be quiet, he thought he could hear something... I shivered as I heard singing in the distance. When it reached the French officers they climbed out of the trench and ran off, shouting orders at their soldiers, who were left alone.

I was confused. As the voices got louder, it sounded like they were singing in Polish which I recognised because my parents sometimes spoke it to each other, usually when they didn't want us to understand what they were saying. We heard marching too. There was a bend in the road so we couldn't see them yet but the French soldiers who were still in the trench seemed to know who was coming. They picked up their guns and ran away. You could hardly blame them; their officers had already left. The French army was clearly in bad shape.

The singing soldiers marched into sight along the main road from the opposite direction in which the French soldiers had only just disappeared. When they reached the railway station, just before the school building, they were ordered to halt and stand to attention while one of the officers made an announcement in badly spoken French.

'The village of Sarry is now under the occupation of the German army,' he bellowed. An orderly nailed a document on the outside wall of the railway station's ticket office, then the officer shouted another command and they marched off down the road. A handful of locals came out to witness the occupation of their village, though most chose to watch from inside their homes, through the curtains. Sarry was so small there was no reason for the soldiers to hang around for more than a few minutes and then continue their 'occupation march'.

When the soldiers were out of sight, Claude, Little Louis and the other younger kids came out. Little Louis's father had seen the soldiers and come up to meet him. Meanwhile, I grabbed Claude and we ran home to tell everyone what we had seen.

'Maman, Papa. There were German soldiers in the village, but they were singing in Polish!'

'So, they're here already. We know what they think about us Jews, so we must be careful,' warned Papa.

'Don't worry,' Claude said. 'They've gone! They only stopped in the village for a few minutes and then they left.'

'That, at least, is good news,' said Maman. 'Hopefully they'll leave us alone. We don't look any different to the gentile families in the village. No one is going to know we're Jewish just by looking at us so, as long as we don't give any German soldiers reason to question us, we shouldn't have any problems.'

'But why were they singing in Polish?' I asked.

'They are Volksdeutsche,' explained Papa. 'There were many people from German families living in Poland. Since the Nazi occupation last year they have been forced to join the German army.'

'They are forced to fight for the Germans who are destroying their homes in Poland. That is madness,' said Pierre, who seemed to better understand what was going on than I did.

'What's madness is anyone wanting to go and live in Poland!' said Bubbe from her seat in the corner of the room.

'You're not wrong there,' agreed Papa. 'I think now would be a good time to tell the boys what happened when I went back to Poland for my father's funeral.' He looked at Maman, who nodded in agreement. 'Do you remember that I went by myself? It must have been three years ago now, before the war started. After the funeral, a policeman grabbed me and told me I had to join the Polish army.'

'What did you do, Papa?' We were all fascinated.

'I told him my home was in France now and I was going to join the French army. Well, he didn't much like that answer and started to lead me away.' He paused for a moment.

'Don't stop now! What happened then?' we all shouted.

'I kicked him in the shin and then hit him with all my might, in the stomach and the chest and the face. I hit him as hard as I could, as if my life depended on it. I guess I did a good job of it because he fell to the floor.'

'Did you kick him when he was down?' I asked, with a cheeky grin.

'No, Son. I turned and ran away as fast as my legs could carry me. Sometimes you have to fight and other times you have to run.'

'Thank goodness you got away!'

'Of course he did. No one is stronger than Papa!'

'I don't know about that,' said Papa, smiling, 'but perhaps I escaped thanks to my strength and fast thinking!'

'And your modesty?' added Maman who had been sitting quietly, watching us as we listened to our father's great adventure.

'Modesty won't save your life,' said Papa, turning serious.

'Then what happened?' demanded Claude, desperate to hear more.

'I went straight to the train station and came home. A couple of months later I received a letter from the Polish government telling me they'd taken away my citizenship because I'd refused to join the army. Now that we're at war it's important we register to become French citizens. Pierre, you have your citizenship. I will arrange for the rest of us to go to Poitiers to apply.'

'I don't see why I have to go,' I said. 'I was born in France, I speak the language, I go to school and when I'm old enough I'll fight for France. Isn't that enough?'

'Sadly not,' said Papa.

****

We went to Poitiers by train. As we left the station, I could hardly believe my eyes. The town was full of German soldiers. They weren't taking any notice of us, thank goodness; we were just an ordinary-looking family and they were busy watching the pretty girls walk past as they sat outside cafes drinking coffee and smoking.

It looked like the German soldiers were enjoying the war. The girls looked happy too. I saw them smiling and giggling and doing that funny walk Pierre had told me about, the one when a girl is pretending to ignore a boy but really wants him to notice her. Maman looked at them disapprovingly and muttered, 'Shikshas.' That's what she called the non-Jewish girls she didn't like. I wasn't interested in girls, but I was sure Pierre was. *He'll be sorry when I tell him what he's missed*, I thought to myself. I knew Pierre was suddenly desperate for a girlfriend!

To apply for citizenship, we all needed to have physical examinations. Papa had asked neighbours for the name of a sympathetic doctor. Doctor Savatier was recommended and we made our way to his surgery. Although they hadn't said, I knew my parents were worried about my health. If the doctor noticed anything wrong with my lungs it was unlikely he would sign us off as fit and healthy. Why would he risk his own safety for a family he had never met before? Thank God the months we had been away from Metz had been good for me and the doctor didn't even blink when he listened to my chest. My lungs were clear, and we all passed with flying colours.

Doctor Savatier made a joke about getting Georgette and Henriette mixed up and Maman laughed nervously. Claude and I had strict instructions to be on our best behaviour. There was a lot of paperwork to fill in and the two of us sat totally still the whole time; my idea for us to play 'frozen statues' in the doctor's office worked well. When the forms were completed, we each had to sign our own. Neither Claude nor I were used to signing our names and we both did so with much care. My brother was jealous because I have a 'S' in my name which I was able to loop and squiggle while Claude didn't have the chance to do anything so fancy with his signature. He complained about his name the whole way home. My little sisters were only two, so Papa signed for them. We were told our forms would be sent off for processing and we would hear back by post.

****

On our way home from school Claude and I passed the house of Monsieur Petis, a friendly old man who waved to us from his garden. He had an old dog called Pippin who would run out to greet us. Claude and I really wanted a dog, but

Papa said it was hard enough to get food for ourselves these days without having an extra mouth to feed. We would stop to play with Pippin and Mr Petis would ask us about school. He told us he was a retired army officer who had lived in Sarry for many years, and nowadays he spent his time looking after his fruit trees.

As the summer approached, Monsieur Petis asked if we could help him pick grapes from his vineyard during the school holidays, which we were happy to do. In return, he gave us some of the fruit to take home, as well as telling us stories from his years in the army. As we walked home with our grapes I had a brilliant idea.

'Claude, let's make our own wine. We learnt about it at school. Wine is made from grapes. We just need to squeeze the juice out, leave it for a few weeks, et voila! We can give some grapes to Maman and still have plenty left over to use.'

Claude usually did whatever I told him to, so it didn't come as any great surprise he thought my idea was a great plan. When we got home we left a couple of large bunches of grapes on the kitchen table for the family, grabbed two empty wine bottles from the cupboard and took them, with the remaining grapes, to a quiet place behind the barn. We set everything down on the ground and started to make our wine. I picked up a grape and squeezed it between my fingers, managing to get one or two drops of juice in the bottle with the rest landing in the dust. It reminded me of my first attempt at milking a cow. Claude picked up a grape and copied me, just managing to collect a couple of drops of juice.

'This isn't working,' I said. 'Let's put the grapes into the bottle and squeeze them once they are inside. That way we won't lose any juice.'

I took a bottle and started to stuff grapes in, one by one through the narrow opening. Claude copied me. When the bottles were full we picked up the cleanest-looking stick we could each find, pushed it inside our bottle and smashed up the grapes. We stuffed a few more in and did it all again. In the end we managed to use most of the grapes and replace the corks tightly in the bottles. We found a corner of the barn to hide them.

'I'm going to stick a stone in my cork, so we know which bottle is mine,' said Claude. 'Now what?'

'Now we wait for the grape juice to turn into wine.'

'How long does it take?'

'A couple of weeks, then we can taste it.'

A few weeks later, towards the end of the summer and just before we were due to go back to school, my brother and I returned excitedly to the barn to try the wine. Claude picked up his bottle with the stone in the cork and handed me the other.

'The bottles are really warm.'

'That's good, it means the wine has been cooking,' I said.

We pulled the corks out.

Claude made a face. 'What's that smell?'

'It's the wine, silly!' I said as I lifted the bottle to my lips and took a sip. Ugh! The wine was fizzy and tasted awful. It took all my efforts not to spit it out in disgust. Claude watched me drink and then did the same. He grimaced as he swallowed the first mouthful, but neither of us would admit our wine was revolting. We drank a whole bottle each, then lay down on the grass in the sun with our eyes closed.

A while later, Maman called us indoors. 'Samuel! Claude! Come and wash before supper.'

We both scrambled up. The ground was swaying.

'Woah, I feel dizzy!' said my brother.

'Me too.'

'Do you think the wine was bad?'

'I don't know.'

We stumbled into the house and managed to get up the stairs, falling over each other on the way.

'What is the matter with you two?' asked Maman.

'I don't feel so well, Maman,' said Claude, on the verge of tears.

'Me neither,' I said.

'What's the matter?'

'I don't know,' we both replied.

'Are you hungry?'

'No.'

Maman was instantly worried.

'Let me feel your foreheads. Hmmm, a little warm but you have both been outside most of the afternoon. Go and lie down for a bit.'

Maman came in to check on us half an hour later.

'Boys, are you feeling any better?'

'No, my head hurts,' I said.

'Mine too,' said Claude.

'Oh my, it must be a virus!' said Maman.

'It sounds to me more like they're drunk!' said Bubbe, who had been listening to the conversation.

'Oh, Mame, don't be silly!' replied Maman.

Neither of us was concentrating on what they were saying. The room was spinning, and our heads were banging. They left us to rest... and then the cramps started. It felt like I was being stabbed in my stomach.

'Sam?'

'Huh?'

'Sam. My tummy really hurts. I need the toilet.'

'Me too. We should go outside.'

We were unsteady on our feet but helped each other out of bed and down the stairs moments before the diarrhoea started. The stomach cramps were unbearable. There was only one WC and we both needed to go at the same time! We staggered into the woods at the back of the house to relieve ourselves and stayed there for hours until we felt it was safe to go back home.

We confessed to our parents about drinking the home-made wine, and Maman's reaction turned from worry to relief to anger to amusement. Claude and I suffered from stomach ache and diarrhoea for several days. We got no sympathy from our family; they laughed at us. We had learnt our lesson; no more home-made wine.

Pierre

I had never been to Paris. I had always wanted to go and even planned what I would do there: visit the Eiffel Tower and walk through Montmartre, but now it seemed unlikely a trip would happen any time soon and I stopped myself from thinking of such frivolities. The Maginot Line had proved itself a worthless defence; France surrendered to Germany following a swift and humiliating defeat. On 14 June the Germans occupied Paris. I turned fifteen a month later, on Bastille Day. I was too young to fight for my country, but I would do everything I could to look after my family.

After the invasion, a large convoy of cars and trucks came through Sarry on the Route Nationale 10, along with French police and military motorcyclists. They drove at high speed straight through the village. It was the French government fleeing from Paris to Bordeaux, and they were not the only ones to leave. There were also civilians, mainly women, children and older folk who arrived but all continued on their way as there was nothing in the village for them. Thousands of people left the capital but only a small number made it this far; some found refuge on the way, others were forced to abandon their cars when they ran out of fuel, and then there were those who fell victim to the German air raids.

Our radio told us what was happening in the rest of France and Europe. Philippe Pétain, the same World War One hero who had been the innovation behind the useless Maginot Line, was appointed prime minister – prime minister in such important times at eighty-four years old! It was crazy to have such an old man in charge. He wasted no time signing an armistice with the Germans and split France into two with a 1,200-kilometre demarcation line. The northern side was to be under German control and the southern side to be under control of Pétain and his French government, which, after fleeing Paris, had relocated again from Bordeaux to the spa town of Vichy. We were mere kilometres from the demarcation line, but on the German-occupied side. What would this mean for us? Also part of the armistice agreement was that Alsace and Lorraine were now under German administration, so unless the Germans were defeated, we were unlikely to return to Metz.

Papa and I left our jobs in the foundry when it became clear it would be taken over by the Germans and we helped out a local stonemason instead, but there really wasn't a lot of work for us. All other Jewish families were in the same situation. Most of the men were tailors or merchants who'd left their businesses in the east of the country. Everyone had brought money with them and received the stipend from the government, used to buy food from farmers, and most of us were also growing our own vegetables which, at least, gave us something to do.

****

A new radio station, Radio Londres, was now being broadcast from the BBC studios in London. It was the talk of the village and we invited neighbours to listen in our house. The station was run by the newly formed Free French Forces led by Charles de Gaulle and opened with the comforting words, '*Ici Londres! Les Français parlent aux Français...*' 'This is London! The French speaking to the French...' I felt proudly patriotic as I listened. They promised to speak to us every day. De Gaulle's speeches were inspiring; he urged us not to give up and to support the Resistance. When I heard him I vowed to join the Resistance at the earliest possible opportunity. The war for France was not over yet and I would not allow Pétain or Hitler to determine my fate.

Pétain didn't waste time in blaming the Republic for the French defeat and demonstrating how he planned to return France to Nationalist glory. At my old school I had been taught the three Republican ideals of *Liberté, Egalité, Fraternité* (Liberty, Equality, Fraternity). Now my younger brothers were taught the Nationalist ideals of *Travail, Famille, Patrie* (Work, Family, Fatherland).

In July, Radio Londres reported the Vichy government had passed a law allowing the denaturalisation of anyone granted French citizenship since 1927. Half a million naturalisations would be reviewed. Papa looked crestfallen when he heard the news. No one dared say it out loud, but everyone was thinking the same: how would it affect their applications for French citizenship, and would I have mine taken away?

****

It was time to celebrate Rosh Hashanah, but there was no synagogue in Poitiers for us to celebrate the New Year. Instead the community was offered a room in the town hall to use. This year, more than ever, we wanted to celebrate with our neighbours but due to the size of the room and the number of families now living in the area, only the men would attend. Papa and I went with Uncle Isaac, cousin Gabriel, and Leon, cousin Simone's husband.

The service was led by Rabbi Epstein. He stood in front of a small wooden cabinet which served as the ark. The Torah scroll, brought to Poitiers from the synagogue in Metz, had been placed inside. At the beginning of the service the precious scroll was carefully taken out of the ark, the velvet cover and silver breastplate removed, and the delicate paper opened at the correct reading on the table which had been provided as our makeshift altar. During the Rosh Hashanah service the shofar is blown one hundred times. 'Tekiah!' called the rabbi repeatedly, as one of the congregation took a deep breath and blew into the ram's horn, creating long blasts sounding like cries of distress; 'Shevarim!' followed by patterns of three shorter blasts to signify wailing; 'Teruah!', the call for nine rapid blasts of alarm and, finally, 'Tekiah HaGadol!'; one last blast for as long as the breath would allow.

I remembered the competitions at school in Metz to see who could blow the Tekiah HaGadol for the longest. In those days it had seemed like a game but the significance of the blowing of the shofar had never seemed more relevant than it did now.

At the end of the service, when the Torah scrolls had been returned to the makeshift ark, Rabbi Epstein stood in front of us to give his sermon. Nobody knew what to expect. He shifted from one foot to the other and fidgeted with the tassels on his prayer shawl.

'Shana Tova. Happy New Year. My friends, my neighbours, we can't know for sure if these wishes for a good new year will be fulfilled. I have been asked to pass on an announcement from the office of Pétain which has chosen today, Rosh Hashana, to pass a new law, the Statut des Juifs.'

****

As soon as the service finished, we returned home. Maman and Aunt Dora had prepared lunch in celebration of Rosh Hashanah: poached gefilte fish followed by chicken cooked with apples and plums with braised cabbage. They had saved rations for weeks to be able to serve such a feast. At the end of the meal they put out slices of cake, made with honey from a nearby farm, to symbolise our hope for a sweet new year. Maman was disappointed she couldn't get any cinnamon, part of her traditional family recipe. I had little appetite following what I had heard that morning, but I forced myself to eat what was put in front of me.

We decided on the way back from Poitiers that we would wait until after lunch to share what we had learnt. We knew this could be our last festive meal for some time depending on how long it would take to defeat the Germans, and we were determined not to spoil it for the others. Once the meal was over, the young children were told to leave the table. It was now time for Papa and Uncle Isaac to pass on the terrible news.

'How was the service?' asked Aunt Dora. 'What did you men get up to without the women there making sure you behaved yourselves?' The women laughed.

'The service was fine, but Rabbi Epstein's sermon wasn't what we were expecting to hear,' said Papa.

'Go on,' urged Maman, the joy draining from her face as she registered the look of despair in his eyes.

'He told us Pétain and his anti-Semitic monkeys have given us a present for Rosh Hashanah. It's called the Statuts des Juifs.' Papa's voice shook with anger as he explained. 'From today, as Jews, we have lost all our rights.' He stopped again and looked around the table. The men were silent. Maman, Aunt Dora and my cousins Anna and Simone looked confused.

'What does that mean?'

'Well, as an example, any Jew who still has a business has had it taken away as of today.'

'What? That's madness. How can they steal someone's business?' demanded Aunt Dora.

'They can do whatever they want because they are doing it to please the Germans. But wait, there is more.'

'What else?'

'Jews may only shop during certain hours in the afternoon.'

'You mean when there will be nothing left to buy!' said Bubbe.

'Jews won't be allowed to go to the cinema. There will be a curfew and we're not allowed to go out after dark.' At this point Papa stopped to take my mother's hand in his. 'Rosa,

Jews are banned from going to public parks, like the one we went to when we were courting and where I asked you to be my wife.' We knew the stories of how my father would 'accidentally' bump into my mother on the street near where she lived and take her for walks in the parks of Metz. Tears filled my mother's eyes and I was furious that those bastards had made her cry.

This was the moment when I understood nothing would ever be the same again. We were used to being blamed for the lack of work in France and the state of the economy, being called dirty Jews and chased home from school. Yet the Statuts des Juifs marked the nadir in our lives.

The radio continued to be our best way of finding out what was going on in the world. Radio Londres kept its promise to broadcast every day, sending messages of solidarity from across the Channel and urging the French not to give up hope and to join the fight for freedom, but there was little news of what was happening to the Jewish people.

****

The last three months of the year passed slowly. There was no work for a fifteen-year-old Jew. My irritation at having nothing productive or helpful to do was affecting my mood and I found myself miserable much of the time. Meanwhile, Samuel and Claude were happy enough at school: their teacher Madame Noyer was kind and they had each other and their friends to help pass the time. Samuel had Ernst while Claude had Little Louis, such a sweet kid!

Maman had her hands full with the twins – now running everywhere but bringing everyone much joy as they did so – and having to be incredibly inventive with the limited supplies available. When we left Behonne, Papa had been forced to abandon most of his clothing merchandise. Thankfully he had the foresight to strap a few rolls of material to the roof of the car which Maman was now able to use to clothe us.

Maman was also resourceful when it came to feeding the family as food became scarce. Although she hated it at the time, she now missed the days when Papa had arranged for a shochet to come from Poitiers every few weeks to slaughter chickens in the kosher manner. When we first arrived in Sarry, we had to find a way to continue this tradition.

'Where will this slaughter take place?' Maman asked when Papa first announced his plans. 'There is no abattoir in the village.'

'I thought we could do it in our barn,' he said matter-of-factly.

'Albert, please. We have enough screaming and crying from my mother and the twins. I don't want to listen to screaming chickens too. What of the mess and the smell?'

Maman was determined not to allow the chicken slaughter to happen at our home and instead Papa found a barn near the school to use. It was my job to visit the families and tell them when to bring their chickens. When a chicken is slaughtered in the kosher way it doesn't die instantly and it was normal to see chickens running around with their heads hanging to the side. People would argue about which chicken belonged to whom as the birds ran around in circles making it hard to keep track. One chicken ran across the street and I had to catch it and bring it back. We laughed a lot at the expense of the poor chickens.

Now there was little left to slaughter and the Statuts des Juifs meant the shochet could come no more. It was a blow to our morale but we thought we could find another way and went to Poitiers to see Rabbi Epstein.

'The kosher slaughter of animals has been banned,' confirmed the rabbi.

'What shall we tell our neighbours?'

'God will allow us to eat non-kosher meat to save our lives and after the war we will resume our kashrut laws.'

When we returned home we asked Maman what to tell Bubbe.

'We can tell her what the rabbi said, or we tell her nothing and she will have no reason to think the meat is not kosher,' Papa said.

'I think we should tell her the truth. If this is the worst they can do to us, then let it make us stronger,' I said.

'I agree with you, Son. But I'm not sure this is the worst they have planned for us.'

Samuel

Sarry
November 1940

Monsieur and Madame Klein, Little Louis's parents, were a young couple from Metz. Little Louis was six and his younger brother Victor was the same age as my sisters and would sometimes play with them. Monsieur Klein had the brightest red hair I had ever seen; it made him look almost like his head was on fire! The Klein family were allocated a home near the school but on the opposite side of the Route Nationale 10. The road was downhill to Sarry and it was not unusual for cars to pick up speed as they passed through the tiny village. At first Monsieur Klein came to school after class to collect Little Louis and walk him home but after a while he allowed him to walk by himself. Then Monsieur Klein would wait on the side of the road outside his house and tell Little Louis when it was safe to cross.

One cold autumn afternoon we came out of school after our lessons and a priest was waiting for us. Sarry was too small to even have a church so he only came to teach catechism in a house across the street. The local Catholic boys went, as instructed, but us Jewish kids started to walk away.

One of the Catholic boys must have told the priest my name because he called out to me:

'Samuel! I am talking to you. Come here!'

'No, I'm Jewish. I don't need to learn catechism,' I shouted back.

'I'm going home before the priest calls my name,' declared Little Louis, running off towards home. 'Bye, Claude, see you tomorrow!'

'Bye!' replied Claude.

When Little Louis saw his father waiting on the other side of the road he ran towards him. He didn't hear the German officer's jeep approaching at high speed, nor did he hear his father warning him to wait and not cross. The jeep hit Little Louis as he ran across the road, the dull thud of the impact stunning us into silence. His small body was lifted up by the collision, twisting in the air like an acrobat and then falling fast like a sack of grain into an awkward pile on the road. His father and school friends watched helplessly; I pulled Claude to my side to protect him from the horrific scene. Monsieur Klein rushed over. He knelt down in the road and lifted Little Louis's head on to his lap. His cap had fallen off, but his face looked untouched except for one line of blood trickling slowly down his forehead, as red as his father's hair. Monsieur Klein sobbed as he held the lifeless body. Madame Klein emerged from the house holding Victor on her hip to see what the commotion was and stopped in horror when she realised it was Little Louis lying dead in the road. I looked at the Germans in the jeep. They seemed irritated by this inconvenience, which was delaying their journey. The officer in the front seat shouted at the mourning father, 'What is your name?'

'Baruch Klein,' he whispered, unable to find his voice in his state of shock.

'I said, what is your name!' demanded the officer.

'His name is Baruch Klein and that is his son,' answered one of his neighbours.

'Oh well, one Jew less,' announced the German and drove off, picking up speed again and without looking back.

****

The next day, Papa told us the Klein family had left Sarry, afraid of repercussions from the German officers. Poor Claude was still traumatised by the sight of his friend being hit by the jeep.

'But why? Those poor people, haven't they suffered enough?' asked Maman.

'The Nazis could return to make sure there is no one to make a complaint against them,' said Papa. 'No one wants to draw attention to themselves. They are scared for Victor's sake. Rabbi Epstein made arrangements for them to stay elsewhere.'

'But the funeral? The shiva? They should sit and let us help them through this,' said Maman, who knew the comfort neighbours and friends could bring at times of such sorrow.

'The rabbi has promised to say prayers for them all week. I said goodbye to the family from all of us. Please God we will see them again when the war is over.'

Pierre

Jews who had the chutzpah to think we had endured enough discrimination were soon proven wrong. Pétain and the Vichy government established Le Commissariat Général aux Questions Juives (The Office for Jewish Affairs) after the Germans announced plans to set up a similar department in Paris. The French were not trying to protect us by putting themselves in charge – they wanted to keep control rather than handing it over to the Germans. Xavier Vallat was appointed commissionaire. He was instantly recognisable; he wore a black patch over one eye and had a wooden leg due to injuries sustained in the last war. Vallat was responsible for Jewish affairs on both sides of the demarcation line. Bubbe said it was more like he was responsible for anti-Jewish affairs. One of his first actions was to order a census of all the Jews in France.

****

When we first came to Sarry we were surprised by the wild boar that came out of the woods to forage at night. They came right up to the house, practically knocking on the door. My brothers enjoyed seeing the animals so close to our home; a few years before they would have run away from a wild boar, but now they wanted to keep one as a pet. At that time our family had no interest in eating this treif, but as the war progressed and food shortages became a way of life, we were tempted to eat non-kosher meat. As it happened, we never got the chance as hunting went from being a hobby to a survival technique. There were fewer and fewer wild animals. The local game warden, Monsieur Auger, was kept busy patrolling the area to ensure no snares were set or poaching was going on.

We were surprised one evening when there was a knock at our door – few people ventured out after dark anymore.

'Who can it be?' asked Papa, rising from his chair. He was at the kitchen table attempting to carve a small toy farm animal from wood, despite not being particularly skilled at woodwork.

'I don't think we should answer,' said Maman, grabbing his arm. She always seemed nervous these days. I'm sure I wasn't the only one to notice that my dear mother appeared to have lost her *joie de vivre*.

'Perhaps it's an emergency, a friend who needs our help,' replied Papa and he went downstairs where Uncle Isaac had just had a similar conversation with Aunt Dora. They opened the door to find the game warden waiting. People in the village were already suffering from the effects of food rations and difficult living conditions, but Monsieur Auger appeared to be thriving. His tummy hung over his belt and his cheeks were red as if he had recently enjoyed a good meal with plenty of wine. As if that wasn't proof enough, he even had the nerve to burp when he spoke to us – that enraged me so much I had to stop myself from hitting him straight in his fat gut.

'Bonsoir,' he said.

'Bonsoir, Monsieur. How can we help you?'

'I have been asked to compile a list of everyone in the village. You must give the names of all the people who live in this house.'

'What is this list for, Monsieur?'

'The gendarmerie has asked for it and given me full authority to obtain the information,' said Monsieur Auger, with an air of arrogance.

'We are law-abiding people and we have nothing to hide. I will give you the information you ask for.' Papa listed everyone who lived in our house.

'From where are you relocated?'

'We have all come from Metz.'

'And, finally, you will tell me what religion you are.'

'Who is this nosey person asking all these questions?' shouted Bubbe from inside.

'Mame, sshh!' said Uncle Isaac.

'Why do you need to know that?' Papa asked the game warden.

'Just tell me!'

'We are Jewish.'

Monsieur Auger recorded the information in his notebook, said good evening and left.

When he was sure the front door was securely shut, Uncle Isaac said, 'Albert, I hope we have not made a mistake this evening.'

'Surely we won't be punished for telling the truth…' But his tone was uncertain.

****

That summer a second Statuts des Juifs was passed, forbidding Jews from working in certain professions. This didn't affect our family as we were simple folk, merchants and labourers rather than doctors or lawyers.

'Let us not be under the illusion this is all down to Hitler. These laws have been brought in by Pétain,' said Papa. 'No doubt he's looking to pass on the blame for his defeat at the hands of the Germans. We can be sure he is no friend of ours.'

****

Rabbi Epstein came to visit. 'It will be Rosh Hashanah and Yom Kippur soon enough. We're not welcome to congregate in the town hall as we did last year. All other venues we have used since our relocation are now closed and I'm at a loss as to what to do.'

'We could hold the service here,' said Papa, without a moment's hesitation. 'It's out of the way and would not attract attention from the authorities. If we empty the house, we could fit in over a hundred people.'

I looked over to Maman to see what her reaction would be. Unlike the time when Papa had wanted to turn our barn into a chicken slaughterhouse, this time Maman nodded in agreement. 'That is an excellent idea, Albert. I would be happy to offer our home for the holy day services.'

Uncle Isaac was equally enthusiastic. Everyone agreed it felt good to offer a practical solution and to do something, anything, that would help the community in these hard times.

'Rabbi, what do you know of what is going on? What is happening to our people?'

'What I have heard is bad. Thousands of Jews have been arrested in the past few weeks.'

'For what reason?'

'There is no reason. Only for being Jewish refugees.'

'We are Jewish refugees!' exclaimed Maman.

'But we have lived in France for over twenty years and we have applied for French citizenship,' said Papa. No one mentioned that the applications had been made nearly a year ago and we hadn't heard anything yet.

'Do you know of the camp de la route de Limoges?' asked Rabbi Epstein.

'The camp just outside Poitiers?'

'Yes. It is an awful place, taken over by the Germans but being run by the French. They've split it into two. One half is full of gypsies and the other is full of Jews. I've asked the authorities if I may visit the Jewish prisoners – the official name is "internees", but I think we all know these people are prisoners – but they've refused me entry. Thank God for my friend Father Samuel Bisset, the priest of College St Augustus in Poitiers. Father Bisset is permitted to enter the camp every day to visit the gypsies and he has offered to visit the Jewish camp too, even though he doesn't have permission to do so. He has been there on numerous occasions now and brings me news of the prisoners and takes letters to their families in and out. He is a wonderful man.'

'He is indeed a prince among the French people,' agreed Papa. 'But why are you telling us this? Is there anything we can do to help?'

'There is nothing at the moment, but perhaps there will be some way soon. Just knowing that you are offering to help is a comfort. Now, let's discuss the arrangements for the holy days.'

****

Papa took his bicycle and rode to Rabbi Epstein's house in Poitiers, with a wicker bread-basket strapped on his back.

'Albert, welcome. Come in quickly.'

'What a delicious smell!'

'The rebbetzin has been busy baking but we need the baguettes as a disguise. I'm afraid you can't eat them yet.'

Rabbi Epstein led Papa into their modest kitchen where his young wife Rivka was clearing away after her morning baking session. Even with her face smudged with flour, she was a very pretty woman. 'Many people were happy to spare some of their rations so I could make enough bread,' Rivka explained with a sweet smile. It was easy to understand why few would have denied her request.

'Come, come,' the rabbi said, 'let's get this done.' He knelt on the floor, opened one of the kitchen cabinets and took out the bowls and plates. When the cabinet was empty, he pushed firmly on the back wall which came away to reveal a secret space from which he carefully extracted the Torah scroll. It was protected by a royal blue velvet cover, decorated in gold thread with a crown and Hebrew lettering. The rabbi held it in his arms and kissed the cover gently as he would a small child before placing it carefully in the wicker basket while whispering a blessing. 'Let us cover it with the baguettes,' he said, placing loaves in the basket around the scroll. He broke the last in half to cover the top so that the velvet was completely hidden. 'Now, Albert, cycle carefully home and please hide the Torah somewhere safe. I will come on Rosh Hashanah and Yom Kippur, as arranged, to take the services. I have told the congregation; we should have a full house.'

I waited outside our home for Papa to return. He cycled straight into the barn when he arrived. We had already prepared a hiding place, a wooden crate placed in a hole dug into the ground in the far corner of the barn. This corner was also where we hid our money, brought with us from Metz. Papa had buried it a while ago and told me and Samuel where to find it, should we ever need it. I helped my father carefully take the precious cargo out of the basket and lower it gently into the crate. We put a piece of wood on top as a lid to stop the Torah from getting dirty and covered that with a layer of earth. When the job was complete, we took the baguettes into the house and shared them with our cousins.

****

When Rosh Hashanah came, we emptied the house at the last possible moment to minimise the risk of being noticed by the gendarmerie, or by a collaborator like the game warden – anyone who might be snooping around and wonder why our beds were in the barn. Time was of the essence and everyone in the family helped. We left the tables and chairs but everything else was taken out – our beds, our clothes, the kitchen equipment – nothing remained from either our home upstairs or Uncle Isaac's downstairs. Only Bubbe complained when she had to get out of bed early so it could be taken outside.

Rabbi Epstein arrived an hour before the service was due to start and we retrieved the Torah scroll from its hiding place in the barn. We used a kitchen cupboard as the ark to hold the scroll during the service and the kitchen table as the altar. And then people started arriving, dozens at a time. The women went upstairs, and I joined the men downstairs. The children stayed outside because there was simply not enough room for everyone. The mood was sombre. The Jewish New Year is when we think about the year that has passed, ask for forgiveness for our sins and look forward to the year which is beginning. No one could imagine what the new year would hold for us, but we suspected it was going to be just as difficult, if not worse.

Rabbi Epstein led the service. The doors inside were open so his voice would travel all through the house. People were crammed into every possible space, including the hallways and the staircase. When it was time for the Torah reading the rabbi turned to me to get the scrolls. We had covered the kitchen cupboard with a tablecloth to make it something like a proper ark, so Papa held the cloth to one side as I opened the cupboard door. I carefully took the scroll and held it in my arms while Papa removed the blue velvet cover, then we placed it gently on the kitchen table and Rabbi Epstein unrolled it to reveal the reading for Rosh Hashanah.

God visited Sarah. On this day we read of Sarah and Abraham and how God gave them a child when Sarah was ninety years old and Abraham was one hundred years old. God fulfilled his promise to them, to relieve their distress of not being able to have a child. God did not forget them, and He will not forget us. He remembers us His people and He will redeem us just as he did Sarah and Abraham.

After the morning service, Rabbi Epstein helped us bring the furniture back into the house. Normally he would hold a service on the following day too, but these were not normal times so one day would have to suffice.

As he helped Papa carry a bed up the stairs, the rabbi told us of what he had learnt recently. 'There are a number of Jewish children in the camp de la route de Limoges who were arrested along with their parents. Father Bisset sees them when he visits the gypsies in the camp. He has spoken to the families, and they've asked us to help their children. We have a list of the names and ages of their sons and daughters and we intend to get these children released and placed with other families until their parents are freed. We have false documentation for all the children under the age of fifteen…'

'But how? From where?' interrupted Papa.

'Don't worry about that, Albert. What we need are remote homes away from the eyes of the gendarmerie where the children can be looked after.'

'We don't have much room, but we can take in two children. I'm sure they could attend the school too, the teachers are sympathetic. I will find out if they are willing to help.'

'Thank you.'

'There is no need to thank us.'

'Rabbi, I would like to help too. What can I do?' I asked. 'I'm not afraid. Tell me what I can do.'

'Pierre, Son, look after your family. That is the best thing you can do.'

This was not what I wanted to hear. I was frustrated at not being able to fight in some way but had no choice but to do as I was told.

****

A week later we emptied the house again, this time for Yom Kippur. Again the people came, over one hundred adults inside and the children outside. They prayed and cried and asked why, but there were no answers. I didn't usually fast over Yom Kippur, but this year I made an exception, willing to try anything that might help protect my family in the year ahead. I realised that I would need to call on my faith to get me through the hard times. I asked for forgiveness on this Day of Atonement and for God to inscribe the names of my little sisters and brothers – too young to ask for themselves – in the Book of Life. As on Rosh Hashanah, Rabbi Epstein gave me the honour of helping with the Torah scroll and from my position at the top of the room I looked out at the faces of the downtrodden men who came to our house to pray with us. Everyone prayed, whether they believed or not. Everyone had been questioned for the census and their names put on a list. No one had been asked if they believed in God. We were all Jews, whether religious or not, and the camp at Poitiers was filling up with our people as each day passed, arrested at the whim of the French police.

My father invited Rabbi Epstein, his wife and daughter to stay and break the Yom Kippur fast with us at the end of the day. 'I'm sorry we can't offer you a feast like the ones we used to have before the war,' said Maman.

'Nonsense, Rosa, it's really tasty,' said Rivka. 'You're very clever making everything so delicious with the few ingredients we can get these days.'

Maman blushed. She was a proud hostess and it was difficult for her not to provide for her guests as she had in the past.

'We talked about the children from the camp,' said the rabbi. 'There are two sisters I would like to bring to your house, if you are still willing to take them?'

'Absolutely. Can I ask their ages?'

'Eight and ten.'

'The poor little things,' said Maman. 'When will you bring them?'

'Father Bisset has the false papers and is going to the camp tomorrow. He is well liked by the French guards and they have no reason to distrust him. This was his idea; he is a wonderful person. God will protect him.'

'Then let us raise our glasses to Father Bisset,' said Papa, lifting his empty glass.

****

The following day Rabbi Epstein brought the girls to our home. He introduced them as Francine and Ella. 'These are their names now and they have to get used to them as soon as possible,' he explained, smiling kindly at them. He handed Papa their new identification papers. We were not told anything of their family. The girls were thin, pale and filthy; their clothes full of holes gnawed by rats in the camp. They clung to each other and wouldn't look at us. When we spoke to them, they didn't answer. They only whimpered and sobbed for their parents.

Maman set about immediately arranging for the girls to be bathed. She heated water while Samuel and I brought in the metal tub from the barn. We were sent out of the house while the ladies got to the not-insignificant task of washing our guests. Soap was almost impossible to get, so the girls had to be scrubbed with rough washcloths and have their hair painstakingly combed through to remove the head lice. It would have been easier to cut their hair short, but that would have added to their trauma, so Aunt Dora and cousin Simone did their best with a comb. Afterwards they rubbed on eucalyptus oil to kill any lice that remained. In the past they'd used gasoline, but there was none to be had, which was probably a blessing in disguise.

Maman scrubbed their clothes and tried to mend the holes as well as she could. Unfortunately, there wasn't much we could offer them from our own clothing. But we gave them our bed and Samuel and I slept on the floor. Maman sat with the girls and spoke softly to them. She tried to stroke their newly washed hair, but they moved out of her reach. We told ourselves that it was to be expected. They were traumatised by what they had lived through at the camp and by being separated from their parents. But their silence conveyed a terrible fear, far worse than any words could express.

****

After a few days which the girls spent clinging to each other and crying, cowering in the farthest corner of the house and having nightmares all through the night, Rabbi Epstein came to take them away. He had found another family in Vichy France, considered to be a safer area, who would take care of them. We all felt a sense of relief once they left... and then guilt for not having tried harder.

****

'But, Papa! Please try to understand.'

We heard shouting downstairs and Maman sent me to find out what was happening. Cousin Simone and her husband Leon were sitting with my aunt and uncle around the kitchen table. They all looked distressed.

'Never!' shouted Uncle Isaac. Then, noticing me, he lowered his voice, 'What do you want, Pierre?'

'Maman sent me down to ask you not to shout so loud, you're upsetting my sisters.'

'Of course. Wait... do you know of this madness?'

'What madness?' Everything seemed mad lately.

'Simone and Leon plan to cross the demarcation line.'

'We didn't tell Pierre yet,' said Leon.

'So tell him your brilliant idea!'

'Your cousin Elias in Lyon said we would be safer in Vichy France. Innocent Jews are being arrested and put in that camp in Poitiers for no reason. Whole families are being kept there. Simone and I have our two children to consider. Things are only going to get worse. Now is the time to leave.'

Aunt Dora was silent. She looked down at the dishcloth in her hands, tears falling onto the kitchen table.

I kept quiet, but I admired my cousins for trying to create their own fate. I considered asking to go with them but realised I could never leave my family, particularly my mother and sisters.

'You know it is not permitted to cross the demarcation line. Anyone caught crossing is arrested, and then you will surely end up in a camp like the one at Poitiers – or worse. You're crazy! The Vichy government are the ones responsible for introducing the anti-Jewish laws, what makes you think you'll be any better off over there?' said Uncle Isaac.

'Elias told us. I can assure you we have not taken this decision lightly. Simone and I have discussed it at length, and we will be leaving soon. I know someone who will help us cross. Anyone who wants to come with us is welcome, but no one will stop us leaving.'

****

Uncle Isaac and Aunt Dora were distraught at the thought of their daughter and her family leaving; their only consolation was that Elias would help them settle in Lyon once they completed the five-hundred-kilometre journey. My aunt and cousin spent the rest of the day weeping at the prospect of being separated. We were all worried about them going; only Bubbe and the youngest children were oblivious to what was happening.

Simone, Leon and their two children left early the next morning.

'When will I see you again?' sobbed Aunt Dora, clinging to her daughter before hugging her grandchildren.

'I don't know, Maman,' wept Simone.

'We promise to get word to you as soon as we arrive at Elias's house,' said Leon.

'But how…?' asked Uncle Isaac, but they were already halfway down the path, Simone holding her children's hands tightly, head bowed and not once looking back.

Once safely over the demarcation line, they would travel by bus to their destination. If everything went according to plan, we would receive message of their safe arrival within days. We were told that the same people who would help them cross over would also deliver the message. I was desperate to find out more of these people who were helping others in the fight against the authorities, but Leon refused to tell me anything 'for my own good'.

Three, four, five days passed and no message arrived. We told ourselves it was still early and nothing to be concerned about. After a week Uncle Isaac and Aunt Dora were besides themselves with worry. They wrote to Elias and, weeks later, received a reply with the news that his sister had not reached Lyon and Elias had not heard anything from her. We didn't know who to speak to. Leon was the only person in the family with any connection to the people who were to help them cross, and no one contacted us.

Uncle Isaac drew another blank after asking around in Poitiers. I was shocked to see him unable to hold back his tears as he reported back to us; we all relied on him and Papa to be the strong ones who would see us through these terrible times. 'Word is there was a crackdown on security at the demarcation line around the time they left. Prior to that, people had been crossing freely for months. The Germans decided to post more guards at the border with strict instructions to arrest anyone who tried to leave without a visa. We don't know if they had visas, but Leon was very secretive about everything. Damn him!'

This may have been the first time I heard my uncle curse.

'Oh my darlings. Will we ever see them again?' cried Aunt Dora.

'We must hope they crossed the border and settled somewhere else,' consoled Uncle Isaac, composing himself as he held his wife's hand. 'Yes, I'm sure that's what happened and they're all fine.'

Over the following months we still hoped for some news of our cousins. Papa asked Rabbi Epstein if he could find out anything, but nothing came back. Elias wrote again asking if any news. It was as though they had simply disappeared.

Samuel

Life felt different. Claude and I went to school as usual and played with our friends, but it was difficult to have fun when our cousins had vanished. I got angry with my pals who carried on as normal, but they hadn't lost anyone from their families. Simone's children were younger, and I used to get annoyed when Maman told us we couldn't leave them out of our games and had to play something gentle so they could join in, but now they were gone and I really missed them. We were all worried about them. My aunt and uncle were so upset, Aunt Dora cried all the time. What had happened to them, and would it happen to me next?

We had even less to eat. The Germans took their pick of the crops and livestock that the farmers had managed to keep till now. There was a pond that was used to farm carp, looked after so carefully by the farmer. Claude and I had always enjoyed seeing the fish swim up to the surface with their huge mouths wide open in the hope we were there to feed them. Some luck that would be; we hardly had enough to feed ourselves. We'd watch the farmer when he came to open the sluice and catch the carp in his nets as the water ran from the pond into the nearby stream. He would carefully return the smaller fish to the pond and take the big ones to the fish market in Poitiers. Sometimes he'd let me help him, when there was a particularly wriggly fish looking for an escape!

A group of German soldiers passing through the village discovered the pond and noticed the fish. The thugs threw a grenade into the water and collected the dead fish that floated to the surface. How I wished I could throw a grenade back at them.

We were all hungry. Claude and I would go with Maman to keep her company as she waited patiently in line to try to buy food and did our best to cheer her up when we were forced to return home empty-handed. The black market was thriving. People were spending their life savings on feeding their family. Jewellery and valuable heirlooms were sold for a fraction of their worth for a chicken or piece of cheese. Papa told us, 'Survival is the only thing that matters now.'

****

'For goodness sake!' said Maman, sucking her finger where she had stabbed it with a sewing needle. Claude and I had arrived home from school and found her sitting under the cherry tree with Bubbe. Our sisters were playing with their rag doll Bernadette, handed down by a cousin. They shared everything, and I had never seen them fight with each other, unlike Claude and me – we loved a good spat! It was a warm and sunny afternoon in June, yet the mood seemed dark. Maman had her sewing kit next to her, at least what little was left of the buttons, needles and threads after darning and altering our clothes since we had first arrived in Sarry. She was working on some yellow patches and appeared to be having trouble with them.

When Maman saw us arrive she seemed to brighten a bit. 'Hello, boys. How was school?'

Claude gave our mother a hug and kiss, as he always did. 'Madame Noyer said my reading is getting good, but I need to practise more at home if I can. She told me I can take home books from school if we don't have anything for me to read.'

'You're very lucky to have such a nice teacher. Next time I get the ingredients I shall bake some biscuits for you to take her,' said Maman, although she had not been able to get any sugar or butter for ages now.

'What are you sewing?' asked Claude.

'Oh, it's nothing,' said Maman with a strained smile. 'We have to wear one of these silly things on our clothes. Right here, over our heart,' and she placed her hand on her chest.

'Ha! No one is going to tell *me* what to wear!' announced Bubbe.

'What is it?' asked Claude.

'It's a Star of David,' Maman said as she held up one of the yellow patches for us to see. Her hands trembled.

'What does it say?'

'You tell me. You're the one doing well with your reading!'

'OK. J-U-I-F. *Juif.* Jew? Why do we have to wear that?'

'You know what, these days it is better not to ask why. This is the law now and if we do what we are told then we will be fine. If the Germans want us to wear a yellow star on our clothes, then we will. What harm can it do us? Now, hand me your jackets please so I can sew on these stars. I have a lot to do. Thank goodness I don't have to worry about your sisters' clothes too.'

'Why not?'

'It's only the law for adults and children over six years old.'

'Not fair!' exclaimed Claude.

'No indeed,' agreed Maman. 'It really is not fair at all.'

The next day, Claude and I went to school with a yellow star on our jacket pockets, as did the other Jewish children. Madame Noyer called us into class.

'Good morning, children.'

'Good morning, Madame,' we all chorused.

'This yellow star has no place in my classroom and I won't allow it to be worn here. I suggest all of you take off your jackets – yellow star or no yellow star – and put them under your desks next to your gas masks.'

We did as we were told.

'Be careful not to put your dirty boots on your jackets or I will have your mothers coming to see me! In my classroom all my students are treated the same. Religion does not make a difference to your schoolwork and therefore I do not need to see any stars other than the stars I put in your workbooks for excellent writing! And *that* is the end of the subject.'

When it was time to go home, I put my jacket back on, but, before leaving the classroom, Madame Noyer called me up to her desk.

'Samuel, I suggest you throw that yellow rag away.'

'But Madame, Maman only sewed it on yesterday and it made her quite angry to do so. I don't want to upset her by removing it; she might need to sew it on again.'

'Very well. We do not want to upset your mother but if you leave it on please make sure you take your jacket off before you come into my classroom. I shall tell the same to all the children.'

'Yes, Madame. I don't care about wearing it anyway. We all know who is Jewish and who isn't, but we're no different.'

'That's right, Samuel. You may leave now and please send my regards to your mother.'

Samuel

Sarry
July 1942

When school finished for the summer, Claude and I were sad to say goodbye to our wonderful teacher. The school in Sarry was to close, so Claude and I would go instead to school in nearby Cerneux, where I would graduate to high school. I hoped my new teacher would be as kind. Meanwhile, I looked forward to the long summer break.

It turned out to be a pretty hot summer after what had been a freezing winter. On one particular day the temperature hardly dropped at all after the sun went down. Supper was the usual cabbage soup with a few carrots and potatoes and the added treat of a tiny piece of chicken mince which Maman had queued for hours to buy. She paid for it with one of her few remaining pieces of jewellery; money was practically worthless now. I promised Maman I would buy her new jewellery when I was older. After supper the twins went to sleep while my brothers and I played a card game. Maman read a book she had borrowed from a friend and Papa sat looking at an old newspaper which had been passed on by a neighbour.

We missed our radio terribly. We had been forced to turn it in to the Germans a few months earlier. Signs had been posted outside the ticket office of the railway station announcing that all radio sets were to be handed in to the authorities and threatened severe punishment for anyone who didn't follow the order. Papa had suggested hiding ours so we could listen to it in secret.

'But, Albert, why risk our safety because of a radio? It's not worth it. Please just get rid of it. We'll still have each other, and that is all that matters.' And, as usual, Papa did as Maman asked.

It was hot indoors, but our house was so isolated we felt safe keeping the windows open, so there was at least a slight breeze.

Claude and I were playing the best game of hide and seek. I found a little cupboard to hide in and he had been looking for me for so long that I was beginning to get bored. Then someone started banging on the cupboard door and I heard shouting. I woke up and realised it was the middle of the night and I had been asleep. I was in bed and the game of hide and seek had been nothing more than a dream... but the banging continued as did the shouting.

'Öffne die tür!' 'Open the door!'

Papa was out of bed.

'Stay here,' he said to us all.

He went downstairs as Uncle Isaac came sleepily out of his ground-floor bedroom. They opened the front door together. Bubbe and the twins hadn't woken, but the rest of us watched from the top of the stairs as two German officers with rifles barged their way into our home. Through the front door I could see German soldiers and French police waiting by a truck right outside. It was one of those military trucks that drove along the Nationale 10 which we could hear in the classroom so I couldn't imagine how this one hadn't woken us. They must have turned the engine off and coasted down the driveway.

'I am looking for Jankiel Laskowski,' one of the officers said in a harsh voice that made me flinch.

'That's me, but my name is Albert now.'

'Jankiel Laskowski,' repeated the officer, 'I have a warrant for your arrest. You must come with me now.'

We were shocked and looked to Maman for reassurance, but her face was unreadable. She was hardly breathing.

'But I have done nothing wrong, Monsieur. I am an honest and law-abiding citizen.'

'That is a lie. Our records state you are Polish…'

'I was born in Poland, but I've lived and worked in France for over twenty years. My life is here, my children were born here. My application for French citizenship is being processed.'

'THAT IS ENOUGH! None of this is of any interest to me. Your application for French citizenship was denied. You disobeyed an order to return to Poland and join the army, so your Polish citizenship has been revoked. You are now stateless and, as such, you're considered a threat. You may pack a small suitcase to bring with you – I suggest you bring some warm clothing as it can get very cold where you are going.'

'Do you mean he will be away all winter? Where are you taking him?' demanded Pierre from our viewpoint at the top of the stairs.

Maman grabbed him and begged him to be quiet.

'Don't worry, Son, I'll sort this nonsense. It must be a mistake,' said Papa.

A dreadful silence followed, quickly broken by the German officer shouting, 'Now! You have five minutes to pack your belongings or you won't be allowed to bring anything.'

The soldiers outside took a step closer to the house, their rifles raised in the air. I couldn't believe what was happening. Papa hurried upstairs followed by the two Germans. As they entered the bedroom, Papa spoke quietly to the officers and he gave them items which they stuffed in their jacket pockets. Then he turned to us. There were so many things to say, so many questions to ask, but there was no time. Maman recovered her composure first and helped Papa pack. 'Take this photograph of us all,' she said, with tears on her cheeks.

'When will you come back?' asked Claude, usually the quietest of us but now the only one who managed to find his voice.

'I'll be back before you know it. Pierre, you help Uncle Isaac look after the family until I return.'

We all kissed and hugged him. The twins were half-awake by now. They didn't understand what was going on but their eyes were big as they looked around at us all weeping. Only Papa didn't cry. He held us tight and then, when one of the officers shouted, 'Come now!' he stood up, holding his head high and put on his jacket with the yellow star on the pocket. Taking his small suitcase, he walked down the stairs, nodding to Uncle Isaac and Aunt Dora on his way out of the door. Flanked by the policemen, he was led into the back of the truck. They started its engine and drove off, leaving the outside of the house in darkness as we stood there in stunned silence.

Finally Uncle Isaac spoke. 'There is nothing we can do tonight. Go to bed and, first thing in the morning, Pierre and I will go to Poitiers and sort this out.'

'What on earth is all this racket about? Some of us are trying to sleep!' boomed Bubbe, who had at last woken up but was without a clue as to what had happened.

****

Pierre and Uncle Isaac went as soon as the curfew was lifted, while the rest of us waited anxiously at home. It was another hot day but Maman begged Claude and I not to leave the house and we did as she asked. We spent most of the time sitting at the table, not knowing what to do with ourselves, apart from Maman who walked constantly, to and fro.

My brother and uncle came back at midday.

'We went to the police station and they told us that Albert is being held in the camp de la route de Limoges. Then we went to see Rabbi Epstein who promised to speak to Father Bisset. He'll try to find out what is happening. There were quite a few people with the rabbi: Albert wasn't the only one arrested last night. There have been arrests all over France.'

'I don't know what to think. Does that make it better or worse, that Albert wasn't the only one?' said Maman, pacing up and down as she had been doing all morning.

'Better, I think,' said my uncle, although he did not sound very sure.

****

Rabbi Epstein came to our home the next day.

'It's not good, I'm afraid,' he said. 'Albert has already been taken from the camp at Poitiers. A large group of men and women were put on buses and driven away. We haven't been able to find out where they were taken. I'm so sorry.'

We were stunned by this dreadful news. I had been planning to go to Poitiers to see if I could spot Papa through the barbed wire. We'd written letters to him in the hope they could be smuggled into the camp. Now all we could do was wait for him to get a message back to us, from wherever he'd been taken.

Maman was so distraught she could hardly speak. Aunt Dora tried to lighten the mood: 'It'll be like old times in Metz when your papa was always going away. We can pretend he's away on business and coming home soon.' Maman just stared at the wall.

Pierre

The news was that thousands more Jews had been arrested: 13,000 men, women and children in Paris had been taken on the same night as Papa. Maman was inconsolable and while it was my priority to look after her and my brothers and sisters, I was desperate to find a way to both bring Papa back and fight the Germans.

Four weeks after Papa was arrested, the German officers and French police returned to our house. It was the middle of the night again, the same loud knocking and shouting at the front door instantly striking fear into our hearts. I scrambled out of bed, told Maman and the children to stay upstairs, pulled on a pair of trousers and went downstairs to open the front door with Uncle Isaac. With Papa gone I was now the head of our family. The same two German officers stood there with their stooges waiting behind them by the backed-up truck which, once again, we had not heard arrive.

One of the officers said, 'We are here for Anna Hofman and Gabriel Hofman.'

Aunt Dora wailed from inside their ground-floor bedroom.

Uncle Isaac said, 'Why them? They are only young. Take me instead. I am strong. I can work hard.'

'That is not possible. Anna Hofman and Gabriel Hofman. Are they here?'

'Yes, we're here.' My cousins came to the front door.

'NO! I won't allow it!' Aunt Dora pulled her son and daughter back.

'Maman. It will be OK. We have done nothing wrong,' said Anna.

'No, please. Not them.' Aunt Dora put herself between her children and the Germans, who were tiring of this family drama and motioned to the armed French police to come closer. They were instructed to forcefully grab hold of Anna and Gabriel. The officers stood in the doorway, holding back my helpless uncle and aunt in the house. Aunt Dora fell to the floor, sobbing hysterically as her children were taken away and when Uncle bent down to comfort her, one of the officers hit him on the head with the butt of his rifle. Aunt Dora screamed as her husband fell to the floor next to her. Meanwhile, Bubbe had started singing loudly some sort of prayer which only led to the confusion. Before we knew it, the truck had gone, and my cousins with it. Uncle Isaac recovered from being struck, but he was a broken man. There was no logic to this cruelty. We couldn't understand why Anna and Gabriel had been taken.

The following days were sheer torture. Cousin Simone and her family, Papa and now Anna and Gabriel too had been taken. I wondered who would be next. We thought about leaving, but where would we go? Nowhere was safe now, and we should stay in case the others returned.

Several weeks passed as the excruciating dissection of our family continued. The officers returned, this time with a list.

'The following people will come with us now: Isaac Hofman; Clara Hofman; Dora Hofman; Rosa Laskowski; Georgette Laskowski; Henriette Laskowski.'

I waited for my name to be called, but the officer continued: 'You are to come with us. We will give you a few minutes to prepare your belongings.' I turned to Uncle Isaac but he had already gone to organise his wife and elderly mother. I looked up the stairs and saw Maman and my brothers staring down at me in confusion. I ran up to them.

'What is happening? Why are they taking you, Maman?' whispered Samuel.

'Why are they taking the twins and not us?' asked Claude. 'I want to go with you too,' and he grabbed hold of her tightly around the waist.

Maman gently released herself from his hold and gathered us around her. 'Listen to me. I don't know why they didn't call your names, but we must thank God for that. I'm sure they will take us to be with Papa, then he can look after us and you boys must stay here and look after each other. Now, help me get the twins ready.'

We helped our little sisters get dressed, while Maman packed a small suitcase. The girls each held a hand of their beloved doll Bernadette. 'Make sure you don't pull Bernadette too tight,' Claude said, 'you wouldn't want to pull her arms off!'

'We promise,' said the girls sweetly in unison, each releasing their grip on the doll slightly.

'Maman, this is madness. I won't allow you to go. I promised Papa I would protect you,' I said.

'We can't refuse to go. I'll send a letter as soon as I know where we end up. Let's say goodbye here,' said Maman, 'I don't want them to see us.' She hugged Claude and Samuel and then last of all me, whispering in my ear as she held me tight, 'Look after your brothers, Pierre. I know you will.'

She went downstairs with the twins following closely behind, clumsily and sleepily climbing down one stair at a time. I told Samuel and Claude to stay upstairs while I went down to watch our mother leave. The Germans just ignored me; my name was not on their list and so they had no interest in me. It was inexplicable – why weren't the rest of us on their list? Maman walked silently out the front door with the girls in her arms. The policemen nodded towards the back of the waiting truck. Maman lifted my little sisters, one at a time, onto the vehicle before she climbed on herself and disappeared behind the tarpaulin.

Isaac, Dora and Bubbe hadn't come out so the German officers went inside to hurry them up.

I heard screaming and crying from inside the house. One of the Germans rushed out looking agitated and barked at two of the policemen to come in with him, leaving the other two guarding the truck. Uncle Isaac and Aunt Dora were pushed out through the front door, wearing their hats and coats and carrying a small suitcase each. Aunt Dora was crying. They were ushered onto the truck, but Bubbe was still in the house, sitting in her chair and refusing to leave.

'Madame Clara Hofman, you must come with us now!'

'I am not going anywhere!' she screamed, her blindness sparing her the knowledge that there were rifles pointing at her.

'Madame, I order you to get out of that chair!' shouted the police officer, but it only fuelled her fury.

'NEVER! You can go to Hell!'

'Men, carry this woman to the truck!' came the order.

As well as being senile, Bubbe was incontinent and she soiled herself in the stress of the moment. As the smell reached the policemen, looks of disgust spread across their faces. They struggled to lift her due to her size, eventually having to call in a third policeman to assist. When they carried her outside she kicked and spat, swearing in Yiddish at her captors. Somehow, they managed to get her onto the truck. We could hear her tirade even after the engine started up and the truck drove away.

Then there was silence. Only the three of us were left, and we had no idea why.

****

There was no time to waste; I'd learnt that when Papa was arrested. As soon as the sun rose, I ran to a neighbour to borrow their little trailer which I hooked on to the back of my bicycle and rode as fast as I could into Poitiers. I left Samuel and Claude at home and ordered them to stay hidden and not to leave the house or answer the door for anyone.

In Poitiers, I went directly to the headquarters of the Special Police. I was fuelled by adrenaline and acting on instinct. I left my bicycle in the street and asked the German guard in the doorway to look after it while I spoke to the officer in charge. The guard looked startled, but nodded and told me to go upstairs. I ran up the stairs two at a time and knocked on the door.

'*Entrée*!'

I opened the door without hesitation and went into the office. 'Good morning, Monsieur,' I said, taking off my beret. He was younger than my father, of average height and slim with short fair hair. He didn't look particularly evil. He looked puzzled, or perhaps amused, to see me in his office.

'What do you want, young man?' He had a strong German accent.

'My mother and two sisters were arrested last night. I think they were taken to the camp de la route de Limoges. I would like you to release my sisters, please. They are so young.' I was speaking very quickly.

'I see. Sit down. Now, tell me. Where do you live and what are the names of your sisters?' The officer spoke slowly and purposefully.

'We live in Sarry and my sisters are Henriette and Georgette Laskowski. They are twins. Just four years old.'

'Hmmm. Yes, that is very young... Let me think what I can do.'

As the officer sat at his desk, I looked around the room for the first time. There was a framed photograph of Hitler on the wall behind the desk and a large red and black Nazi flag hanging from the ceiling. The officer himself wore a red and black swastika armband. I realised he must be quite a high-ranking Gestapo officer. My heart, already racing, lurched as it suddenly occurred to me that I might have just put myself and my brothers in danger.

Finally he spoke again.

'There is a restaurant in town called Café du Jet d'Eau. Can you tell me what it would be called in German?'

It seemed an odd thing to ask.

'That name in German would be der Wasserstrahl.' I wasn't sure if it was correct, but I hoped so.

'Bravo! Your German is very good – you've earned a reward. But I can't help you. I didn't arrest anyone, it was the French police so now you must go and ask them to release your sisters.' He got up and walked towards the door. It seemed he had tired of his little game. I muttered some thanks and quickly left. I ran down to the street, grabbed my bicycle and cycled to the French police station to tell them what the German officer had said.

The policeman on duty looked unsure, but wasn't going to take a chance on acting against the orders of the Gestapo, and so he wrote a note stating that he would release my sisters. 'Now you have to get this note authorised by the German officer… otherwise it is worthless,' he said.

For a moment, I hesitated. I'd been so relieved to get out of the Gestapo office, now it seemed terrifying to have to go back there. It felt like they were using me to play tennis, with me as the ball. I headed straight back without giving myself more time to think.

I ran up the stairs and knocked on the office door again. When he called me back in, I put the note down in front of the Gestapo officer.

'Excuse me, Monsieur. Here is the note from the police saying that my sisters can be released. Can you please authorise it?' I tried to sound as respectful as I could, unsure if this would work and now certain of the danger I was putting myself in.

He picked up the note to read it. He put the paper down again, looked at me curiously, and then opened the top drawer of his desk. I expected him to take out a pistol and arrest me, or shoot me on the spot, but instead he lifted out a block of wood and rubber, placed it first on a red inkpad and then stamped the note authorising the release of my sisters. He picked up the paper again, and I held my breath – I wouldn't have been surprised if he had picked up a cigarette lighter and burned the note in front of my eyes... but he didn't. He just held it out for me. 'Thank you, Monsieur,' I managed to utter.

I grabbed the paper and ran out. I retrieved my bicycle and rode to the camp de la route de Limoges. It was only now that it occurred to me that I had no proof that my mother and sisters were even there. Could the episode with the Gestapo officer and French police have been a farce for their amusement? I blanched at the thought. I was drenched in sweat from the effort of the morning. I hadn't thought to eat anything, and started to feel dizzy.

When I got to the camp a French guard came out of the gatehouse at the entrance. I handed over the stamped piece of paper. He glanced at it and told me to wait. He went back into the gatehouse and left through a door at the back to walk over to a small nearby building. In a panic, I paced up and down outside the double fence of barbed wire. From where I stood I couldn't see anyone inside, but I could see the beginning of the barracks: dozens of buildings with wooden walls and corrugated-iron roofs that stood in long rows.

Suddenly I caught sight of figures in the distance. As they approached, I could make out a woman and two small children, along with a guard. Maman was marched to the gate with Henriette and Georgette doing their best to keep up. They were still holding their doll between them. Maman seemed to have aged years in the few hours since her arrest. Her face was ashen, and her beautiful almond-shaped eyes had lost their sparkle, but when she spotted me waiting, I saw a glimmer of hope return to her. My sisters started running towards me. 'Careful, girls. Don't touch the fence, the spikes are dangerous!' I called.

They stopped and returned to the safety of our mother's shadow.

'Pierre, my darling. How are you? How are your brothers?' Her voice was strained.

'They're fine, Maman. How are you?'

'I'm alright,' she said, though she didn't seem it.

I was overjoyed in that moment, but then just as suddenly the joy was taken away when the guard pushed the girls through the gate and locked it behind them with Maman still on the other side.

Henriette and Georgette immediately started crying for their mother, reaching out towards the vicious wire that separated us. They hadn't even had an opportunity to say goodbye.

'Excuse me, sir. These little girls should not be separated from their mother. Can you please let her go too?' I asked the guard.

'The order only permits the release of the children. You should consider yourselves lucky even for that,' he replied.

'Hush, girls. Go with your brother now. Everything will be fine. Pierre, you've done well. Take good care of your sisters. I love you all!' Maman shouted to us over her shoulder as she was roughly pushed back towards the barracks and out of sight.

****

'They're back!' shouted Claude from the upstairs window as I cycled down the path to the house, with our sisters sitting in the little trailer behind.

'Well done, Pierre!' cried Samuel, running out of the house and rushing over to give the girls a hug.

Samuel and Claude helped their sisters out of the trailer. 'Where is Maman? Is she walking home?' asked Claude.

'Maman is still in Poitiers. They only let the girls out.' I was crushed with the guilt of only having asked for my sisters to be released. I had saved the twins, but at what cost? I had abandoned my own mother.

'So, we're all alone,' said Claude.

'At least we're together, and we have each other,' said Samuel. We agreed that was the most important thing at that moment.

A few days passed. I was so busy I didn't even have time to write to Maman. We were hungry and the girls needed help with almost everything. I knew our parents would want me to make sure that my brothers continued going to school, which left me to take on the roles of both breadwinner and homemaker. It was an impossible task, so I called a family meeting.

'Madame Leblanc has agreed to help us by looking after Henriette and Georgette. I found work with a mason preparing bricks and roof tiles and I will pay for their keep with the money I earn. They will be close, practically next door, and we can see them every day.'

The girls went to live with Madame Leblanc – the miller's wife – and her daughter Marcia, who promised she would look after the girls as if they were her own sisters. It was the best arrangement possible under the circumstances. I hoped Maman would approve.

****

After our cousins had been taken away it didn't seem right to go downstairs and use their things, except for food left behind which would have gone bad or been eaten by mice. We struggled to keep our part of the house clean and tidy so, after a while, we decided to move downstairs. By the time Rabbi Epstein came to visit a few weeks later, the whole house was a mess.

'How are you managing?' he asked, looking around at the chaos.

'Probably not as good as I should,' I admitted.

'Anyone would find it difficult under these circumstances. You did incredibly well to get your sisters released and looked after by a neighbour. I'm sure your parents will be proud when they hear how you've managed.'

I flinched when he spoke of my parents, as if he'd slapped me across the cheek.

'Pierre, I have some news about your family from Father Bisset. It's not good, I'm afraid. They have all been moved from Poitiers to Drancy, a large camp outside Paris.'

'What will happen to them now?' I asked.

'I don't know. The minute I have more information I will tell you.'

This was terrible news. I had been to the camp in Poitiers a couple of times to see if I could spot Maman or maybe my aunt or uncle through the barbed-wire fence, but I hadn't been able to see anyone. I had planned to go and try again that week.

Rabbi Epstein continued. 'I am rabbi for the Union générale des israélites de France, the UGIF, in the region. What do you think of asking them to help you look after the boys? They can find a foster family for them to stay with.'

I thought about it for a moment. 'The UGIF was set up by the Vichy government. Why should we trust them?'

'That's a good question,' said Rabbi Epstein. 'The organisation was set up by the government, but it's run by Jews to help Jewish people in circumstances like yours. They can be trusted.'

As Rabbi Epstein left that day I promised him I would consider asking the UGIF for help. Everything was so uncertain. The first few days after the arrests we were expecting everyone to come home and tell us it had been a terrible mistake. What reason could anyone have for arresting my mother, my grandmother, my aunt, uncle and cousins? It was crazy. And why did they leave us boys but take the girls? It didn't make any sense at all. We were sure it was an error someone had made on one of those damn lists.

I wanted to ask Papa or Maman what to do – they always knew best – but they had been taken away and I was left in charge at just sixteen years old. Georgette and Henriette were thriving with Madame Leblanc and I reasoned a similar set-up could work well for Samuel and Claude too, allowing me to concentrate on earning enough money so we could all live together again soon while waiting for the rest of the family to come home. I decided I would go to the UGIF for help.

My brothers were not happy with this idea. Samuel insisted he was old enough to look after himself and Claude and the home while I went to work. He put up a convincing argument, but I knew that our parents would want him to concentrate on his schooling and he knew that, as the eldest, I had the final say.

Samuel and Claude were placed with a Catholic foster family, the Laurents, in nearby Cerneux, and their keep paid by the UGIF. The family seemed nice and the boys had recently started school in the town and were going there most days anyway. It was agreed they would make the one-hour walk back to Sarry each Sunday and we would all spend the day together with Henriette and Georgette. I was sure I had made the right decision and that our parents would be pleased when they came home.

Pierre

On a cold February morning Rabbi Epstein was arrested, along with his wife and daughter. This was a terrible blow for the Jewish community although, by that time, there were practically no Jews left in the area. Most had disappeared during the night, so it was hard to know if they had escaped for their own safety or been arrested. There were a few children left, mostly staying with foster families arranged by the UGIF. This arrangement worked well for us until May, when a letter arrived. I was surprised to read that my brothers and sisters were to go to Paris. The letter stated that they should be taken to a UGIF children's home in Montmartre. I was devastated by the idea of them going so far away. It would be difficult for me to travel such a long way to visit them and almost impossible to find work that would allow me to live nearby, but I had to trust the UGIF knew best with so many children in its care and that I would find a way to see them.

The following day I went to Cerneux after work. The boys were happily helping Madame Laurent with some chores and excited to see me. I was invited in and, as we sat around the kitchen table, I was given a cup of something which had been offered as coffee but tasted like warm water.

'This arrived yesterday,' I said, pulling the letter out of my jacket pocket.

'Is it news of Maman and Papa?' asked Claude.

'Unfortunately not,' I said. My brothers both looked deflated. 'This letter is from the Jewish Agency and it says you must go to Paris.'

'Will the girls go too?' asked Samuel.

'It says that all of you must go together.'

'And you, Pierre?'

'It only says that you four must go. I'm seventeen, not a child anymore. I have to stay and work.'

'I'm not a child either,' said Samuel. 'I am past bar mitzvah age and I am a man!'

'Yes, dear, but you still need someone to remind you to wash behind your ears sometimes,' said Madame Laurent kindly.

'Ha ha! But seriously, Samuel, I think you should go so you can look after the others,' I said.

'Yes, you're right!' he replied proudly. He was clearly pleased with this new role of guardian to his younger brother and sisters.

'I shall be sorry to see you boys go,' said Madame Laurent, her voice quivering slightly. 'It has been lovely having you here. Does the letter say how you are to travel to Paris? It's not that easy to get there these days. I believe the only way is to go on the night train and Jews are not allowed to travel outside the region or go out after curfew!'

'I hadn't thought about it yet, but that is going to be a problem,' I said.

'Let me speak to my brother who is a policeman,' said Madame Laurent. 'Maybe he'll have some ideas. Come back in a few days and I'll tell you what he says.'

****

I went to see Henriette and Georgette the following evening. It was nearly their bedtime when I arrived, but I played with them for half an hour, refreshed by their innocent company. They didn't ask about our mother and father and I didn't mention them, relieved not to have to disappoint them with the lack of news. Madame Leblanc looked after them well. She had encouraged them from the beginning to call her 'Maman' and they happily did so. One month before, we had celebrated their fifth birthday together; although difficult to find the ingredients, Madame Leblanc had made a cake and lemonade for the gathering.

After I helped put the girls to bed, I told Madame Leblanc of the letter from the UGIF. 'It says the girls must go to Paris with Samuel and Claude.'

'Well thank goodness they won't be by themselves, the poor mites,' she said, wiping away a tear with the corner of her apron. 'I will miss them very much. They are like two rays of sunshine in this horrible world. They are happy here and now they are to be moved again. Who knows what this place in Paris will be like? Why don't you leave them with me? I will look after them as if they were my own. Who will realise they are not in Paris? There will be hundreds of Jewish children there whose parents have been arrested.'

'We already know too well about the lists of names which the French police kindly compiled for their German friends,'

I said bitterly. 'My worry is that the boys will be punished if the girls are not with them. I appreciate how upset you are – I am too, but they will be together and well looked after by the Jewish Agency.'

'Hmm, not as well looked after as they would be with me,' said Madame Leblanc.

'No indeed, Madame. I cannot thank you enough for your trouble. I don't know when they will be leaving yet so I would be grateful if they can stay here until we have made the travel arrangements.'

'But of course! What do you think, that I would throw them out into the street?'

****

I returned to Cerneux after Madame Laurent had spoken to her brother, as promised.

'He said I should travel to Paris with the children on the night train,' she said.

'But, Madame, I can't ask you to do that. I should go.'

'It would be extremely risky for you to travel. It is going to be difficult enough to get the children there safely, but it will be easier for me than for you.'

'Madame, I can't allow you to do this for us. It's too much to ask.'

'And if you get caught? No, I will take them and that is final.'

She was right, of course. 'Thank you,' I said.

'Do you have money to pay for the tickets? My brother also said I should take some tobacco to give to the police on the train. They are sure to ask for our papers; doing the

120

Germans' dirty work but happy to look the other way if there is a bribe on offer.'

'I'll take care of it.' The time had come to use the money Papa had hidden for emergencies, as my modest wages would not cover these expenses.

I returned to the house in Sarry. It had ceased being a real home some time ago. I was the only person living there now and, although I didn't spend much time at home, the nights alone were difficult. Sometimes I thought I could hear Maman humming as she cooked and cleaned and more than once I had to look twice having imagined Papa sitting at the kitchen table drinking a glass of wine.

I took a lamp and went into the barn. I found the spot in the corner at the back and dug up the box of money. It was a relief to find there was more than I needed. I left the rest in the box and reburied it for whatever the future might bring. It was a pity we hadn't been able to persuade Bubbe to hide her money there too. I smiled to myself as I remembered her carrying all her wealth in a bag tied around her waist, hidden under her skirts, before the war. When the war began and before senility took hold of her – or perhaps because of it – she entrusted her treasure to Rabbi Epstein. She was convinced her bag of money and jewellery would be safe with the rabbi and he committed to give it back it to her after the war. I hoped they would both get to return one day, and the rabbi could fulfil his promise to Bubbe.

****

With the money safely in my pocket, I went the next day to buy the train tickets and had little problem finding someone

121

to sell me a carton of tobacco on the black market at an exorbitant price.

I collected the girls from the mill where Madame Leblanc bid them a prolonged and emotional farewell; this time there were no guards with rifles hurrying us. I wished Maman had had that same opportunity to say goodbye. Madame Leblanc tried to put on a brave face so as not to upset the girls, but without much success, and the girls wept too. This was the second 'Maman' they had been forced to leave. Then it was time to put them in the bicycle trailer. I rode them over to Cerneux where Samuel and Claude were ready to leave. Now it was my turn to say goodbye. I couldn't stop thinking of Maman's last words to me, 'Take good care of your sisters.' She had entrusted them to me and now I was sending them off to Paris. I hoped I was doing the right thing.

We were already running a little late because of Madame Leblanc's endless hugs, so I kept my farewell brief. I hugged my brothers and sisters in turn, squeezing them tight and kissing their cheeks. I breathed in the smell of their skin as I whispered my love to each of them. I handed over the tickets and tobacco and my gratitude to Madame Laurent and watched as they walked towards the train station. It was too dangerous for me to even go to the station now and I had to return to Sarry before curfew. I cycled home without looking back. Now I really was alone.

Samuel

Paris
June 1943

We had to change trains at Poitiers and wait for the overnight to Paris. The twins were tired and irritable and the rest of us were anxious. Pierre had reserved seats for us, so we were able to settle the girls down and they soon went to sleep, using each other as pillows. Claude dozed off but woke every now and then, asking if we had arrived yet. I couldn't sleep. Thick blinds covered the windows while inside the train the lights were cold blue, but thankfully dimmed.

I sat fidgeting and wondering what this children's home would be like. Claude and I had been happy staying with Madame Laurent, who had treated us like her own family. Claude sleepily asked – again – if we had arrived yet and Madame Laurent said we were about halfway to Paris. Suddenly our carriage door opened. Two French police entered, demanding to see everyone's papers. It was ridiculous. We'd been ordered to go to Paris by an organisation set up by the government, but we still needed to bribe the police to allow us to travel. Madame Laurent was prepared as she handed over a carton of tobacco and the police walked on.

The train arrived at Gare Montparnasse early in the morning. My first impression of Paris was not a good one. Nazi flags were flying everywhere, and crowds of German officers sat in the cafes drinking coffee and smoking cigarettes like they owned the place. The street signs were in German, and the blackboards outside cafes advertised their menus in German too. There had been flags and German officers in Poitiers, but not as many as here. We went quickly down to the metro station, where the walls were plastered with posters telling us the wonders of Hitler and the Third Reich and warning of evil Jews.

We caught the metro to Montmartre. Had we been travelling under different circumstances, this would have been a fantastic adventure; our first time in Paris and our first journey on the metro! As it was, Claude and I couldn't enjoy the moment, but put on a brave face for our sisters.

We made our way to the children's home, as we had been told to do in the letter from the Jewish Agency. It was a giant house which looked even taller than its four storeys at the top of a steep hill only a few metres away from Sacré-Cœur. Madame Laurent tearfully handed us over to the director and left, but not before she made Claude and me promise we would write to her and come back to visit one day, 'when this sorry mess is over.'

I was assigned a bed in a top-floor dorm along with other boys my age, and I was happy to see a few children I knew from Metz. Claude was on the floor below and the girls were on the first floor. The home was run by Jews, although German soldiers came regularly with their lists to check up on us. Most of the children had only recently arrived and the people in charge were trying to find local school places for as many of us as possible.

On our first day there, I was in the garden with my new roommates.

'Look at that wall,' said one of them. 'It must be less than two metres high.'

'Last time I was measured I was a metre and a half tall although I'm sure I've grown since then,' said another. He walked casually over to the wall and lent against it. It was not even as tall as him.

'We could easily climb over,' said the first boy.

'And where would we go?'

'Back to Sarry,' I said. 'Our house is big enough for all of us, and it's empty now except for my older brother, Pierre. It's out of the way and there are some good hiding places in the barn in case the Germans come. We could go there.'

'Great idea,' my friends agreed.

'We would have to take my brother Claude and our sisters with us,' I added. We decided to have a think about the details, but the plan was to leave as soon as possible.

****

'Hey, guys, come and look. They're doing something to the wall!'

It was the morning after we had been in the garden planning our escape. We ran downstairs.

'What's that for?' we asked the workman. He had a bucket of broken glass bottles and some wet cement and was sticking shards of glass to the top of the wall – our way out!

'To stop you running away!'

Later that day we were in the garden with some of the older kids. The oldest was Jacqueline Goldstein. She was sixteen and had been at the children's home for four weeks. Jacqueline noticed the glass on the top of the wall, and we told her of our conversation from the day before.

'Someone must have overheard you and told the people running the home. They will get in trouble if any of us escape.'

'Wouldn't you like to get out of here, Jacqueline?'

'I'm allowed out to go to school and I can visit my grandmother here in Paris as long as I'm back by six. If I disappear, the authorities will punish my grandmother. I could never do it.'

'Your grandmother is still here?' The adults in all our families had been arrested by now.

'Yes, thank God. She still lives in her apartment. My parents and I were arrested and sent to Drancy back in January. I got sick with diphtheria and had to go to hospital, then my grandmother arranged for me to come here instead of going back to Drancy. She wanted me to live with her, but I wasn't allowed. At least I can visit her from here and this is a million times better than Drancy. But my parents…'

'What is Drancy?'

'It's a huge building outside Paris that's been turned into a prison camp. Most of the prisoners are Jews, mainly French but some from other countries too.'

'What's it like?'

'Terrible. It's *really* terrible. The building is only half-built. There are no doors, so the wind blows through everywhere and you have no privacy. People sleep together in large rooms on planks of wood. The toilets and bathrooms are disgusting, and the food is horrible. There is nothing to do except walk round and round the courtyard. There are too many people crammed in, and a lot of disease. That's why I got sick.'

'I think my family went to Drancy. Did you meet a woman called Rosa Laskowski or a man called Albert Laskowski? Those are my parents. Or maybe my cousins, Gabriel and Anna Hofman?'

'I don't remember meeting anyone with those names. There were a lot of people. Thousands were constantly coming and going.'

'The people who leave. Where do they go?' I asked. 'Maybe my parents left.'

'I don't know where they go, but I don't think it's a good place. Everyone calls it "Pitchipoi" – the unknown place – because they don't know what or where it is. There were lists of people who were transported. They had to send people away to make room for the new arrivals.'

'Who makes the lists?'

'Some of the Jewish prisoners. At first they chose only the old and sick, but then the guards realised what they were doing and forced them to make new lists of young people too. Lists were put up all the time and we would have to see if our names were on them. No one wanted to find their name on one of those lists.'

That night I had another vivid dream. This time I was in Drancy. I saw my mother check the lists for her name. I tried going to her but there were too many people between us – I couldn't get through them all. I called her name, but my voice was lost in the noise coming from the sky. All I could do was watch her from afar. The noise got louder and there was an almighty bang. I jumped out of bed. I was torn between the joy of seeing my mother and disappointment when I realised it had all been a dream.

The air raid sirens were sounding as I heard the planes flying overhead. My roommates were looking out of the window and I joined them. We heard an explosion far away followed by flashes of light. The city glowed in the distance. The allies were bombing Paris! We cheered them on while hoping they wouldn't bomb us. One of them hit something nearby; I think it was a gas tank because it lit up the whole sky. Thank goodness they still had the chutzpah to fight back, unlike the French.

****

After a couple of weeks they told me I was too old to stay at the children's home and I was to move to the trade school in Le Marais, the Jewish quarter, to learn a skill. I was desperate for something to fill the long days, but I wasn't happy to leave Claude, Henriette and Georgette. Our family was slowly being ripped apart – first Papa, then Maman, then us from Pierre, and now I had to leave the little ones. I told the director of the children's home my concerns, but he had little sympathy. He said that my siblings would be well looked after and that I should go and learn a trade so I could provide for them in the future.

Claude was devastated that I was leaving. 'Sam, please take me with you. We always stay together, you and me,' he said.

'I know, but I have no choice. It won't be for long, I promise,' I said, praying it would be true.

Although older than me, Jacqueline was to remain at the children's home. Only the boys were sent to the trade school; the girls stayed to help look after the younger children. She was fond of Henriette and Georgette and promised to look after them for me. Likewise, they had attached themselves to her. While the girls had each other, I was more worried for Claude, who had never been away from me. I begged the director to let him come with me, but at only eleven he was too young. I explained to Claude that the responsibility of caring for our sisters was now being passed on to him. He would have to be brave and strong for them, and one day soon we would all be together again.

****

Three of us from our dorm were to attend the trade school, which was close to Notre Dame. We were given metro tickets and told to get off at Saint-Paul station. Excited at the prospect of learning a trade, we didn't even think about running away, and how could I go without my siblings? Besides, we had no money, only a few personal belongings, mainly clothes and a photograph or two. I also had a book about music I had brought with me from Sarry, given to me by Madame Noyer. I wasn't enthusiastic about music, but with so few things to my name it was one of my most treasured possessions.

When we climbed the stairs at Saint-Paul metro, I was surprised to find the streets empty. The shops were shut and there was an eerie silence. We were almost at the trade school when we finally saw a man walking past us.

'Excuse me, sir. Where are all the people?' I asked him.

'They've all been taken away. Last summer they came and took everyone to the Velodrome. No one came back. They are still taking people. Be careful,' he warned us, and hurried away.

The door to the school was unlocked. We walked in and someone in the office at the entrance wrote our names in the register book. We were to turn in our wicker suitcases to the laundry, pick up two sheets and a blanket and then find an empty bunk. That wasn't a problem as the place was half empty. We were a bit shaken by what the man in the street had told us. Everyone here seemed to be on tenterhooks. We were looking around the place when one of the guys shouted in my direction: 'Oi, you!'

I looked behind me but there was no one there.

'I'm talking to you!' he declared, pointing directly at me.

'What do you want?' I asked.

'Want ta fight?'

'Not really,' I replied.

'Ya scared?'

'Yes, I am,' I said, and the guy started laughing. 'Scared of hurting you!' I continued. That wiped the smile off his face! He rushed at me, trying to knock me to the ground, but he didn't know my father had been a champion amateur wrestler in his youth and had passed on a few tips to me. I beat that guy well and good and he never bothered me again.

All the boys at the trade school seemed to have recently arrived, coming from one children's home or another. The school was also run by the Jewish Agency so we should have been safe, but something didn't seem right. Rumours were flying all over the place. The Germans were giving the French quotas to fill. If they didn't hand over enough Jews, the Germans would take them at random. Someone said the school was waiting for there to be enough of us to fill a truck, and then we would all be taken off to Drancy. We were told the prisons and reform schools were being emptied to fill the quotas and that the trade schools would be next.

There was a group of older boys, around sixteen years old, who hung out in the piano room at the back of the building. They would close the door and play music so we couldn't hear what they were talking about. One day they disappeared. Someone said they had been arrested, taken outside of Paris and shot as saboteurs. We checked the register, but their names had disappeared.

We collected bricks and stones on our balcony to throw down to the courtyard should they come to arrest us. We cut a hole in the ceiling of our dorm to escape through and decided we would jump off the balcony if it came to that.

I wasn't planning on hanging around to see if the rumours were true or if our escape plans would work. I wrote to my older brother:

Dear Pierre,

It was a terrible mistake coming to Paris. I have been moved to a trade school near metro Saint-Paul and I had to leave Claude and the girls at the children's home. Everyone says they are going to arrest all the Jewish children. Please come as soon as possible. Come and get me and we will get the others together.

Your brother, Samuel.

Seven days later, he replied:

I'm coming. Meet me at metro Saint-Paul at 4 p.m. on 11 August.

Georgette

Paris

June 1943

Samuel left. I don't think he wanted to go. They told him he was too old to stay here. He had to go and learn to make things so he could look after us later. I think that is a bit silly because it's the maman and papa's job to look after the children.

Samuel said he wasn't going too far away. I hope he's going to have fun, like Henriette and I do. We play a lot. Sometimes we play with the other children and sometimes we play with each other. I feel sorry for the boys and girls who don't have a twin. Being a twin means you're never alone and that is something that makes us feel better, even when we are a bit sad, like when Samuel left.

Claude is still here. He comes to say hello every day but then his friends drag him away to play football. There are lots of children and there is always someone to play with. The older girls like Jacqueline help us with getting washed and dressed. And then we spend the day playing. We are happy.

****

'Henriette!'

'What?'

'Stop tickling me!'

'I'm not!'

It felt like she was tickling me, and it was getting annoying. I had never slept in a bed by myself, so I was used to feeling an arm in my back or a foot on my leg during the night, but this felt different; itchy.

Next day, the monitors told me off for scratching. I didn't even know I was doing it but soon it felt like there was always someone telling me to stop.

All the girls from our room were taken down to the medical room. We'd been there before, when we first arrived, and a kind doctor had looked in our eyes and mouths and made sure we were well. He wasn't there now though. A lady wearing an overall and gloves, and with a scarf covering her hair, scowled at us. She wielded a sharp-looking comb as we stood in line and she came to check our hair. 'Yes. Yes. Yes,' was all she said in an angry voice as she looked at each of us. I was standing there scratching my head, so she didn't even bother looking in my hair.

'YES!' She almost spat out the word as she walked past and pointed at me.

'OK, girls, come in one by one,' said one of the monitors. The first girl in the queue was taken into the medical room.

'What are they going to do to her?' someone asked. Before anyone could answer, we heard crying coming from inside. The door was open allowing the girls who were next in line to peer in to see what was happening. They gasped in horror! Henriette grabbed me, and we hugged each other tightly. What was this horrible thing they were doing to that girl?

Were they going to do the same to us? When the girl came out of the room we stared at her in horror. She had gone in with pretty curly dark hair, but she came out with just fuzz on her head. Her pale face was streaked with tears and she stared down at the floor refusing to look anyone in the eye. We tried to smile to make her feel better but we were all upset because we knew we were next.

Henriette and I had worn our hair in the same short bob since we were babies. Lots of girls had this hairstyle but people tended to make a fuss over us because we looked the same. We enjoyed the attention that came with being identical twins.

When it was our turn we had to be dragged into the medical room. I sat down first, trembling as the angry lady came towards me with the clippers in her hand. She told me if I didn't keep still I would be tied to the chair, so I closed my eyes and pretended to be a statue. It was a game we used to play with our brothers. I felt the cold metal of the clippers against my head and the hair brushing my face as it fell to the floor.

It didn't take long. I got up and Henriette sat down instead. There was no mirror, but we didn't need one to see what we looked like, we only had to look at each other. Our beautiful hair gone. I reached up to touch my head. It felt strange, like a soft, furry ball. I quickly pulled my hand away, worried in case I broke this new delicate part of me. It was easier for Henriette and I to touch each other's heads than our own, and we each told the other it didn't look so bad after all.

****

A week after Samuel left the children's home, Jacqueline ran into our dorm early one morning.

'Girls, get dressed and pack your things as quickly as possible. We need to leave right away.'

'Are we going home?'

'No, but it's not safe for us to stay here now. Please hurry!'

Pierre

Sarry

June 1943

With my siblings gone to Paris, I set my mind to working as much as possible, trying to save up some money for the family. I had to stay home in the evenings because of the curfew, so I wanted to keep busy during the day to stop myself from going stir-crazy. I was nearly eighteen and totally alone. When I had nothing to do, I felt guilty for being the only one in my family who hadn't been arrested or sent away. Why me?

The loneliness exacerbated my desire for a girlfriend. You would think there would be plenty of opportunities, with most of the men away at war. I wasn't bad-looking and I knew my manners, but I didn't know how to speak to girls; the only girl my age in the village had been my cousin Anna. Samuel had had better luck with girls than I had, for goodness sake.

And so it was work that kept me busy. I was still working with the mason, preparing bricks and roof tiles for urgent repairs to buildings damaged in air raids.

At the weekend I would meet up with the few friends who were still around, mostly Jews born in France to immigrant parents who had been arrested. One Sunday three of us decided to go into Poitiers. If we didn't get the chance to speak to girls, at least we would see some walking around or having coffee in the terrace cafes. We wore our jackets with the yellow star and carried our papers stamped 'Jew' in red ink.

'Those Milice bastards,' said one of my friends, spotting a table of young French men sitting outside a cafe wearing the Milice uniform of brown shirt, blue jacket and wide blue beret. They were catcalling after girls and generally acting like a bunch of yobs.

'When I join the Resistance I'll teach them a lesson,' I said quietly, aware that any one of the ordinary French citizens walking around could be a collaborator. I was desperate to join the forces working with de Gaulle, but I hadn't yet been able to find a way to contact them. I suspected that Rabbi Epstein had been working with them, but he had been arrested months before and there was no one else I could think of to approach.

'The Milice are more dangerous than the Boche,' said one of my pals, spitting on the ground. 'They arrested one of my neighbour's relatives in Limoges and he never came back. They say he was tortured to death. They were after names of the Resistance. He was a farm worker; I doubt he knew anything.'

'I have no idea who's a freedom fighter. If I knew, I would beg them to let me join,' I said.

My friends walked on while I took a moment to light a cigarette. One of the young Milice spotted me and called me over. I walked up to him. I wasn't worried. The Milice only operated in Vichy France. We were mere kilometres from the demarcation line, but Poitiers was out of their jurisdiction. As I got closer he shouted to me to get off the sidewalk.

'Why?' I asked.

'You're a Jew. We don't want you here.'

'You're the one not wanted.'

He jumped up, grabbed my lapel and dragged me inside the cafe. 'This Jew was walking on the pavement. What should I do with him?' he said to his officer, who was sitting at a table.

'He has done nothing. Let him go on his way and finish your coffee,' the officer said indifferently without looking up from his newspaper.

The young Milice looked furious, but led me back outside and pushed me away. I walked away quickly and caught up with my friends, heart thumping. My plan of meeting girls couldn't have been further from my mind now. We carried on walking and got to the plaza behind the cathedral. We stopped to smoke a cigarette and I was telling the guys what had just happened to me when I saw two men walking towards us. They weren't in uniform but I was worried they might be more Milice idiots.

'We are Freemasons. Be proud to wear that,' they said, pointing to our yellow stars.

I didn't know any Freemasons, but I knew they were being targeted by the Nazis, like us. I wasn't eager to start a conversation with strangers, so I said politely, 'Merci, Monsieur,' and we walked away.

'What was that about?' my friend asked.

'Who knows? Best to keep to ourselves.'

'I've heard Freemasons are enemies of the state. Apparently, there's a Jewish–Masonic conspiracy going on.'

'Pity no one told us about it! People are crazy. Are we going to get the blame for everything?'

****

I was desperately lonely. I wrote to Papa's good friend Henri Reiss, who lived in Le Blanc in Vichy France, some seventy kilometres from Sarry. Henri's son Adam was a friend of mine and I hoped they could help me. I wrote:

> Everyone has gone. I'm living in Sarry by myself. Could you help me find work so I can come and live near you?

When Adam wrote back, he told me to come over and they would see about finding me a job.

I went round the house and collected up the last of our belongings – Maman's handbag, a few family photographs, some clothes – there really wasn't much, but what I found I hid in a box under the floorboards. *Let the Germans take the kitchen utensils!* I packed my suitcase, locked up the house and left on my bicycle.

The demarcation line was now mostly unguarded. The Germans were too busy fighting the Russians in the east. I crossed into Vichy France without issue and arrived safely at Adam's home in Le Blanc.

Adam and his father gave me a warm welcome. They took me to meet Monsieur Deschamps, a crop farmer who agreed to give me a job. I had never worked on a farm before, but I would give it my best shot. It turned out farm work was more difficult than I had imagined. It didn't help that my new boss was a misery to work for. It soon became clear he didn't want me around. He spoke only to shout orders and then tell me I was doing it wrong. After a few days, he told me not to bother returning. I felt bad for Adam and his father who had gone out of their way to find me the job. I apologised to them for messing up the opportunity, but they agreed to help me once again.

They put me in contact with Monsieur and Madame Masson, who had a farm in Bazaiges, around forty-five kilometres east of Le Blanc. When I arrived at their door I instantly liked them; they were friendly and kind. 'There is plenty of work to do on the farm. Which crops do you know about?'

'I haven't worked on a farm before, but I'm strong and healthy and a quick learner. If you give me a chance, I promise I will work hard for you,' I said.

'I admire your honesty,' said Monsieur Masson. 'Let me be honest, too. The work is not difficult to learn, but it is hard-going. My son Lucas worked on the farm with us, but he was taken to the German work camps.' Madame Masson sighed at the mention of her son's name. Monsieur Masson held her hand to comfort her. 'Now, now. We know that Lucas is alright. We get regular letters from him. He can't tell us what work he's doing but he says he's fine and he has plenty to eat. He's a strong lad. But how near-sighted to take all our young men without thinking about who is going to work the land when they're gone. Then the Germans will want our crops. Don't they realise if we had our young men to help us then we could produce more food for them?'

'No, Monsieur, the Germans don't think like we do.' I could have said more, but I was learning to keep my opinions to myself.

'So, we have a lot of work to be done but not much money to pay you. We can offer you somewhere to sleep and food to eat and maybe a few francs. We have a friendly bunch working here and I think you'll fit in nicely.'

'Thank you.'

'Ah! Here is our daughter,' said the farmer. I turned to the door and caught my breath at the heavenly sight in front of me. She was about my age, dressed for farm work, her hair tied up in a scarf with a few curls hanging down over her cheeks, smudged with dirt. If there had been any doubts about taking the job before, there were certainly none now.

'*Bonjour, Mademoiselle.*'

'Aimee, this is Pierre. He's thinking of coming to help us on the farm, even though we can't pay him much at all,' said the farmer, stressing the latter.

'Don't worry, Monsieur. I'm grateful for the work and I think I'll be happy here. Thank you for the offer, I accept the job.' We shook on it.

'Aimee, can you show Pierre to the barn, please?'

'It will be my pleasure, Papa. Come on, Pierre. This way.'

Wow, I couldn't believe my luck! As we walked out of the farmhouse, I frantically tried to think of something to say to stop myself looking like a fool, but I needn't have worried as this lovely girl started asking me questions. Where was I from? Where were my family? The conversation flowed until we reached the barn. The other farmhands had just arrived back from the fields.

'Here we go. Martin, Jules, Henri… this is Pierre. He will be helping us on the farm. Please show him the ropes.'

'Sure, Aimee, anything for you!' said one of the guys. 'Come on, Pierre, let's find you a bed.'

'Yes, let's find Pierre a bed!' said another.

'Here you go. This bed is perfect for you. Try it on for size.'

'Thanks,' I said as I went to sit down and ended up in a heap on the floor. There was no board under the blanket. Everyone, including Aimee, fell about laughing.

'Sorry, pal. It's the broken bed gag. All the new guys get it. Nothing personal!' They all came to shake my hand and pat me on the back.

'Oh, Pierre, your face when you fell on the floor!' said Aimee through tears of laughter.

I was mortified, but put on a brave face. 'Oh yes, ha ha! Great joke, guys!'

****

That first night I convinced myself that Aimee didn't like me because she had walked me straight into the broken bed gag. I thought it best to avoid her from then on, but she worked with the rest of us on the farm and it was impossible not to see her. From my first morning working in the fields she was charming to me; chatting, sitting next to me during our breaks, and even giving me a bit extra when she helped her mother serve the food. I wasn't sure if she felt bad for her part in my humiliation, or was perhaps setting me up for another fall, so I was a bit wary. The other guys noticed and eventually one of them said to me, 'Pierre, you fool. Can't you see the girl's sweet on you? What's the matter, she not good enough for you?'

'What? No, no, she's great. Do you really think she likes me?'

'You don't know much about girls, do you?'

'Is it that obvious?'

'I think Aimee must find it charming. Yes, she likes you!'

'I thought maybe one of you guys…'

'You have our blessing, *mon ami*. Aimee is a nice girl, a bit too nice for us lads, if you get my drift.'

I thought I knew what he was talking about. I smiled and nodded, keen to bring the conversation to a close. I wished Papa was here and I could ask his advice.

****

My family were always on my mind. Where were my parents and when would they come back? Would they come back at all? How were my brothers and sisters doing in Paris and had I made the right decision to let them go? These were questions I couldn't answer, but that didn't stop them tormenting me. I knew though, that none of this was my doing and no one would blame me for making the most of my time on the farm. I allowed myself to make some good friends and they helped turn me into a farmer. The days were long and hard, but we spent the evenings together talking and laughing. Aimee worked as hard as the men, and she helped her mother cook for everyone too. She lit up the room when she walked in and everyone liked her, especially me. I was awkward around her at first, but she was just like one of the guys and we soon became good friends. We talked about our lives before the war and what we would like to do when this madness was over. I was desperate to ask her on a date, maybe go for a walk or something, but I was afraid of being rejected and I didn't want to upset her parents, who had been so good to me. Then again, if I didn't act soon she might grow tired of waiting…

****

We were in the fields and Aimee smiled at me. My heart started beating quickly. It was a hot day so my flushed face and sweaty palms didn't give my feelings away. When we stopped for a water break, I sat down on a log and she sat next to me, so close our legs were almost touching. After a long moment of silence, I made up my mind to ask her to take a walk with me.

'Hi,' I said.

'Hi,' she said back.

'Beautiful day.'

'It is.'

What to say next? Should I say something about her being as beautiful as the day, or should it be the day is as beautiful as she? Yes, it sounded better that way round. I took a drink of water. For God's sake, my hands were shaking! Here goes, I'm going to ask her now…

'Look!' She pointed at a gendarme who was walking across the field towards us. What horrible timing!

'I am looking for Pierre Laskowski.'

I stood up.

'I am Pierre.'

'Come with me,' said the gendarme and he escorted me off the field. As we walked away, I looked back at Aimee who was watching me leave. Our eyes met briefly, then the policeman ordered me to turn around and face forward.

****

The gendarme took me to a cafe in the village. He sat me down at a table and took out his notebook.

'Pierre, you have not been arrested. That is why I have brought you to the cafe and not a police station. Do you understand?'

'Yes, sir.'

'Where do you come from?' He was reading from his notebook.

'I was born in Metz, but my family were relocated to Sarry, near Poitiers.'

'What is your father's name?'

'Albert.'

'Who is Jankiel?'

'My father's Polish name was Jankiel, but when he settled in France he changed it to Albert.'

'Show me your identification papers.'

Everybody carried their papers with them all the time – you couldn't be found without them. I handed mine over.

'You may return to the farm now but tomorrow you must come to the police station and I will give you back your papers.'

This didn't sound good. I had no idea what he wanted with me, but I had to do as he said. By the time I walked back to the farm everyone was finishing work for the day. I went to the field and looked for Aimee among the group of guys, but she wasn't with them. Some of them came up and asked me what had happened. I told them what little I knew. Then I went to knock on the farmhouse door and Aimee answered. Her face lit up when she saw me. 'Pierre! Are you alright?'

'Yes, thank you. I'm fine. I need to speak to your father, please,' I said.

She looked disappointed. 'Oh, yes of course. I'll call him for you.'

'But, Aimee, I wanted to see you too. I was going to ask you if—'

'Pierre! What happened to you?' Monsieur Masson came to the door and ushered me into the house. 'Come in!'

'Thank you, Monsieur,' I said. While we stood in the hallway of the farmhouse I told him what happened. 'I'm sorry but I need to go back to the police station tomorrow to pick up my papers,' I said. 'I will go first thing in the morning and come back to work as soon as possible.'

'Of course. That's fine. We're happy to see you back. We were quite worried for you, weren't we?' He turned to smile at his daughter. 'I will see you later. Aimee, please see Pierre out.' And he left us alone.

'Pierre, what were you going to ask me?'

'What?'

'Just then, when Papa came. I thought you were going to ask me something.'

'Oh, yes. Sorry. I was going to ask if you… if you would like to take a walk with me after supper this evening.'

'Oh!' said Aimee, in surprise.

'Actually, it's a stupid idea. Forget it,' I said and went to open the front door.

'No! It's a lovely idea. I would be happy to go with you. We should have time for a quick walk before the curfew begins. We don't want to get you in more trouble!' she said.

'That's true. Well… see you later!' I practically skipped out of the front door like a little kid!

****

After supper I waited for Aimee outside the farmhouse. She didn't keep me waiting long. When she came out of the front door she looked so beautiful I could hardly believe she was interested in me. I was very nervous; what if I had got it wrong and she just wanted to be my friend?

'Let's walk down to the stream,' she said, and off we set. 'Were you scared today, Pierre?'

'No, not really. With all the terrible things that could happen to any one of us these days, going to a cafe with a gendarme didn't seem too awful!'

'Ha! I hadn't thought of it like that. Yes, you're right. We had a letter from my brother Lucas today. He said that conditions are getting worse in Germany and the French workers are being pushed harder and harder. There is a lot of illness there too and some of his friends have died.'

'That's terrible. I'm very sorry to hear it.'

'My mother is really upset. This stupid war just gets worse and worse. Everyone is suffering and all because of that idiot Hitler.'

'I agree. My family has been torn apart and I don't know if I will ever see my parents again. My little brothers and sisters are alone in Paris...' My voice faltered as I thought of my siblings and I realised Aimee was the first person I had been able to share my thoughts with. 'I'm happy on the farm but I should be doing something to help. I feel so useless.'

'Don't say that,' said Aimee as she stopped and faced me. She took my hands in hers. 'You are helping to feed a lot of people by working here.'

'But I should be fighting to defend my family and good people like you and your parents.'

'Pierre, you're a good person too. You are honourable, and I'm sure you will always do the right thing. Now the most important thing is that you get your papers back tomorrow.'

'No, you're wrong,' I said impulsively. Aimee looked surprised. 'This is the most important thing right now.' I pulled her towards me and kissed her softly.

She put her hand on my shoulder and kissed me back.

****

I walked Aimee back to the farmhouse and, checking no one was in sight, kissed her goodnight.

'I'm going to the police station early in the morning, so I'll see you when I get back.'

'OK, be careful. See you tomorrow. I had a lovely time this evening, Pierre.'

'Yes, me too,' I said. What a day!

****

First thing next morning I rode my bike to the police station in Bazaiges and presented myself to the sub-officer sitting at the front desk.

'My name is Pierre Laskowski. A gendarme came to see me yesterday and took my papers away. I was told to come here today to get them back.'

'I'll call the sergeant and we'll see what he has to say,' the sub-officer replied.

He picked up the telephone. 'Pierre Laskowski is here. What do you want me to do with him? What? Oh, I see.

OK.' Turning back to me he said, 'Pierre Laskowski, I am arresting you.'

'What for? I'm not a criminal. I work on a farm!'

'You crossed the demarcation line without a visa. That is a criminal offence.'

'But yesterday the gendarme said he was not going to arrest me! What is going on?'

The sub-officer offered no further explanation as he led me to a cell at the back of the police station. I was the only prisoner. Me – in prison! With no one to talk to, my mind was free to conjure up all kinds of scenarios. I had been arrested just like my father and mother had, and my grandmother and aunt and uncle and cousins, and none of them had come home. Would that happen to me? And what about Aimee, what would she think when I didn't return to the farm ? I picked up a newspaper that was lying there. It was the fascist rag, *Je Suis Partout*, but I read it to distract me. True to form, it was crammed full of anti-Semitic propaganda which did nothing to calm me down. After what seemed a long time, the gendarme from the day before returned.

'Monsieur, please let me go. I'm needed on the farm. It's a busy time, the crops will be ruined without me to help,' I pleaded.

'One more day will make little difference. Tomorrow I'll take you to see the judge and ask for you to be released,' he said.

I was shocked. 'Why are you helping me?' I asked.

'I have a son a little older than you. He has been sent to Germany as slave labour. I can't help him but maybe there is a police officer in Germany who will treat him fairly, as I'm doing for you. However, you crossed the demarcation line without a visa and I can't let you go without the permission of the court.'

****

The words of the gendarme gave me hope that the world might not be so bad after all. In the morning the gendarme took me to the courthouse. Instead of going to the court-room we were directed to the judge's office.

'Now, who have we here?' asked the judge from behind his desk.

'This is Pierre Laskowski, your honour,' replied the gendarme on my behalf. 'He has been detained for cross-ing the demarcation line without a visa. He has no other convictions and is an honest and hard-working young man. I request he is released to his employer, Monsieur Masson, who needs him on the farm. The hay season approaches.'

The judge looked down at my papers on his desk.

'The law dictates that this matter needs to be decided in court, but this young man is not yet eighteen so I cannot allow him to go through the court system.'

I couldn't believe my luck. It seemed like the gendarme and the judge were both going to let me go.

'You are only two weeks away from your eighteenth birth-day on... let me see... 14 July. Ah, Bastille Day! Very good. Until that date you shall go to the local children's home and then return here before me.'

'But, sir...' I started. The judge looked at me sternly. It was clear I shouldn't speak.

'That is all. I will see you in two weeks, young man, when you will be just that… a young man!' said the judge, to his own amusement.

When we left the office the gendarme said, 'It is only two weeks.' He probably thought, as I did, that it was ridiculous taking me to a children's home when I could be working on the farm instead. I was not a child. I had been living on my own for months now and working like any other man. I even had a girlfriend now – well, for a day at least. Trust my luck! After showing Aimee I was the man for her I was to be locked up in a children's home!

****

There were around one hundred children living at that home. Most were there because their parents had been sent to Germany as forced labour. I don't think any of them were Jewish. I was by far the oldest; most other children over the age of fourteen in the area lived and worked on farms. The supervisor in charge was cruel and the conditions were terrible. Were Samuel, Claude, Henriette and Georgette being treated this badly? The thought of my poor brothers and sisters suffering like these children made my blood boil.

The children hardly spoke. There was no one to show them any kindness or fight for them. Although I planned on keeping my head down, I couldn't ignore the way they were being treated. The place was squalid, the children and their clothes were filthy, and the food was disgusting, served on rusty metal plates like a medieval workhouse. After mealtimes the smell and taste of those metal plates were difficult to forget. All but the youngest children were expected to work full days in the vegetable gardens, but no fresh vegetables were served to us.

I could have run away but then it would be impossible to return to Aimee and my job on the farm, so I stayed and did what I could to help improve the lives of the younger children. I complained about the food at every mealtime. I asked why it was necessary to eat from metal plates which tainted the already revolting food. I showed the children how to wash their own clothes. I 'borrowed' a broom, bucket and mop and arranged a cleaning rota. I taught the children how to tend to the vegetables (after all, I was a farmer now) and, more importantly, I showed them how to pocket a few of the vegetables which could be eaten raw without the supervisor realising. All this kept me busy but it didn't stop me worrying about what would happen next. Once I turned eighteen, would I be sent to a camp and disappear like my parents?

When my court order was delivered to the children's home, the supervisor worried I would tell the judge about the awful conditions. She offered to accompany me to court as I was under her responsibility, but the official said that wouldn't be necessary.

My birthday came soon enough. Another birthday with no celebration and this year none of my family with me. It was almost a year since I had last seen Papa. So much had happened in such a short time. Would he be thinking of me on this special day? Would we all get to celebrate our missed birthdays and anniversaries when we were reunited again? I would not allow myself to think any other way.

When I was called to enter the courtroom I was surprised to see three judges sitting on the bench, not only the one I had met before.

'Ah, Monsieur Laskowski. You are now an adult and therefore responsible for your own actions. Can you tell the court why you crossed the demarcation line without a visa, when you knew this was forbidden by law?'

'Your honour, I was trying to save my own life. My parents have been arrested and my brothers and sisters taken to Paris. I am all alone. There was no work for me in Poitiers, no way to make a living. I came to this area to work on a farm. I'm working hard to help produce food for France.'

The three judges conferred.

'We are not unsympathetic, but you must realise there are certain rules and laws which have to be abided. It could have been extremely dangerous for you to cross the demarcation line without a visa. You should consider yourself lucky that it is this court dealing with you as others may not be so understanding.'

'Yes, sir. Thank you.' I thought of my poor cousin Simone and her family, who had disappeared after trying to make the crossing and had not been heard of since.

I was fined three hundred francs, not an insignificant amount; if I could get back to Sarry I could pay it with the money still hidden in the barn.

'Don't be caught again or next time we'll be putting you in prison,' one judge said. Dammit. How was I going to get to Sarry and back without crossing the demarcation line – twice?

'I won't, sir,' I said.

I was allowed to leave. I ran to the Masson farm where I was warmly welcomed back by my sympathetic employers and their beautiful daughter.

****

I worked hard back at the farm. I felt bad for the extra work the others had been lumbered with while I was stuck in the children's home. Naturally, the guys had a good laugh when they found out where I had been. I pushed myself to the limit. I started earlier and finished later. I stopped only for quick water and food breaks. I ran back and forth all day long.

In the evenings I had just enough energy to sit with my beautiful Aimee. Being together felt so right and, while I was still fuming at having been treated like a child, our time apart only made me want to be with her more. It was almost possible to forget about the war and be happy. Would I ever get the chance to tell Maman about my sweet girlfriend?

Keen to not risk my future on the farm (yes! I finally had a future to think about), I knew I had to settle the three hundred francs fine. It would take years to pay out of my low wages and I was too proud to ask Monsieur Masson for a loan. The other guys had no money so my only option was to return to the house in Sarry and collect some of the hidden money in the barn. This time I would be careful crossing the demarcation line and not be seen. My plan was to go and return to the farm straightaway, but that all changed when I arrived in Sarry and Madame Leblanc came rushing over with a letter in her hand.

Georgette

Paris

July 1943

It was easy to pack our things. There wasn't much to take; one change of clothes each and a toothbrush. Our hairbrush had been burned after they found the head lice. We didn't need it now anyway. And, oh yes, we had our darling doll Bernadette, packed in Henriette's case for safekeeping.

Jacqueline said she was really proud of us when she saw how quickly we got ready. She told us to wait in our room until she came to get us. The other children were running noisily down the stairs. I climbed up on the bed to look out of the window and saw a bus driving up the road, stopping outside the building. A group of older children piled on and scrambled to get the best seats. They looked excited, like they were going on an adventure. I couldn't remember ever having been on a bus. I had been in a car, a train, in a trailer on the back of a bicycle being ridden by Pierre... I started to think of Maman for the first time in a long while. I remembered being in that horrible place with her and then Pierre coming to get Henriette and I. Where was Maman now? I tried desperately to remember her face, but I couldn't picture it. I was about to ask my sister if she remembered, when Jacqueline came back and told us to make our way downstairs. We didn't run down the stairs like the older children. We walked carefully, holding on to the handrail as we went. Soon enough we were boarding the bus and leaving the children's home.

Henriette and I were, naturally, sitting together, but I sat next to the window and as we drove out of Paris I was fascinated by what I could see. The children's home was on a high point of the city and there was a fantastic view as we drove away.

As we continued on our journey the streets narrowed, and we saw fewer people and buildings until the bus turned off the road, up a gravel driveway and stopped in front of a big house with a walled garden.

We were taken through the gate to our new home. Only some of the children came with us and, most importantly, Henriette, Claude and Jacqueline were with me. And Bernadette, of course.

Pierre

Paris

August 1943

The letter waiting from me at Sarry was from Samuel, warning me the children were not safe in Paris. I sent a hurried reply and made plans to go there immediately. I would collect Claude, Henriette and Georgette and then we would meet Samuel at Saint-Paul metro station and leave Paris together. We would come back to Sarry and live as a family once more. I thought about the Leblancs, and Aimee in particular, but the safety of my brothers and sisters had to take priority.

As I walked up the last part of the steep hill in Montmartre, I could tell something wasn't right. It was morning, but the courtyard was silent, not what you would expect from a large building of young children. Where was everyone? I tried to open the front gates but they were locked, the home was deserted. I began to panic. Was I too late; had the children been taken? I sat on the wall on the other side of the street, not knowing what to do, when a man walked up, stopped at the gate and took out a key to unlock the door.

'Monsieur, can you help me please? I'm looking for my brother and sisters who were in this home. Do you know where they've gone?'

The man looked at me. He wore a yellow star on his jacket pocket, but I wasn't wearing mine. I had stopped wearing it after the incident with the Milice that Sunday in Poitiers, besides I wouldn't have been able to travel to Paris on the night train wearing it. I did have my papers with me though, so I took them out of my pocket and showed him the 'Juif' printed in red ink.

'What are their names?'

'Claude, Henriette and Georgette Laskowski. See on my papers? They are my siblings. Claude is eleven and the girls are five-year-old twins.'

To my huge relief the man said, 'Yes, I know them. Come in and I'll tell you more.'

We went into an office and he explained that all the children had been taken outside the city for safety. 'It's rumoured the gendarmerie have been given huge quotas to fill by the Germans. Before, French Jews and children were off-limits, but not now. Your brother and sisters are being well looked after, don't worry.'

'I need to see them. Can you tell me where they are?'

'I'm sorry but that information is classified. We need to keep the new locations secret.'

'I understand, but I beg you to tell me where they are. I have risked everything to travel here to see them,' I pleaded.

'I'm sorry, Son,' he said.

'Please, Monsieur. My little brother and sisters. Who knows when I can see them again?'

'I can't—'

'Monsieur. Everyone has been taken away from me. I just want to see the children. Do you still have your family with you?'

The man looked like I had struck him. 'Alright, Son. Let me see where they are.'

He unlocked a drawer and took out a ledger.

'What was that surname again?'

'Laskowski.'

'Ah yes, here they are. They've been taken to a suburb west of Paris called Louveciennes. The address is 1 Place DreuxRoux. You can get a bus there, it's not too far. You should be safe to travel, although these days it's a risk to go anywhere.'

'Yes, I know.'

****

As the bus drove into Louveciennes, we passed grand houses. It was different from a dirty city like Metz, a tiny village like Sarry, or the farmlands of Bazaiges. Here there were mansions, country estates and even castles. When I got to the gate at 1 Place DreuxRoux I noticed a large sign outside: Orphelinat. Orphanage. It stopped me in my tracks. It was only a word, but the difference between 'children's home' and 'orphanage' stung. Is that what we were now? Would we ever truly know?

I rang the bell.

'Can I help you?' asked a young woman who appeared at the gate.

'I have come to see my brother and sisters,' I said. 'Claude, Henriette and Georgette Laskowski.'

The woman smiled when she heard their names. I took out my papers and pointed out my surname.

'Come in,' she said.

She accompanied me to the large building at the end of the drive and to the office of the director, Monsieur Denis. I introduced myself and asked if I could see my brother and sisters.

'I don't think that is a good idea. The children are settled and there would be no benefit in them seeing you,' said Monsieur Denis. He was a small, thin man. He didn't seem to have any warm qualities which seemed strange, considering his job. I took an immediate dislike to him.

'I'm eighteen and old enough to take responsibility for my family. I will be looking after them now.'

'Your intentions are most admirable,' he said without sincerity.

'So, if you can ask for them to get ready, we will leave immediately.'

'I don't think so—'

'But I really must insist. It would be the wishes of our parents.'

His tone changed and with impatience he said, 'That is totally out of the question. The children will stay here. They are being well looked after and this is the best place for them. Did you not see we moved them all from Paris recently because it was no longer safe? I can assure you that the well-being of the children is our top priority.'

'I understand and I appreciate what you say, Monsieur Denis. However, I would at least like to see my brother and sisters now that I'm here. We've been apart for months, and who knows when I'll be able to return.'

'At the risk of repeating myself, Monsieur Laskowski, I think it would be better...*for the children*... less unsettling, if you didn't see them.'

This is getting me nowhere, I thought. *Let's try flattering the old toad.*

'Monsieur. I'm so grateful for all you have done for my family. Under the circumstances I can't imagine a safer place for the children, and I'm sure it's all thanks to you. My parents will be so happy to know their youngest are being cared for so well. I beg you to please let me see them before I leave.'

That did the trick. The loathsome man finally agreed, and I was taken to see my siblings. They were finishing lunch in the dining hall. There was happy chatter going on and they appeared to be well. Claude was the first to see me; he did a sort of double take and then came running over and grabbed me tightly.

'Pierre! It's so good to see you. What are you doing here?'

'I came to see you, of course. How are you?'

'Oh, alright I suppose but I would rather be with you and Samuel. Have you seen Samuel?'

'No, not yet. Hopefully later today. Where are the girls?'

'Over there,' Claude said, pointing to one of the long tables. We went over to them. My sisters jumped up when they noticed me.

'Girls, where are you going?' said an older girl, sitting at the head of the table.

'It's our brother!' said Claude.

'Pierre!' Henriette and Georgette hugged me.

'Let me see you both,' I said, loosening their grip on me so I could hold them at arm's length and see their faces. 'Look at your short hair!'

'They had to cut our hair off because of the bugs,' said Henriette.

'Oh dear. Did the bugs crawl all over your body like this?' I said, tickling them so they squealed with delight. It was so good to see them chatting and laughing. After a few minutes the older girl came over to us.

'Hello. I'm Jacqueline. I'm a monitor here, and I look after your lovely sisters. They've told me a lot about you. It's good to meet you.'

I spent an hour with the children. They showed me where they slept and where they played. Claude introduced me to some of his friends and then someone came to tell me to return to Monsieur Denis's office.

'So, Monsieur Laskowski, are you satisfied now, knowing the children are well looked after?'

'It's good to see they are well, and I met Jacqueline who they seem to like very much.'

'Indeed, all of our monitors are excellent. Jacqueline is in a similar situation to the children; her parents have been arrested and we think it helps her to be occupied. It also helps her charges to have someone who understands what they are going through. Jacqueline looks after nine of the youngest children, including your sisters.'

'However,' I insisted, 'anyone would agree they would be better off with their own family and that is why I must take the children with me now. They are my responsibility.'

'Unfortunately that is just not possible. I have to account for every child to the German soldiers who come weekly. If anyone is missing, the rest of the children – and staff – will suffer the consequences.'

'I won't leave without them.' I held my ground.

'In that case I have no choice but to call the police and have you arrested, Monsieur Laskowski. I'm sure they will be curious to know why you have broken the law to travel outside of your region.'

He went to pick up the telephone on his desk. I wasn't sure if he was bluffing. Would he really do that to me: did he really want the police coming here? He was unreadable. I had no choice, as I couldn't risk being arrested again.

'I'll be back for them,' I said as I was escorted to the gate without being allowed to say goodbye. I was desolate and tried not to think about how my brother and sisters would feel once they realised I had gone.

Samuel

Paris
August 1943

It was the day I was to meet Pierre. Getting away from the trade school wouldn't be a problem; we could come and go as long as we signed the register and were back by curfew. I was desperate to leave but I also wanted to carry on studying. I was learning woodwork and how to be a draughtsman. In class I sat next to Paul Segan, who had become a close friend. Paul was from Paris and his parents had only recently been arrested. He was a nice guy and I didn't hesitate to ask him if he wanted to come with me.

'We can leave after class,' I said. 'I've arranged to meet my brother Pierre at the Saint-Paul metro station at four o'clock. We need to get our younger brother and sisters from the children's home so we might not be able to leave Paris tonight because of the curfew. I'm hoping Pierre has thought of a place where we can stay.'

'I can help. We can stay at my parents' apartment,' said Paul. 'It would be better if you and I don't leave at the same time. You go first, then I'll go later. Take the metro to Rue Résal and we'll meet at the apartment. I can walk there, I know shortcuts. It'll take me around an hour, but you'll probably arrive before me and it might be dangerous to hang around outside. I'll give you the key to the apartment. Oh no! I just remembered the door was sealed when my parents were arrested.'

'Not a problem. In my woodwork class one of the boys showed us how to break a seal and then make it look like it hadn't been touched.'

'We have learnt some useful stuff! Great, so you can wait inside the apartment, it'll be safer. Make sure you don't put the lights on, the police have Jews patrolling the streets and if they see there's someone inside, they'll report it.'

'Unbelievable! How can people do that to their own?' I said.

'Fear brings out the worst in some people.'

'That's a kind way of looking at it, Paul. We'll keep an eye out; we won't let them ruin our plan.'

'Pretty sure we've thought of everything. Great work!' said Paul.

****

After class Paul gave me the address and key to his apartment. I asked the laundry for an extra change of clothes, saying that mine were dirty. I bundled them up with a few other belongings, like the music book I had brought from Sarry, but left everything else so it didn't look like I had left for good. When it was nearly four o'clock I waited in the dark corridor behind the entrance until the supervisor finally left for his break, then I walked casually out the door, without signing the register.

I ran to the metro station. I was relieved to see Pierre waiting for me. As I caught my breath at the top of the stairs, he told me German soldiers had been shot at and blockades put up all over the area to catch those responsible. They were stopping everyone and checking papers. I didn't have any; my only form of identification was my ration book and I'd left that at the school. A German soldier rounded the corner and we ducked down the stairs to avoid him, but before getting to the bottom we heard a voice from behind us.

'You. Come here!' We'd been spotted!

We turned round to face a rifle aimed directly at us. We made our way back up the stairs and the soldier pointed to the package I was carrying.

'What do you have there?'

'Only some clothes,' I answered nervously.

'There is something else there. What is it?'

I looked down and realised a corner of the book I'd taken was sticking out, covered by a shirt. 'It's a book,' I said.

'Let me see!' And he held out a hand while the other firmly gripped his rifle.

I fumbled around with the clothing and took out the book to show him.

'It's about music,' I said.

He seemed disappointed I was telling the truth, and annoyed to waste his time on something so trivial.

'OK, you can go,' he said, hurrying us away before one of his fellow soldiers came over and saw the book that had prompted the search. We went into the metro before the German had chance to realise he hadn't asked to see our papers. When we arrived at Rue Résal, we found Paul's apartment and managed to split the door seal as quietly as possible. We shut the door behind us and breathed a sigh of relief. We had made it.

The curtains in the sitting room were half open and enough light would come in for a while yet, long enough for us to get our bearings before it got completely dark. We peered round the curtains down at the street below. Patrols of Jews were walking up and down, accompanied by the French police, looking up at the windows to see if there were signs of life in the apartments owned by their Jewish neighbours who had been taken away. Pierre was exhausted. He had been travelling for twenty-four hours now, but I couldn't let him sleep without him telling me first about Claude, Henriette and Georgette. I hadn't wanted to ask until we were safely in the apartment with no one to overhear.

'It's good they've moved the children away from the centre of Paris and that Jacqueline is looking after them, but is there no chance of us going and sneaking them out?' I asked, after he told me what happened.

'I can't see a way. There is a big wall around the garden. It's much too high for the girls to climb over. The director promised me they are safe there. I didn't like him much, but I think he was being honest, and they seemed happy,' said Pierre. 'We have no choice but to leave them where they are for the time being.'

We settled down for the night in the sitting room. It didn't feel right sleeping in the beds of people dragged out of their homes. As night fell we drifted to sleep, waiting for Paul.

Sounds from the street below woke us. It was morning and people were able to leave their homes, but there was no sign of Paul. Pierre and I agreed we needed to leave Paris as soon as possible. I wanted to wait for my friend but it wouldn't be safe to stay much longer – maybe he had changed his mind and stayed at the school? I also worried about Claude and the twins, but Pierre reassured me they were safe in the orphanage. We left the apartment, hid the key under the mat and put back together the seal on the front door. Then we started back on our way to Poitiers.

Georgette

The dining room at Place Roux is the biggest room I've ever seen. Dinner is my favourite time of the day; not because of the food, which is pretty horrible, but because everyone eats together at the long wooden tables, so we get to see Claude. We sometimes see him during the day too, but he's usually off playing with other boys his age. Henriette and I sit with the other five and six year olds. There are eight of us girls and just one boy, Tommy, who is the youngest. Tommy is really sweet and we all love playing with him. Jacqueline collects our food from the kitchen and sits at the end of our table to eat with us. She always tells us to make sure we don't spill anything because that would be a waste. We all know food is precious.

It's a long time since we left Maman in that awful place and went home with Pierre. All the children have similar stories; their parents are gone, but almost no one speaks of them. In our little group only Corinne cries for her maman, and she does this every day. Her pain is so bad that one of the monitors usually takes her to a quiet spot so she doesn't upset the rest of us, giving her a moment to 'get it out of her system'.

Our days at Place Roux soon become all we know. Our group share a dormitory; Henriette and I share a bed, of course. In the morning Jacqueline wakes us up and helps us to dress, then we go downstairs for breakfast, which is a bowl of porridge. Sometimes the porridge is watery and other days it is thicker, but it is usually enough to stop our stomachs from rumbling too much, except for Rosette, who is always hungry. Jacqueline helps clear away after breakfast and then she disappears for the rest of the morning to study. She told us she used to go to school in Paris but now she has to study by herself as there is no school nearby.

When the other monitors leave for their homes in Louveciennes at the end of each day, Jacqueline watches them and sighs. As the only Jewish monitor she has no choice but to stay here with the rest of us.

Once a week German soldiers come with a list of names to make sure we are all still there. Jacqueline is the only monitor whose name is on the list. Each monitor counts up the children in their group and then goes to tell the soldiers there is no one missing.

'Some of my friends speak of running away,' Claude told us.

'Please don't go,' Henriette and I begged.

'I promise I'll never leave you.'

We also have Jacqueline, who we all love. She gives us cuddles, never tells us off and shares the parcels of food her grandmother sends from Paris.

'Come, children, I have a surprise for you,' she said, when the first parcel arrived at Place Roux.

'What is it, Jacqueline?' we asked.

'My Bubba has sent us a package.'

'But I don't know your Bubba,' said Tommy.

'Neither do I,' said Corinne. 'Do I?'

Rosette, who had an idea there might be food in the package, quickly said, 'Let's open it and see what she has sent.'

The package was wrapped in brown paper and tied with string, which Jacqueline carefully took off and put to one side. Brown paper and string were things to treasure. Underneath were layers of newspaper that were also kept to one side. The older children liked to read the newspapers, they said it was their only way of finding out what was happening outside the orphanage. Monsieur Denis had a radio but he didn't let anyone else listen to it. At last we could see what was in the package – bread, apples and a small piece of dried sausage. Jacqueline shared it with us; everyone got a small piece of something and it tasted wonderful.

There was never enough to eat although this was how it had always been since I could remember. Maman always said Henriette and I were born small and we were still small compared to some of the other children our age. Not everyone seemed to have such a bad time though. Madame Bolon, the cook at Place Roux, looked like she was getting plenty to eat! We didn't see her much, she mainly stayed in her kitchen making the porridge for breakfast and potato soup for lunch and dinner. Sometimes a piece of meat would give the soup a bit more flavour or pieces of carrot or turnip would appear in our bowls.

'Madame Bolon should give us more meat to eat but she keeps it for herself and to sell. She should help us instead of being so mean, because she's Jewish,' Claude told us.

'Are we Jewish too?' I asked him.

****

Monsieur Denis lived at Place Roux with his wife and their daughter Michèle. They had their own private rooms but they ate in the large dining room with us, at their family table. It was easy to see their meals were bigger and better than ours. After the meat rations stolen by the cook, and the extra portions served to the Denis family, there wasn't much left for the rest of us. Monsieur Denis didn't seem at all worried that we were going hungry, in fact he didn't seem to like children very much, and that included his own daughter.

Michèle was six, only a bit older than Henriette and me, so we would have been her friends, if she wasn't so nasty. She didn't care that no one liked her. Michèle enjoyed reminding us she was the only child at Place Roux with parents. She wore the prettiest dresses and the biggest bows in her hair, and often had a lollipop in her mouth or a handful of sweets. She liked nothing more than showing off to the rest of us. Jacqueline invited Michèle to join our games, but her mother wouldn't allow her. Sometimes I would see Michèle looking sad as she watched us having fun, then she would realise I was looking at her and run to her mother to give her a big hug, and her mother would reward her with another piece of candy.

****

Pierre came to see us! We were in the dining room, had just finished lunch and in he walked. What a lovely surprise! He told us about the farm he was working on and his girlfriend. Her name is Aimee and she's very pretty. Henriette and I were excited to hear about her, but Claude didn't seem that interested. Pierre told us he was going to see Samuel too. I hope he brings Samuel with him next time. Claude asked about our maman and papa, but Pierre said he hadn't been able to find out anything yet. I said I could hardly remember what they looked like and Pierre said he had a photo of the whole family back on the farm and he was going to bring it to show us next time.

Mostly Pierre wanted to hear about us and how we were, what we did during the day and who were our friends. Claude told him about school; Henriette and I told him how we play in the woods or in the garden. But then he left, and he didn't say goodbye, which made us sad. Jacqueline said she was sure he would come back soon and maybe he had to rush off to catch the bus, because people aren't allowed to be outside late anymore. That night Henriette and I hugged each other tight and cried a little. Claude cried too, but he had no one to hug so we let him borrow Bernadette.

Pierre

Samuel and I took the train back to Poitiers, travelling third class, the cheapest ticket available. I felt defeated. It was as if the police and soldiers on the train knew I wasn't even worth bothering with, and we weren't questioned. I had failed the children. I couldn't stop thinking about them and how I left them without saying goodbye, but I reassured myself they would be well looked after at Place Roux.

Meanwhile, Samuel and I had no plan. I'd thought of going to the house in Sarry with all the children but as it was only Samuel and me, I thought it better that I return to the farm. I probably needed to get back anyway in case the police came to check up on me. Samuel would not be able to stay on the farm with me; there was no room for him and I thought it better he be with boys his own age. There was a children's home in the south run by the Jewish Scout Movement, Éclaireurs israélites de France. He took some convincing. He asked if it made sense for him to escape one home to go willingly to another, but I was sure he would be safe with the scouts and eventually he agreed.

At Poitiers we went to collect my bicycle, which I had left hidden in a disused garage. I was relieved to see it was still where I had left it, but I hadn't realised the terrible conditions of the tyres. We looked around and found a length of old rubber hose. 'That should do the trick,' said Samuel. He removed the tyres, which practically disintegrated when he handled them, and made replacements out of the hose.

We set off, me on the saddle and Samuel hanging on for dear life behind me. Around halfway we gave up on the rubber hose tyres, which had been a great idea but were, in fact, completely useless. We cycled as far as our backsides could take on metal frames and then walked the rest of the way. After many hours we arrived in Châteauroux, one hundred and twenty kilometres east of Poitiers and right on the demarcation line. By the time we arrived, it was night. We had to get off the streets. We walked in the shadows of the tall buildings until we came across a convent and knocked on the door. The Mother Superior opened it just enough to speak to us.

'What can I do for you?'

'We are two Jewish boys and we need somewhere to stay for the night,' I said.

The nun opened the door wide enough for us to enter. She looked shocked. 'Come in quickly!' she said. 'Do you know where you are?' She took us to the window. 'Look there. That is the Gestapo headquarters!' The door of the building opposite opened almost immediately. A guard came out and stood to attention, directly across the street where we had just been standing. A few seconds later and he would have seen us.

'Our Lord Jesus is looking after you,' said the Mother Superior. 'You may stay tonight but you will have to leave first thing tomorrow. It would be too dangerous for you to stay any longer.'

'We're so grateful. We don't want to cause anyone trouble and we'll continue our journey in the morning,' I promised.

'The safest place for you to sleep will be in the attic.'

We followed the Mother Superior up several flights of stairs. When she opened the door to the large attic room the over-powering smell of urine mixed with disinfectant hit us. From the light of the lamp our host carried we could see around a dozen beds, mostly occupied by elderly women. Some were sleeping quietly but others were moaning or crying.

'These women are very ill,' said our hostess. 'The Gestapo are afraid of disease and they would never come up here.'

Samuel and I were pretty afraid of disease too, but the Mother Superior went on to reassure us that no one was contagious. 'But we keep that quiet,' she said, with a hint of a smile.

We found two empty beds and settled down for the night. We were exhausted after our long journey and quickly fell asleep.

****

We got up early the next morning, eager to avoid being noticed by our room-mates, and quickly made our way downstairs. The Mother Superior was already busy with chores.

'Good morning, boys. I hope you slept well.'

'We did. Thank you for allowing us to stay. We're most grateful for your help, Madame.'

'I'm happy we were able to help you, but now it would be best if you leave as soon as possible. I'm sorry we are not able to offer you breakfast. Here, please take this,' and she handed over a box of biscuits.

'Thank you.'

'Let me see if it is safe for you to leave.' She looked out of the peephole in the front door. 'All clear. May God go with you.'

****

We left the convent, carefully crossed the unguarded demarcation line and went to the bus station. I put Samuel on the bus for Toulouse and told him to get off at Beaulieu sur Dordogne and to look for the Jewish Scout Movement. I felt miserable sending my brother away again like this. I had achieved nothing. I had gone to Paris and not managed to get my three youngest siblings out of the children's home. Samuel had escaped by himself, I had done little to help him, and now I was sending him to another home. I was failing my parents terribly. I felt useless and wretched. I headed back to the farm.

Samuel

Beaulieu-sur-Dordogne
August 1943

Another journey and another children's home. I didn't blame Pierre; he didn't know what to do with me. Besides, I was old enough to look after myself. I could have gotten off the bus anywhere and not turned up at the Jewish Scouts, but I didn't much like being on my own. I decided I would go there and give it a couple of days. If I didn't like it then I would run away.

Pierre left me the entire box of biscuits from the convent, which I devoured on the bus. The guy in the ticket office said the journey would take around five hours. I didn't want to tell the driver where I was getting off, in case the police came and started asking questions. The problem was my full stomach made me sleepy, and, anyhow, I had no watch so how was I supposed to know when five hours had passed? I was drifting in and out of sleep when the bus stopped and the driver called out, 'Beaulieu sur Dordogne.' I quickly grabbed my things and got off.

Pierre had said someone from the Jewish Scouts would meet me, but I couldn't see anyone waiting. I hoped I was in the right place. I had no idea where I should go so I waited until I saw someone to ask.

'Excuse me, Monsieur. Do you know where the home for the Jewish Scouts is?'

'That way, to the square,' he said.

As I reached the square I came across two boys fighting in the street. From a distance it looked like quite a brawl but, as I got nearer, it was clear they were only playing around. When they saw me arrive with my small package of belongings, they stopped fighting and ran over to me.

'Are you Samuel, just arrived on the bus?'

'Yes.'

'See what you did?' one of them said to the other, punching him on the arm. 'You made us late to meet him.' Turning to me he said, 'Hey, Sam, please don't tell the director we didn't meet you.'

'It was your fault. You started it!' said the other boy, punching the first one back.

'It's OK. I won't say anything,' I said.

'Phew! I'm Marcus and this is my brother Rudy.'

'Hello,' I said.

Marcus and Rudy Kohn were from Germany. They spoke broken French with a strong German accent, but that wasn't a problem for me, coming from Metz. Marcus was fourteen like me, and Rudy was a year younger. They fought all the time, but you could see they were best friends and I was jealous not to have a brother I could be that close with. Pierre was four years older and Claude three years younger than me, but that wasn't important right now; the only thing that mattered was neither of them were here.

Marcus and Rudy took me to meet the Scout director, Monsieur Gordin. I was assigned a bed in the same dorm as my two new friends, who showed me around. 'This building is for the little girls. This one is for the older girls. This is the dining room; let's go there now, it's nearly dinner time.' That sounded good to me, I hadn't eaten anything except the cookies since lunch on the day I left the trade school.

****

I was happy with the Scouts and any thoughts of running away were soon forgotten. The Kohn brothers and I got along like a house on fire. They included me in everything they did, and we became a close group of three. The children were organised into troops and we spent the days hiking, singing songs and playing games. That was fine for the little kids, but we older boys wanted more so the director arranged for the local blacksmith to teach us tool and die-making. He was a good man, and an avid listener of Radio Londres.

'Do you see those cars driving around with big antennas?' he asked us. 'That is a signal finder and they can track anyone listening to the radio. If you see one near, you must tell me.'

'But how do you listen to London without an antenna yourself?' I said.

'Well, I may not have an antenna, but my wife has a very strong laundry line!' The blacksmith's wife would hang out the washing on a wire rather than a cord.

'*Ici Londres*,' came the message every day, followed by 'La Marseillaise' and a number of coded messages. '*La vache est bleue.*' '*La lune est tombée.*' I sure hoped those messages made sense to someone!

****

Marcus, Rudy and I went to the local bakery every morning to buy the bread for everyone. This had to be the best job of all; getting to enjoy the smell of freshly baked bread every day and being smiled at by the baker's daughter. We would take the loaves to the kitchen in time for breakfast.

'Let's get this sliced,' said the cook one morning. Each slice was weighed so everyone got their fair portion. She picked up the bread knife and tried to cut through one of the loaves. 'Hmmm, I'm having a bit of trouble today. Feels like the baker might have dropped a stone in here by mistake. I can't get the knife through this at all. Let's see what is going on here.' She pulled the bread apart with her hands. There was an almighty scream. 'That baker is going to get it from me. A rat in my kitchen!'

We ran to see and, sure enough, there was a rat baked into the loaf of bread. The wretched creature must have fallen into the dough as it was left to rise. From then on we were given a thin stick and told to poke it through each loaf before we left the bakery to make sure there were no more hidden surprises!

****

The director called the children together. 'It's time for another camping trip. Most of you will have been through this before but please help anyone who has joined us recently. Pack only a few belongings as we'll all need to help carry the camping gear between us. We leave in one hour.'

There were a few cheers and most of the children looked pleased to hear this news.

'What's going on?' I asked my pals.

'The police chief warns the director when he hears of a visit from the Nazis or anyone who might be dangerous for us. Then we all go camping for a few days until it's safe to return,' said Rudy.

'It's good fun,' added Marcus. 'It makes a change from the usual routine. Come on, let's go and get ready.'

Being part of the Scout movement, the home had a supply of decent tents and other camping gear, which was shared out between us to carry. We set off on foot, leaving as quietly and discreetly as possible. We went in small groups, avoiding the busy streets, and we all met up again at the beginning of the woods on the outskirts of town.

After a long day of hiking we reached a small clearing in a dense part of the woods and set up camp. We were on high ground and a rota was arranged to look out for unwelcome visitors. The lookout on duty was given a pair of binoculars and taught a bird song to call as an alarm. Such responsibility! I was excited to be included in the rota and could hardly wait for my turn. I shared my first shift with a Scout leader who showed me what to look out for. My first lookout passed without incident. The rest of the time was spent learning survival skills: how to build a campfire, make a shelter, how to forage for food and to hunt. I was having the time of my life!

After a few days, word came that it was safe to return to town. I was disappointed to leave camp. We packed up and went back as discreetly as we'd left. Next morning, Rudy, Marcus and I went to collect the bread from the bakery, as before.

'Hello, boys. Did you have a good holiday?' the baker asked and winked at us.

****

Word came again from the police chief that it was 'getting hot'. This time we were split into smaller groups. Rudy, Marcus and I were put with some of the older kids.

'Everyone pack their blankets and take some old newspapers for insulation – it's going to be cold where you're going,' the police chief said with a smile.

Those words sent a chill down my spine – it was exactly what they told Papa and Maman when they had been arrested...

This time we travelled by bus. We were going to a camp used by the secular boy scouts, L'Éclaireurs de France – EDF – near the Swiss border. We had been taught their anthem to sing later when we reached the campsite and we would fly the EDF flag.

We arrived and pitched our tents. We went scouting and hiking and played football against the other scout troops. At night we sat around a big bonfire singing and telling scary stories. After a week or so the weather changed and it turned cold. The other EDF scout troops packed up and left. We pretended we were leaving too, but we had other plans. It was late autumn and, reportedly, the German army was in pretty bad shape. Their lines had thinned out, including those guarding the Swiss border. The Scout leader gathered us all around. 'Others have made it over the border recently. We will stay and observe for a couple of days and then decide whether to send you over.'

'But what about my family here in France?' asked one boy.

'We all have family here and they would want us to be safe. At this moment I believe it is safer for you in Switzerland than it is in France. As soon as the war ends, you will return home.'

The next day Rudy, Marcus and I left to explore the border. By now the other kids were calling us The Three Musketeers which suited me just fine: it had been one of my favourite books at school. We were told to walk along the border due south of where we were camping. We would be close enough to count the number of guards and to make notes if we saw what looked like a good place to cross, but far enough away to not be spotted. The trees provided cover and shelter for us and we had a pair of binoculars to use. I appointed myself chief binocular holder as we couldn't risk the two brothers bickering over them while we were 'undercover'.

We walked with another small group from our camp in a straight line directly towards the border. When we reached a safe distance the three of us turned ninety degrees to the right and starting walking and observing, while the other small group turned ninety degrees to the left and did the same. This was even better than the last camping trip. We saw some German guards at the border, while making sure they didn't see us. It was an exciting adventure. At the end of the day we compared notes back at camp and made our suggestions for the best places to cross. The Scout leader chose one person from each group to show him their recommendations and to avoid sibling rivalry, I was chosen.

We left at first light the next morning: me, the Scout leader, and a boy from the other group. I'd left some marks on trees and counted steps and I easily found the two places along the border we had thought would offer the best chance of crossing over. Then we turned north and went to see the places chosen by the other group. I had to admit their options were better than ours; more sheltered and easier to stay hidden. Our leader agreed and, after observing the area for a couple of hours, decided to send a group over the following day using one of the northern spots. When we returned to camp, he gathered everyone together.

'We've found a good place, but there will always be an element of risk. Three of you will go tomorrow, then three more each day until you're all safely in Switzerland. I'll take you to the border and when you've crossed you'll be met by friends of the Jewish Scouts who will guide you. I suggest the group of three who found the spot go first. Is that alright with everyone?'

No one objected and the selected three – two girls and the boy I spent the day with – sat with the Scout leader to be fully briefed. I don't know if they managed to sleep but, had it been me leaving the next day, I would have had a sleepless night. They left first thing, while the rest of us stayed at the campsite. We waited all day for the Scout leader to return. When he eventually came back, he looked upset.

'It didn't go well,' he said. I thought he meant they hadn't had the chance to cross and I expected to see the three follow him back. But he was alone.

'What happened?'

'We got to the spot and watched for a while. There were no guards anywhere near, so I told the kids to cross the border. They did exactly what I told them to, moving carefully and watching out as they went, keeping undercover as much as possible. They went over without issue, gave me the "all OK" sign and then disappeared into the woods. I waited for the signal from our people on the other side to tell me they had arrived safely, but it never came. Eventually they sent someone to tell me the children had been arrested by the Swiss police, who called the Germans to collect them. I'm sorry.' And he held his head in shame.

'It wasn't your fault,' someone said. The rest of us were silent. We knew that could have been any one of us today.

'We have to leave. We'll trek down to a town called Ville-la-Grand. It's not too far away. We'll start now, stop when it gets dark and carry on tomorrow,' said the leader.

'Shouldn't we wait to see if the others come back?' said one of us.

'There are people nearby to help should they return,' the leader said.

We all had more questions but we didn't ask them; we packed up in silence and left without our three companions.

****

We reached Ville-la-Grand the next day and went straight to the Catholic school, a large two-storey building practically on the Swiss border. Two priests hurried us into a classroom on the ground floor and invited us to sit and rest while our Scout leader went off down the corridor. We took our boots off for the first time that day.

'Look at that blister!' said Rudy.

'That's nothing. Look at mine!' said his brother.

We all had blisters and sores on our feet. Our socks were threadbare, and our boots didn't fit properly. Someone came to bring us water and told us we would be given dinner soon. We had walked all day in a grey mood but now we started to feel a bit brighter and it wasn't long before we were slinging our smelly socks at each other.

'Ahem!' The Scout leader came back with a man in a black robe and tried to get us to quiet down. 'Boys, girls, please. This is Father Boccard.'

'Hello, children,' said the priest. 'Please gather around. Welcome to The Fathers of St Francis. If anyone asks, you are students here. We are next to the Swiss border, in fact our garden wall is practically on the border and that is why, with God's will, we hope to help you cross into Switzerland. I know you may be nervous. I have been told how three of your friends were captured yesterday so we are going to make sure it is safe before we try anything.'

Father Boccard told us to follow him up to the attic. At the top of the stairs was a door. He said, 'When I open this door I want you to go through in silence, two or three at a time, and walk over to the window. From there you will see Switzerland on the other side of the garden wall, a barbed-wire fence and, most probably, German and maybe Swiss border guard patrols. Observe what you see carefully – for two reasons. Firstly, so you will be confident in us telling you when it is safe to go over the wall and, secondly, so you know what you will find on the other side. There is a place directly in front where you can get through the barbed-wire fence. Make sure you see it.' He opened the bedroom door and we entered in small groups.

Sure enough, it was exactly as he said it would be. We saw the wall, the barbed wire with the gap, and the border guard patrols. When we were all back downstairs, Father Boccard continued to explain the plan. 'There appear to be extra guards on patrol, perhaps because your friends were caught yesterday. We will need to wait until the guards go back to their usual routine which leaves a gap of just over two minutes between patrols for you to climb over the wall and run to safety. Many have already done this and there should be ample time for young people like you to manage it.'

'Father, how do you know when it is safe?' one of us asked.

'That is a good question. Our friends from the village wait with you by the wall. I watch from the upstairs window.

187

When it is safe I take off my beret as a signal. A ladder is quickly put up and over you go, running to the gap in the barbed-wire fence and over to safety in Switzerland.'

'What if we get caught?'

'Nobody has been caught yet by the German patrols, although some have been caught by the Swiss guards. Once through the fence, they've only ever been brought back to our village. No one has been arrested for trying, but that's because the Germans aren't aware of what we are doing. It will be fine if you follow our instructions: stay silent, only go over the wall when you're told it is safe, and move quickly.'

'We have people on the other side who will show you where to go,' said the Scout leader.

'And we have some incredible neighbours who help. Ah, here is Marcel!' he said as the classroom door opened and in walked a young man.

'*Bonjour*, Father Boccard. Who have we here?'

'Some new Jewish children needing our help. We've been through the procedure, but perhaps you can show them the signs?'

'No problem. Listen, kids, when we are waiting by the wall we need to be completely silent so we communicate with our hands and faces instead of our voices. Has anyone seen a Charlie Chaplin movie?'

We all put our hands up and agreed Charlie Chaplin was the best.

'Me too. He's the one I got this idea from,' said Marcel. 'After the war I want to be an actor like him, but for now I use my silent acting to help you. So, this is the sign for stop,' and he held his hand out abruptly. 'This is the sign for go,' and he waved his hand in one direction. 'This is the sign for

get ready, and this one means we have to wait a while…'
And so he went on, amazing us with his easy to understand
signals and testing us on what they meant.

'I have a signal too,' said Rudy. 'This means I need to pee!'
And he locked his knees together and doubled over with a
pained look on his face. The whole room fell about laughing.

'And this one means I need to take a dump,' said Marcus, who wasn't going to be overshadowed by his brother. He
screwed up his face into one of horror and put both hands on
his backside while running around the room.

'Shh, boys and girls. Quiet now, please.' Even the Scout
leader had been laughing, but he soon brought order back to
the room.

'Indeed. Thank you everyone and thank you, Marcel,'
said Father Boccard as the young man waved us an animated
goodbye.

****

We stayed at The Fathers of St. Francis for a couple of days
until it was obvious the extra patrols showed no sign of being
lifted. We would need to abandon our plan of crossing into
Switzerland.

I wasn't sorry. I didn't want to leave France while my
brothers and sisters were still here or for when my parents
came home. I think most of us felt the same.

'No one will be returning to Beaulieu-sur-Dordogne,'
explained the Scout leader. 'It's not safe anymore. We've been
told to close the home and move you all to safer areas. As
Switzerland is now not an option you will instead be given
new identities as Catholic children.'

This news came as a surprise and we all had many questions. How would we know how to act? Would people know we were really Jewish?

'We'll give you as much information as possible. Let me look at the list… Samuel Laskowski, Marcus Kohn and Rudy Kohn, you are going to a trade school in Tonneins. There are other Jewish boys there already, but trust no one, boys or teachers. Samuel, your name is now Samuel Chastain and you are from Orléans.'

'Why Orléans?'

'Because its city hall has been bombed and all the registrations lost. There is no way of checking if your papers are false. Rudy and Marcus, you are now Rudy and Marcus Gauthier. You were born in Alsace, hence your German accents. Samuel, you must help your friends improve their French as much as possible.'

We were taken to a small room where our ration books were 'sanitised'. Potatoes cut in half were used to absorb the ink from the issuing city stamp, the page was then cleaned with bleach to erase our names and our new name handwritten on.

'Samuel Chastain?' said the Scout leader. No one replied.

'Samuel Chastain!' he said again, looking directly at me.

'Oh yes, sir! I am Samuel Chastain,' I said.

'Here are your papers. Mazel tov, you are now Catholic!'

'My name is Samuel Chastain and, God help me, I am Catholic,' I repeated to myself.

Pierre

Bazaiges
September 1943

After I put Samuel on the bus to Beaulieu-sur-Dordogne, I returned to the farm and to Aimee. The last thing I had said to her was that I was returning to Sarry to get the money for the fine and coming straight back, but that was before I read the letter from Samuel. I was afraid she'd be angry, but when I explained I had to go to Paris to make sure my siblings were safe, she understood and we carried on as if I had never left. Being with Aimee brought a welcome distraction from worrying about my brothers and sisters. She had lots of questions about them and I said she could meet them after the war was over and we all lived together again.

There were still crops to harvest and then plenty of work preparing the farm for the winter months. I was so grateful to the farmer and his wife for allowing me to return. There was no contact from Resistance members in the area, so I kept my nose down and stayed where I was; at least I was able to receive letters from Samuel while I stayed put.

Samuel wrote to me of the adventures he was having; he seemed well and was learning life and survival skills.

Jacqueline Goldstein wrote to me from Louveciennes with updates about Claude, Henriette and Georgette; they were well and happy too. Jacqueline even sent me a photograph of them with some other children in the garden of the orphanage. Henriette's hair had grown longer but Georgette looked like she had been visited again by head lice as her head was freshly shaved. Claude had more hair than both of his sisters! Most importantly, they were all smiling.

Georgette

While Jacqueline studied in the morning we stayed in the big walled garden, free to play hide and seek (there were some really big trees to hide behind) or throw a ball around. If the weather was bad we would stay inside, where there were plenty of rooms to play in. We could do what we wanted, as long as we kept out of the way of Monsieur Denis. His daughter Michèle would sit alone with a beautiful doll, watching us out of the corner of her eye. She looked like she wanted to join us, but her strict parents would not allow it so instead she played alone in her pretty dress with her expensive toys. The few times she asked her maman if she could play with us she was given a handful of candy to convince her she was better off playing by herself.

Whether Michèle played with us or not didn't matter; we had plenty of friends here and lots of space to run around in. In the afternoon we often walked the short distance with Jacqueline into Marly Park. Jacqueline told us it had been the gardens of the Royal Palace, destroyed during the French

Revolution. Henriette and I pretended to be princesses from the royal palace as we ran past the broken statues left lying around. Or we went to Marly woods or to the Louveciennes forest, which were both a short walk away from Place Roux. We played happily in the shade, exploring down little pathways and climbing on the fallen tree trunks. In the evenings we put on shows, singing, dancing and acting out made-up stories.

This was our life during that summer. We knew there was a world outside of Louveciennes as we all had family elsewhere, but we had no idea what was happening in the rest of the world. For us the only terrible things were the food, or rather the lack of it, and the fear in the orphanage when a German soldier or the French police visited.

****

We were talking to our brother about Jewish holidays. Henriette and I had no memory of ever celebrating any Jewish festivals.

'I remember Pesach – that's the best Jewish holiday,' said Claude.

'Why is it the best?' Henriette asked.

'Because that's when you two were born!'

But even for Claude they were a distant memory. Without our parents to explain it to us, we had no idea what it was to be Jewish except it meant the Germans and many of the French hated us. So instead of celebrating the Jewish New Year we celebrated autumn, enjoying the beautiful red, yellow and orange colours of the trees all around us and playing with the piles of fallen leaves, acorns and conkers in the park and forest. One autumn afternoon we were waiting for Jacqueline to take us to the park when one of the other monitors came to find us.

'Children, Jacqueline is not feeling well today and can't take you out. You can join the older children in the garden.'

'What's wrong with her?'

'She has a tummy ache, nothing to worry about. I'm sure she will feel better tomorrow.'

But Jacqueline only felt worse the next day and the day after and, eventually, the doctor was called. He was one of few Jewish doctors who had not been arrested and was still allowed to look after the children. He usually visited each home once a month but came especially to see Jacqueline. She had appendicitis and was sent off to the hospital in nearby Saint-Germain-en-Laye. Jacqueline's best friend at Place Roux was Suzanne Furst, the general supervisor. Mademoiselle Furst walked the six kilometres to and from the hospital to visit Jacqueline every day during the week she was there. She took messages back and forth and gave us daily updates on Jacqueline's progress, promising us that she was doing well and would be back soon.

The only other visitor Jacqueline had at the hospital was her grandmother, who was given special permission to travel from her area of Paris to Saint-Germain-en-Laye, something Jews were not usually allowed to do. Jacqueline told us of her grandmother's visit when she returned to Place Roux and I thought how lucky she was to go to hospital as it meant her family were able to visit her.

'Did your maman and papa come to visit you too?'

'No, Georgette,' Jacqueline said. I felt terrible because now she looked sad and it was my fault; I shouldn't have asked her that. I got together all the children from our group and we decided to put on a show to cheer Jacqueline up and help her feel better. We loved putting on shows. The monitors arranged a stage at one end of the dining room that we used for our performances. We spent the whole afternoon rehearsing. Cook was a bit annoyed because we were making a racket next to her kitchen. When we were ready for an audience, we called Jacqueline to watch.

'Ladies and… ladies,' announced little Tommy, standing in the middle of the stage. 'Welcome to our show!'

Jacqueline clapped enthusiastically. Rosette joined Tommy on stage. 'We would like to sing a song for Jacqueline to make her feel better,' she announced.

Then the rest of us came onto the stage. Mademoiselle Furst had the honour of counting us in 'un, deux, trois' and we all started singing together 'Une souris verte', one of our favourite nursery rhymes about a little green mouse:

A green mouse
That ran in the grass
I caught it by its tail
I showed it to some men
The men said
Dip it in oil
Dip it in water
It will become a snail
Nice and warm.
I put it in a drawer
It said, 'It is too dark.'
I put it in my hat
It said, 'It is too warm.'

As we sang we acted out the story, pretending to catch an imaginary mouse and do all sorts of terrible things to it. It made Jacqueline laugh and clap. When we finished, Henriette and I came to the front of the stage. Holding hands, we announced together, 'Thank you for watching our show,' and took a bow.

'Bravo!' said Jacqueline. 'That was fantastic. Thank you, all.' And we rushed over to give her a hug.

****

When Jacqueline felt better after her operation she took us to the nearby parks and woods again, although it was now early winter and we couldn't go out when the weather was really bad; for one thing we had no way to dry our clothes if they got wet as there was no coal left for the fires. There were still trees in the woods but they were far too big for us to cut down so we had to make do with the twigs which we picked up from the ground and sometimes someone from the village shared their wood with us.

One afternoon, while we were getting ready to go to the park, Mademoiselle Furst came and whispered something in Jacqueline's ear. She looked shocked and hurried out of the room.

'Is Jacqueline alright?' I asked.

'She has a visitor, so I'll take you to the park this afternoon. Is everyone ready?'

'Yes!' we all shouted happily. Mademoiselle Furst was very kind. We liked her as much as we liked Jacqueline. We trundled off to the park for what seemed longer than usual. It was the end of November, and almost dark by the time we returned home. After we took off our coats some of us went to find Jacqueline to tell her about our afternoon, but she was nowhere to be seen. Eventually she came to find us. We could tell she had been crying.

'Jacqueline, why are you sad? Who was your visitor?'

'It was my grandmother who came to see me.'

'Is she here now? Can we meet her?' we asked.

'Did she bring any food?' asked Rosette.

'No, she isn't here anymore. She had to go back to Paris before dark,' said Jacqueline. 'And yes, Rosie,' she added with a small smile, 'she did bring some food.'

'Is this the first time your grandmother has come to visit you here?' asked Henriette. Jacqueline nodded.

'Why doesn't she come more often?'

'It is quite dangerous for her to travel, but she hid her yellow star under her coat and came anyway,' said Jacqueline.

'Why did she come if it is dangerous?'

'Because she had some news for me. News that couldn't wait,' replied Jacqueline and she burst into tears.

Samuel

Toulouse
November 1943

Under our new identities Marcus, Rudy and I took the train to Tonneins with Andre, an older boy assigned to accompany us and make sure we arrived safely. We travelled by train then walked to our new school. Andre left after we signed the register and were told to join the queue to collect our bedding and wash kit.

'Next!' called the man behind the counter.

Marcus walked up.

'Name?'

'Marcus… errr… errr…'

'Don't you know your name?'

'I…' Marcus looked at his brother desperately for help but Rudy looked just as flustered. I realised neither remembered their new surname.

'Hey! Gauthier,' I shouted to Marcus. 'Hurry up!'

'Gauthier! That's my name!' declared Marcus to the man behind the counter.

****

We were enrolled in tool and die-making classes. The black-smith in Châteauroux had taught us some basic skills and we wanted to learn more.

A few days after we arrived, Rudy and I were in the yard when Andre suddenly reappeared. He was at the gate.

'Where is Marcus?' he asked.

'Inside,' said Rudy.

'Get him. We need to leave – RIGHT NOW! Do you have your papers on you?'

We checked our pockets and nodded.

'Good. Don't go back to your dorm. Leave everything else.'

Rudy found Marcus in a minute and we ran out the gate and all the way to the railway station.

'What happened?' we asked Andre once we were far away from the school.

'The school cook called the police to say she suspected there were three new Jewish boys who just enrolled. The police said they would come and pick them up at midnight tonight.'

'How did you find out?'

'The cook told her assistant, not realising he's a Jew who works with us. He alerted me straightaway and I came as fast as I could.'

'So, now where?' I asked.

'Now to the next school. This time in Toulouse,' replied Andre.

It wasn't until we were on the train that I realised I had left my only remaining belonging – the music book I had brought from Sarry.

****

It was late evening when we boarded the train to Toulouse. After an hour the train stopped, and the guard told everyone to disembark. The allies had bombed the track ahead in an air raid; we would have to walk the short distance to the next station and wait until the track was cleared and repaired before we could continue our journey. There weren't many of us, and most settled down to get some sleep on the benches of the station waiting room.

It was past midnight when three German soldiers entered. They wore big breastplates – German Military Police! One of them was over six foot tall. He started on the right-hand side of the waiting room and went around demanding papers. When he got to me, I handed over my 'washed' ration book. He looked at it, then at me. Keeping my book, he did the same to Rudy, Marcus and Andre. He held our papers, then stepped back and stared at us. My heart was racing; I was sure we were done for. Then he stepped forward, handed us back our papers and said, 'Let's go!' At first, I thought he was talking to us and I was just about to stand up and follow him out, but then I realised he was talking to the other soldiers. They walked out the room, not bothering to check any more papers. I'm sure he knew ours were fake. We had no clue as to why he let us go. We'd had two lucky breaks that day.

Early the next morning we were able to continue our journey.

****

We arrived at the Centre Mercier trade school, just past the railroad yard in Toulouse. It was time for Andre to leave us once again. We were met by the headmaster, Monsieur

Fournier, who told us there were already twenty Jewish boys hidden in the school. The other students had no idea we were not Catholic, so we should do our best to not raise suspicion.

'Next door is a reform school for Catholic boys and both schools share the chapel in between our two buildings. There are services every day, but you boys don't need to go; you can stay in school while the others are at chapel. Some of the Catholic boys don't go either, it is not compulsory,' explained the headmaster. He was a kind man and we instantly liked him.

There were classes in gardening, electrical engineering, woodworking, basket-weaving, leatherwork… we were asked what we wanted to learn. I chose woodworking, taught by Monsieur Labitte. He was an excellent teacher, he showed us how to work by hand as there was no machinery.

We were assigned chores by Monsieur Kraft, the school administrator. Mine was to raise the French flag every morning and bring it down every evening. The Germans had outlawed 'La Marseillaise', which then became the anthem of the Resistance, so a new national anthem was created for Pétain – *Maréchal nous voilà!* Marshall, here we are! We sang it while the flag was raised every morning, even though most of us wished the old fool a quick but painful death.

****

Winter arrived and we settled into our new school. We now knew who the other Jewish boys were. The building was old and parts of it were in need of repair, but it provided a safe place for us. There was one huge shower room, the size of a family home, which had a hot water pipe that went all around the walls with half a dozen taps along it. The boiler was fuelled by coal and it needed two stokers to get the water hot enough for the showers. We made sure two Jewish boys were always on the rota to load the coal and then watch the gauges which would be allowed to rise until they were on the verge of blowing, to create the most possible steam. The rest of us were always first to enter the shower room in front of the Catholic boys. Half of us would go to the left and the other half to the right and we would all face the wall. The first boys in would go directly to the taps and open them up straightaway to let out all the steam and then we would wait for it to fill the room before we turned around, our Jewish modesty covered by the vapour! We did this every morning we were in the school and not once did any of the Catholic boys realise there were Jews among them.

****

I woke one morning with a terrible pain in my stomach. I couldn't face breakfast, something that was unusual for any of us as food was scarce and we normally ate everything we were given. One of the teachers noticed me suffering, and I was sent back to bed. During the morning the pain got worse and I had diarrhoea. The school nurse was called.

'You only have a slight fever but along with the stomach pain and diarrhoea it could be appendicitis. I'll call the doctor to see you,' she said.

Rudy and Marcus had been waiting outside and when the nurse left, they ran in to see me.

'What's the matter with you?'

'She thinks it's appendicitis, so the doctor is coming. I might need to go to hospital and have an operation.'

'Lucky!' said Marcus. 'No school for you, and I bet the food is better at the hospital.'

'You idiot!' said Rudy, as he hit his brother around the head. 'Don't you realise the doctors and nurses are going to see that Samuel is circumcised?'

'Oh no, I didn't think about that,' said Marcus, as his brother rolled his eyes in despair. 'What shall we do?'

'There is nothing we can do except hope they are sympathetic,' said Rudy.

The doctor came that afternoon. The appendicitis was confirmed, and I was taken straight to the nearest hospital, which was run by nuns. My symptoms were so extreme by now that I was taken straight to surgery, so I really didn't have time to worry about what might happen.

As the anaesthetic started to wear off I opened my eyes to see the smiling face of a nun, looking down at me. 'Are you an angel?' I asked, in my semi-conscious state.

'No, Son, you're not in Heaven yet. The operation went well, and you're going to be fine,' she said.

My secret was safe; the nurses and doctors did not betray me. The surgeon who came to check on me was also kind and told me the operation had been a complete success despite my appendix being one of the 'ugliest' he had ever seen. I think that was meant as a compliment!

After a few days' recovery, I was sent back to school. Monsieur Fournier called me to his office.

'How are you feeling, Samuel?'

'I have a little pain, Monsieur, but I have some medicine to help that.'

'I heard the operation was a success and I'm sure they looked after you well at the hospital,' he said.

'I was worried the nuns would see I am Jewish, but no one said anything,' I whispered.

'You have a lot of friends in Toulouse.'

'Really? I don't think I know anyone in Toulouse except for the people at school,' I said.

'I meant that the Jewish people have friends here. Do you know of Monsignor Saliège?'

'No.'

'Monsignor Saliège is the Archbishop of Toulouse and has ordered his clergy and nuns to help hide Jews, particularly children. Unfortunately, the priest of the school next door is not sympathetic to any children, whether they are Jewish or Catholic, so I suggest you keep away from him.

'While you are recovering from your operation you should not take part in sports activities, to allow for your wound to heal. As you will have some free time, perhaps you would like to carry out some errands for me instead?'

'Of course. What sort of errands?'

'Mostly delivering letters around town. Nothing strenuous.'

'I would be happy to help, Monsieur,' I said. I was genuinely pleased. The next day, when the other boys went outside to play football, I reported to the headmaster's office. He handed me a small envelope with a handwritten name and address on the front.

'Please take this letter to Monsieur Blanc at that address. Make sure you give it to him in person. He may give you a letter to bring back.'

We were free to go into Toulouse town centre at the weekend, so I knew it quite well and had no problem finding the address. When I arrived I saw it was the government office in charge of food distribution. I went to the front desk and asked to see Monsieur Blanc.

'And why do you want to see him?' asked the lady behind the desk, looking at me suspiciously.

'I have a message for him from the headmaster of my school,' I said.

'You can tell me. I will pass on the message.'

'Excuse me, Madame, I have to deliver it in person otherwise I'll be in big trouble.'

I tried to look scared, as if I was worried the headmaster would beat me if I didn't follow his orders.

'Very well. Monsieur Blanc is in the office at the end of the corridor.'

'Merci, Madame,' I said, hurrying away.

I knocked on the office door and entered. There were four desks, each with a nameplate, but the only one occupied was the desk directly opposite the door. It belonged to Monsieur Blanc, who had been reading some papers but looked up when I approached his desk.

'What do you want?' he asked. I wasn't sure he was talking to me as one eye looked one way while the other stared in the opposite direction, but neither directly at me. How could he see with his eyes crossed like that?

'What is it, young man?' he asked again, and I finally found my voice.

'This letter from Monsieur Fournier,' I said, handing him the envelope. 'Shall I wait for a reply?'

Monsieur Blanc first checked that the letter was sealed, which it was. It hadn't occurred to me to open it. He picked up a letter opener and swiftly slit open the envelope, took out the note and scanned it over, which must have been quite a challenge as he moved the paper from side to side. Having read it he returned the letter to its envelope.

'What is your name?' I paused before replying – it was disconcerting answering someone who looked anywhere but right at you!

'Samuel La... Chastain. My name is Samuel Chastain,' I replied, the distraction nearly making me forget my new surname.

'Well, Samuel Chastain. Thank you for bringing me the letter. There is no reply on this occasion. You may return to school.'

'Yes, sir.' I left the office, still a bit confused by the appearance of Monsieur Blanc. When I got back I reported to Monsieur Fournier.

'Ah, Samuel. Any problems?' he asked.

'No, sir. Monsieur Blanc said there was no reply on this occasion.'

'That's fine. Now you know where his office is, perhaps you wouldn't mind taking any future letters to him for me?'

'Of course.'

'Excellent. Samuel, I have another job for you. Is it correct that you know German?'

'I heard it spoken in Metz before the war,' I said, 'but that was a long time ago, so I'm not sure how good my knowledge is now.'

'I think it would be useful if you tried to retain as much of your German as possible. You never know when it could be needed. We are expecting a group of six Jewish boys who have escaped from Germany and will be staying with us.

I'd like you to help them learn to speak French, thinking particularly about their pronunciation. It is important they learn to communicate with the other boys and try to sound as French as possible.'

'Yes, sir. I already help Marcus and Rudy with their French.'

'Indeed, and you're doing a great job. Carry on.'

As soon as the German boys arrived at the school we started with the French lessons, using the time when the other boys were at chapel and any other free moments we could find. The new boys were eager and quick to learn, and within a couple of weeks they were all making good progress. We all became great friends. They taught us German army songs, and we would march up and down the corridors singing them while the new boys shouted words of encouragement to us in their recently acquired French.

Monsieur Fournier had given one of the Jewish boys a radio and every night we would cram into his dorm to listen to BBC Radio Londres. This was another great way to help my new German friends improve their language skills. We were desperate for some news of what was happening to the Jews who had been deported, but they were never mentioned.

Another opportunity for the German boys to better their French was on our weekend trips into the centre of Toulouse. They would read out shop names and street signs to us and we would correct their pronunciation. On one such trip we saw a group of German soldiers marching down the road towards us. Some of the boys started singing a German army song. One by one the rest of our group joined in until we were all singing along at full volume. As the soldiers approached, they gave us a Nazi salute and we saluted them back as they passed us. When they were out of sight we ran off down the road laughing, shocked at our own chutzpah!

Georgette

Louveciennes
November 1943

Jacqueline's grandmother travelled from Paris to the orphanage to bring her a letter.

Written in tiny writing on a small scrap of paper, it was from her maman and papa. She explained that in the camp where her parents were being held, a list of names would appear every day. If your name was on the list, you would be deported to another place far, far away. Her maman and papa were never on the list, however, because her papa had been an officer in the French reserve army and that made them 'safe'.

But then one day some prisoners were discovered secretly digging a tunnel out of the camp. Apparently one of the other prisoners had told on them. As a punishment, the Germans wanted many, many more names on the list, even the names of people who had been safe before. Jacqueline's maman and papa wrote they were being deported, but where they didn't know. Their letter had found its way through many hands to reach her grandmother.

****

Jacqueline's grandmother returned to Paris before curfew. Jacqueline was helping us to get ready for bed when Mademoiselle Furst came to our room. She went over to comfort her friend.

'Oh, Suzanne, I feel so terrible,' I heard Jacqueline say. 'This is all my fault.'

'How is that?'

'I should never have left Drancy. I should still be there with my parents.'

'But you were sick with diphtheria, you might have died if you hadn't gone to hospital.'

'Then I should have gone back after I recovered instead of going to the children's home.'

'What could you have done? I think your mother and father would prefer you here, safe with us,' said her friend, stroking her hair.

I had always thought of Jacqueline as a grown-up, because she was like a mother to us, but now she seemed like a scared child.

Jacqueline managed to put on a brave face for our sake. Like us, she didn't know where her parents had been sent, which meant she could at least still hope to see them again.

Life at Place Roux became more difficult by the end of the year. Mademoiselle Furst was let go by Monsieur Denis as he couldn't pay her anymore. Jacqueline was told she must work harder for her keep by performing more chores at the orphanage and had to cease her studies. I know she was unhappy and thought of running away, but her grandmother would have been punished for her actions, so she stayed. I think she also stayed for us – we all loved her and needed her so badly.

****

On New Year's Day there was little to celebrate. We were told to pack our few belongings because German soldiers would be moving into the orphanage, and we were to go to a house nearby, 18 Rue de la Paix. The Street of Peace! We would stay in our small group; Henriette and I with the other seven children, and Jacqueline looking after us. At least that was good news. Now Jacqueline would be with us all day and all night as she would sleep in our room too.

Samuel

Toulouse
December 1943

With only a fence to separate our school's courtyard from that of the reform school next door, we often witnessed the brutal punishments handed out by the Catholic priests to the boys, and we considered ourselves lucky to be on this side.

One day, in the middle of winter and despite the freezing weather, some of us were outside kicking a football around when over the fence we saw a priest push a boy into the middle of the yard. He was ordered to take his clothes off and kneel on the ground. The priest held garden shears and began to cut the boy's hair in wild, violent strokes. He filled a bucket from the outside tap and poured the water over the boy's head; the water almost froze on the poor lad, who shivered and began turning blue. The priest returned to the tap to fill up the bucket again and again, to torture the boy. My friends ran inside, not wanting to complicate their lives by getting involved, but I couldn't help myself. I stood and watched in shocked silence, and then disgust took over and I shouted at the priest. I can't remember what I said, it was anger talking, not me. He glared at me and stormed back inside, leaving the boy shivering for a few minutes and then, when he saw the priest wasn't coming back, he ran back inside too.

The next day the same priest came to see Monsieur Fournier. 'Why don't these children come to chapel?' he demanded. 'From now on everyone comes to the services. No excuses. Maybe that will teach your boys some manners and to mind their own business.' So we all had to go to church. It was the first time I had ever been, and I had no idea of what to do. I stayed towards the back of the line so I could watch and copy the other boys ahead of me. As they filed past the font, each boy put their hand in the holy water to cross themselves when they entered the chapel. When it was my turn I put my left hand in the holy water and then crossed myself. The priest came over and slapped me for using the wrong hand, shouting I was a lazy Catholic who hadn't been to services for so long I had forgotten which hand to use. I thought I had got away lightly with a slap, but as we were leaving the chapel at the end of the service the priest grabbed me by the collar and pulled me to one side. 'No you don't, boy. Not so quickly. I have some jobs for you, so you remember to use the correct hand when you are blessing yourself. You will mark out our new volleyball court with stones.'

This didn't sound like such a terrible punishment. 'Where will I get the stones?' I asked.

'You'll make them by breaking the big rocks in the yard using a mallet... with your left hand. That will help you to remember your left hand is for work and your right hand is for God. Pray that the Lord will help you with your task.'

I had my doubts about the Lord helping me.

'You will also clear the trash outside the school kitchen every evening after supper. And, before you ask, you will have the use of a shovel for this purpose.'

It could be worse, I thought, remembering the poor boy from yesterday evening who had the buckets of cold water poured over his naked body. I had looked out for him in the chapel that morning, but I hadn't seen him. He was probably in bed with pneumonia.

'You will give me your shoes now.'

'But, sir.'

'Silence! Take off your shoes.'

By now everyone else had left the chapel. There was no one to help me, but I wouldn't have given him the satisfaction of seeing me ask for help. I bent down to take off my shoes and handed them over. I had only had them for a few months since I grew out of my last pair. Mine had been handed down to another boy and my new pair had holes in the soles when they were handed down to me. Luckily, I attended leatherwork classes and had patched the holes.

Now I had no shoes, only socks which were threadbare and offered no protection at all. The stone floor of the chapel froze the soles of my feet which, at least, protected me from the pain of walking on the gravel once I got outside.

It was Sunday, the day of rest, so I was not expected to work on the volleyball court that afternoon, but I did have to go and clear the trash after supper that evening. The priest was there to check that I was still barefoot, and I suppose he had something to do with the broken glass on the floor by the trash bins. I had to move slowly to avoid stepping on the shards of glass; I managed to miss the large pieces, but I did cut my feet on some of the smaller pieces. After

I was excused, I went straight to the leatherwork classroom and made myself a pair of sandals. I made a pattern drawing around my foot, cut out double soles and straps and sewed them together. They were so good some of the other boys wanted a pair too, so I made some more for my friends. Those sandals saved my feet.

****

The Kohn brothers and I went into Toulouse as usual one Saturday afternoon. As we turned a street corner towards the town centre we noticed German troops and Milice had blocked off the street ahead with their trucks. We stopped to watch from a safe distance. A group of men walking past were called over and the Germans barked something to them, but we were too far away to hear what they said. The group of men stood for a moment, we couldn't see their expressions, but they appeared confused as to what to do. Then the German soldiers pointed their rifles at the men. We thought they were going to shoot, but they just took aim while the officer shouted again. The men unbuckled their belts and lowered their trousers and underwear. The Milice approached them, bending down to look at their private parts. I guess all was in order as the men were allowed to dress themselves and walk away. No papers were shown. We didn't need to watch anymore; we knew we couldn't go any further. Between us and the roadblock was the La Variétés cinema.

'Let's go see what's on,' Marcus suggested.

'Are you crazy?' I said. These days it was only permitted to screen Nazi propaganda films.

'Can you think of anything else to do? I don't want to go back to school so soon. It's well before the roadblock so we should be fine, but we'll need to act really normal walking down the street, so we don't attract any attention.'

'Samuel and I will be fine but acting normal could be a challenge for you!' said his brother, receiving a thump on his arm in return.

The Kohn brothers kept me sane during the war even though their sibling rivalry made me miss my brothers desperately, especially Claude. We walked back around the corner so we could practise our 'normal walking' and when we thought we had got it right we turned around and casually strolled down the street. The cinema was hosting a Milice recruitment drive. Many Milice recruits had come from the jails so they were, in fact, dangerous criminals with weapons; that's why we usually avoided them. Now they needed more men to sign up and fight on the Russian front. There were posters on display with the Milice emblem, the Greek letter Gamma stamping out the Communist red hammer and sickle symbol of the Russian flag with the words: *Milice Française. Contre le communisme.* French Militia. Against Communism.

We went in and up to the front desk.

'We want to join and fight for our country!' we announced.

'How old are you, boys?'

'Fourteen years old, sir.'

'Still a little young to fight, but I admire your spirit. Come back in a few years, or at least when you've grown a bit taller!'

'Yes, sir!'

'Would you boys like to watch our information film? You could learn something they won't teach you at school.'

'Sure,' I said.

'Go right in. The film is about to start.'

We entered the cinema. It must have been smart in its day but, like most of France, it was now rundown and in need of repair.

In the semi-darkness we could see a few of the seats were already occupied by a group of young men, so we sat as far as possible from them. Suddenly a white light beamed through the centre of the room, bringing the screen to life with a fast-moving display of black lines and blurred circles. *Der ewige Jude*. We knew immediately what it meant, but for the benefit of the others in the audience a Milice officer stood at the side and translated: 'The Eternal Jew.'

'Is this a Charlie Chaplin movie?' joked Marcus in a whisper. Powerful, dramatic music filled the room and our translator explained we were now watching 'dirty Jews' in the ghettos of Poland. I was instantly interested! My parents were born in Poland and I might have distant relatives there still. I wondered if I could recognise anyone, maybe someone with the trademark Hofman almond-shaped eyes that me and my siblings had inherited from Maman. I watched intently the images of the streets crammed full of Polish Jews hustling and bustling, while listening to the make-do translator telling us Jews are bartering traders who don't want to do honest work, and are like rats and parasites who benefit from the hard work of others and live in filthy homes despite their wealth. I thought about Papa and Zayde, who had both been traders, so I couldn't argue with that fact. But I also remembered Maman scrubbing our home to keep it spotless, and I was furious this film dared suggest that Jews choose to live in filth.

The next scene was in some sort of nightclub in Berlin. I was fascinated! These Jewish people were so glamorous, wearing fine clothes and having dinner in a fancy setting. I could imagine my beautiful mother wearing an elegant dress and drinking expensive wine in a nightclub like that. I realised this was not a newsreel; this was a film made a few years before and the Jews I was watching probably did not live in such luxury these days.

Next the film jumped to New York and reeled off a long list of Jews who were running Wall Street. This was great news for my aunts and uncles who had gone to New York, and it was also good to know that Jews were so important in America. But if they had as much power as this film said, then why weren't they helping us in Europe?

Next Leon Blum popped up on the screen; the Jewish former Prime Minister of France was in New York? Then Marcus, sitting to my left, knocked me sharply in the ribs with his elbow. 'Did you see that?' he whispered, not taking his eyes off the screen. Our translator now said some rubbish about art while images of naked bodies appeared in front of us. These were sculptures and paintings by Jewish artists being described as 'degenerate and disgusting' – but not in our eyes!

Next were examples of 'filthy pornography'; oh, why did it have to leave the screen so abruptly? Then theatre and film stars, all Jewish. How fantastic! And Charlie Chaplin being greeted by a rapturous crowd when he visited Berlin. Marcus was right, this film did have Charlie Chaplin in it! Could it get any better? Yes! Now we were celebrating Purim at the home of a family in Warsaw. Our translator explained with disgust how this festival celebrated the slaughter of seventy-five thousand Persians, but I was more interested in how the Jewish family were eating, drinking, singing and laughing together at the dinner table and exchanging gifts. It looked wonderful. The next scene was in a synagogue and showed the rabbi carrying the Torah scrolls around for the congregation to kiss. It brought back memories of Rosh Hashanah and Yom Kippur in Sarry when Rabbi Epstein had given Papa the Torah scrolls to bring to our house for the High Holy Day services. That was nearly three years ago now. Bittersweet memories. Finally, back to reality with a final scene of Hitler ranting about the destruction of the poisonous Jewish race in Europe.

The film ended and a light came on at the back of the room. Marcus, Rudy and I sat in silence trying to make sense of what we had seen. Parts of the film had been wonderful, others terrible. We weren't stupid; we understood it was meant to fuel Jew hatred and I had to admit it was cleverly done. Those suffering from hunger and the misery of war would be furious at the sight of Jews enjoying positions of power and luxury. I hoped they had the sense to realise this was mere propaganda; old bits of film put together to make it seem like the Jews were to blame. This wasn't even our war. The Jewish people hadn't chosen to go to war, so why were we being singled out as the evil ones?

Marcus was the first to speak and, when he did, I realised the other people in the room had already left.

'Shall we go and see if the roadblock is still there?'

The film had lasted for around an hour and it was worth taking a look, so we sent Rudy to check things out but he quickly came back to report the Germans and Milice were still blocking our path into town. Making sure we were still alone we talked about what we had watched. We all had similar thoughts. Like me, Marcus and Rudy had relatives who had gone to New York. They could remember celebrating Purim with their families, their father getting drunk 'on the rabbi's orders' and their mother preparing a wonderful meal. We longed for those days again. We boasted to each other about how clean our mothers had kept our homes and how wrong the film was saying that Jews live in filth, then we fell silent, remembering the happy times.

More men and boys came into the room, filling up the seats. A different Milice came to serve as the translator. He didn't know we had already seen the film once or, if he did, he didn't care. And so we watched it again. Thankfully, after the second time, the roadblock was cleared and we were free to leave.

****

My life at the Centre Mercier continued under the protection of Monsieur Fournier. I would carry messages between my cross-eyed friend Monsieur Blanc (for he did become a friend) and Monsieur Fournier. I helped my German Jewish friends to improve their French, and we all successfully hid our Judaism from the other Catholic boys and priests next door. I attended chapel services and crossed myself with the correct hand. I gave no reason for one anyone to punish me. That's not to say I didn't have a few hairy moments.

Toulouse was a popular target for Allied bombing. The Germans stored anti-aircraft artillery near the railroad yard, close to our school, so we survived many air raids. Hundreds of Allied planes would fill the sky above us and shrapnel from the German anti-aircraft artillery would rain down; chunks of steel with razor-sharp edges.

I was running an errand one day, collecting supplies with a small cart, when the air raid siren sounded. I was next to the railyard, too far from Centre Mercier to make it back safely, so I crouched in the gutter behind the cart. The shrapnel was constantly bouncing and ricocheting off the wooden edges; I don't know how I managed to not get hit. That air raid was a short one; the siren sounded again, and I carried on my way, miraculously unhurt.

Pierre

I had been on the farm for a year. I had never worked so hard in my life, which was a relief because I didn't know what else to do. It was impossible for me to travel to Paris to visit Claude, Henriette and Georgette at the orphanage, but I wrote to them once a month and received a couple of replies from Claude saying they were all well. Samuel moved around a bit during the year, but he also seemed to be well looked after. In his last letter, written in May, he told me he was staying on a country estate near the Pyrenees with some other Jewish boys and they were having a great time with no classes and only a few chores. There was still no word from our parents, but it now seemed certain they had been deported to one of the Nazi work camps, probably in Poland. I heard stories of the terrible conditions but no one knew for certain, and while there was uncertainty, there was hope.

The romance between Aimee and I fizzled out. Once the initial spark died we agreed we were more suited as good friends rather than sweethearts and that is what we became. Monsieur and Madame Masson still treated me as one of the family, a surrogate son in the absence of their own. I rarely did anything except work or sleep, which was the easiest way for me to survive, as it deprived me of the time or energy to think of much else. Occasionally I would dream about my family but, thankfully, I was usually too exhausted to even dream.

Every week there was another rumour about the progress of the war. The Germans had been defeated in Italy. The Russians had defeated the Germans. The Germans had suffered terrible losses at the hands of the British. But nothing changed until June. It was a Tuesday and I was working in the fields when I heard excited shouting coming from the farmhouse.

'Come, everyone! Great news!' We dropped our tools and ran over. 'It has just been confirmed on the radio. The Allied troops have landed in Normandy. It's only a matter of time now. They will run the Germans out and the war will be over!'

At last the rumours had come true. We'd all been thinking about this moment every day for the past four years, but the news still came as a shock. We hugged each other joyfully.

****

'With your permission, Monsieur Masson, I'm going to join the Free French Forces,' said one of my fellow workers, a chap called Henri who was only a bit older than me.

I didn't hesitate. 'I would like to go with him,' I said.

'Of course, you must both go,' agreed the farmer.

Henri said we should go to Argenton-sur-Creuse, some forty kilometres away, where the Resistance were stationed.

We packed our belongings and said goodbye to the Masson family.

'Thank you for everything,' I said to these people who had been so kind to me. 'I hope to come back one day with my family so we can all celebrate our freedom together.'

'That would be wonderful, Pierre. I look forward to meeting your mother and sharing some recipes with her,' said Madame Masson, enveloping me in a big hug.

I took Aimee aside. 'I'll miss you,' I whispered in her ear.

'I'll miss you too,' she replied softly. 'You've been a great friend but there are more important things to concentrate on now… so go, help get rid of the Germans, and be safe.'

****

Henri and I arrived in Argenton-sur-Creuse late in the evening; the town was buzzing with people like us looking to join the freedom fighters. As new arrivals we were directed to a barn where we could get food and shelter for the night and told to meet in the town square early the next morning. I had no trouble falling asleep on my bed of hay; staying awake during the night only invited bad thoughts and it was better to sleep, even if that meant having nightmares because you could always escape them by waking up. On this night though the dreams were good ones, of victory and freedom.

****

We were woken at dawn by the crowing of a cockerel and the smell of toasted barley and chicory, the poor excuse for coffee we had been drinking since the beginning of the war; I don't think any of us could remember how real coffee smelt. There was eggs and bread to eat, then we moved to the town square where the Free French forces had set themselves up behind a table and were welcoming anyone who wanted to join. There were no Milice or German soldiers in sight; the Resistance were in charge in this town. We waited in the queue until it was our turn to sign up.

'Name?' asked the man behind the table.

'Pierre Laskowski.'

'Age?'

'Nineteen.'

'Papers?' I took my papers out of my jacket pocket to show him; the Star of David and 'Juif' clearly marked in red ink. He made a note against my name on the list he was compiling.

'Have you ever fired a gun?'

'No, sir.'

'Join the group to the right. Next!'

I instinctively looked to the left and saw a group of men and women being handed guns of various types and sizes. *Damn*, I thought. *I should have lied. Now I'll surely be given some unimportant job to do.*

Reluctantly, I moved to the right. My companion Henri also joined my group and we chatted while we waited to be told what to do next, both regretting our choice to be honest. When the tenth person was sent to join us an armed Free French fighter appeared.

'Welcome to freedom!' he announced. 'Come with me and we'll show you how to fire a gun. Then we'll send you out to round up the Milice and Nazis and to claim back France!'

'Hooray!' someone shouted, and we all cheered.

'Let's go!'

We followed our guide to a nearby field and were each handed a gun, whichever came out of the box next. There were a few pistols, but most got either a rifle or a submachine gun. I was handed the latter and then came the lesson. For the rest of the day we were shown how to take aim and fire and how to reload ammunition, and then we got to practise firing at a target at the end of the field. 'The rest we'll show you along the way,' said our guide. 'If we spend any longer here there'll be nothing left for us to do out there. Get some food and sleep and we'll move out at first light.'

****

Early the next morning two trucks arrived.

'OK, let's mix up the groups from yesterday; we don't want all the rookie marksmen together. Get on the trucks and sit among the hay bales and farm equipment,' we were told.

Henri and I didn't manage to get on the same truck but when we set off, we were travelling in the same direction – south on the Nationale 20 towards Limoges. Along with the ten new recruits in my truck was one Free French officer who explained the situation as we travelled.

'The German battalions of the 2nd SS Panzer Division, Das Reich, have been ordered to head north to Normandy to stop the Allied invasion. They arrived in Southern France from Russia in January, so they've had time to familiarise themselves with the terrain. They are unable to travel by train as the railway tracks have been sabotaged by our freedom fighters, so they are travelling by road. The order is to ambush them at every possible opportunity, whether that means felling trees or building blockades to hinder their progress. We are armed, but we are not stupid. We know the soldiers of Das Reich have the military advantage over us, but we are brave and we cannot be identified. As far as the Germans are concerned, we are regular civilians – at least until we shoot them!'

His words brought cheers from the guys. 'Hide your guns in the hay and look like farmers!' Everyone laughed. I thought that shouldn't be too difficult for me.

When we reached Limoges Henri's truck continued south while mine turned west. It was a beautiful summer day and as we drove through the quiet countryside I drifted off and dreamt of lying in long grass with a beautiful girl by my side. In my imagination the humming sound was the song of crickets, not the engine of the truck. The tickling sensation on my face was my girlfriend teasing me with a blade of grass and not flies attracted to the smell of my sweat. The Allies had landed in France and the war was coming to an end. I could find my family and get on with my life.

We drove through villages which seemed untouched by the war, perfect images of rural France in the sunshine: Verneuil-sur-Vienne, Veyrac, Oradour-sur-Glane, Saint Junien, and we had just passed Rochechouart. I imagined coming to live in one of these villages; maybe Papa and I could run a small farm together like Monsieur Masson with his son, who would soon return from forced labour in Germany.

There was a clearing off the side of the road. We parked a short way in, out of sight.

'Take your weapons and five minutes to stretch your legs,' the officer told us. 'We're getting close to Das Reich. Keep quiet and stay alert.' Then we heard something approaching.

We hid in the long grass and watched a truck of German soldiers pass and continue in the direction we had just come from. We stayed hidden for a while, waiting to see if more German vehicles would follow, but no one else came. Then we heard gunshots in the distance. We gathered together while our officer spoke.

'Walk back into the last village and see if there is anything we can help with before we carry on,' he said. 'Hide your weapons here and walk off in twos or threes. Then come back and report what you find. Don't all walk together, go chatting as if you're farmworkers going to get supplies.'

I paired up with another guy around my age and we were the first to start walking back to the last village. As we walked, we talked about our families and what we would do once the war was finally over. His name was Victor and he was from Grenoble. He had been forced into the Vichy army but deserted to join the Resistance two days ago when he heard of the Allied invasion. While we were walking we didn't hear any further gunshots and everything seemed quiet, but as we came to the first houses of Rochechouart we saw a woman standing by the road. She was crying.

'Madame, what is the matter?'

'The Germans shot my husband,' she said, between sobs. She pointed to the field where we saw three or four bodies. 'They said it was punishment for what the Resistance have done.'

Victor and I looked at each other. Even though we had only joined the Free French forces the day before, we both felt somehow responsible for this woman's grief. If we had arrived just a bit earlier, we might have been able to stop this from happening.

'Is there anything we can do for you?' I asked the woman.

'Please carry my husband and the others into the house,' she replied through her tears.

Victor and I lifted her husband's body between us and carried it through the kitchen door into the farmhouse.

'Where shall we put him?' Victor asked. But the woman didn't reply. She was staring at the body of her dead husband and didn't seem to hear us.

'I think we'd better hurry up and get going,' I said. 'There might be other people who need our help too.'

'Let's put him down and get the others,' said Victor.

We lowered the body of her husband to the floor as carefully as we could. The distraught woman fell to her knees by his side. Victor and I went back outside to return to the field but were stopped in our tracks.

'Halt!'

We put up our hands in surrender to the small group of young SS soldiers who pointed rifles at us. One of them searched us, but there was nothing to find. I started to speak, wanting to explain that we were only farmworkers, but they commanded me to be quiet. They told us to walk around the house back to the road, keeping our hands in the air, indicating the way with their rifles. As we reached the road we saw more soldiers and a group of around two hundred men, women and children. The SS were under orders to round up anyone they saw fit. They pushed us to join the others and marched us all into town.

****

We were made to stand against a wall while the SS pointed a row of machine guns at us from across the street. I could hear them talking among themselves; many of them had an Alsatian accent similar to what I used to hear as a child in Metz. I wondered if any of these Nazi soldiers had been the Jew-haters who had chased and fought me as a child at school; they looked around my age. I recognised a couple of other Resistance guys from our truck in the group of prisoners, but it appeared to be mainly local people. Those bastards had arrested children too, many of whom cried as the hours passed and we were forced to remain standing against the wall. Some fainted and were left where they fell: the Germans ordered us not to help them. People begged for water but none was given. We stood for six hours until ten o'clock in the evening when the SS commander appeared. He was furious and shouted at the officers to report to him immediately. Then two members of the French Red Cross drove up in a jeep and approached the SS commander. 'You must release the women and children,' they demanded.

'No, they are all terrorists and they will be executed,' replied the commander.

'These are innocent civilians,' said the Red Cross.

'Innocent? Have you seen what these *innocent* civilians have done to our soldiers? They attacked the garrison at Tulle this very day. They do not deserve to be treated with the honour deserving of a soldier. They have mutilated and tortured our men.'

'How long have you been holding these prisoners?' asked the Red Cross.

'Since the afternoon,' said one of the officers.

'How then could these people be responsible for those acts today? Tulle is over one hundred kilometres away!'

At this the SS commander went off to speak to his men, but not so far out of earshot that I couldn't hear him. He was irritated by the continued attacks by the Free French Forces they had endured since starting their expedition north. The plan to travel by train had been sabotaged and now the freedom fighters were making the journey longer and more arduous than expected. After a short discussion the commander agreed to release the women and children under fourteen. This appeared to satisfy the Red Cross workers, who went on their way.

The rest of us were marched to a yard. 'You will sleep here. In the morning we will check your papers. Whoever has their papers in order will be free to leave. Anyone who does not have papers will come with us to Limoges.'

I had my papers, but they carried the Star of David and the word 'Juif'. I had to decide whether to get rid of them or not. I passed a sleepless night on the gravel floor of the yard, sharing the space with one hundred other men, while I tried to work out which would be the better option for me.

****

By morning I decided it would be better to show my papers than not to have any at all. I guessed the SS were more interested in getting rid of the Free French Forces than finding Jews right now. The officers came into the yard and kicked the prisoners awake. Those who had managed to sleep opened their eyes to find a rifle pointed at them. We were ordered to form a line and they started to check our papers. Most were happy to get this done as quickly as possible. They went to the front of the queue but we soon learnt no one would be allowed to leave until everyone had been investigated. I began moving further and further towards the end of the line in the desperate hope they might lose interest in checking everyone's papers before it was my turn. My spirit sank when I saw the commander approach me. He had a sub-machine gun slung over his shoulder like a big shot.

'Papers!'

My heart was beating rapidly. I could feel beads of sweat prickling my forehead and I willed my hands to stop shaking as I handed my papers over. The commander unfolded the document and I watched as the blood drained from his face. I can imagine what was going through his mind: how come this Jew has not been deported yet? The commander regained his composure.

'What are you doing here when your papers say you work on a farm far away?'

My mind raced for an answer. 'The farmer gave me the day off and I came to buy a pair of shoes. The soldiers stopped me and brought me here.'

The commander looked down at my worn-out shoes. He kept looking between my face, my papers and my shoes. He must have thought I was either part of the Resistance and too stupid to show false papers, or else I was telling the truth. I was convinced this was the end for me, and my thoughts turned to my friends and family who I would never see again.

'You can go,' I heard him say. The commander handed me back my papers. Now it was my turn to be confused. I went to join the other men who had their papers in order. At the back of my mind I was thinking: *surely this is a trick*. They weren't going to let us go. They were going to shoot us all.

In the end, ten among us did not have papers. The big shot commander made a show of saying, 'These men have been arrested for not having identification papers on their person. We will take them to Limoges. If they can prove their identity we will let them go. The rest of you must wait for one hour and then you may leave.'

The SS marched the ten men out of the yard, shutting the gate behind them and then we heard them drive away. It went quiet. We sat down and waited, firstly in silence then, little by little, we started talking, asking questions to which no one knew the answers.

'What will happen to the ones they arrested?'

'What will happen to us?'

We fell silent again and then heard voices outside the gate. I thought it was the Germans returning for us but then someone recognised his wife's voice and called her name.

'Julia, is that you?'

'Yes, my dear. Are you alright?'

'I'm fine. Are there any Germans out there?'

'They've left. Come out!'

We opened the gate to the yard and walked out hesitantly. I still half-expected there to be a rifle aimed at me but the only people we found were the family members of some of the men, waiting to greet their fathers, sons and husbands with kisses. We were free to leave.

I made my way back to the truck and found most of the Resistance guys regrouped and my weapon still where I had hidden it the day before. I told them about what had happened and they said I had guts. I'd survived my first war story! Later that day word came that the SS had taken those ten men who did not have papers, driven them out of town, made them dig their own graves and shot them dead.

****

It was only five days since the Allies had landed at Normandy but so much had changed. I was now a freedom fighter! We spent most of the day building blockades; choosing to build them on major roads knowing the SS couldn't travel on the smaller roads with their heavy, slow-moving tanks. As we were finishing up, we received news that we were needed back in Oradour-sur-Glane.

As we approached, we noticed an unpleasant smell that got stronger as we drew nearer. By the time we entered the town the stench was overwhelming. I felt nauseous and copied the others by ripping off a part of my shirt and tying it around my face as a makeshift mask. The smell of my sweat and dirt were sweet compared to this overpowering stench.

The few townspeople we met were overcome with grief and it took a while before we could find someone able to talk to us. A man sitting on the steps of a house finally managed to answer our questions about what had happened.

'The SS. Yesterday. They rounded up every single person in the town. Said it was to check papers. Said they were looking for guns and ammunition. The men were taken away. The women and children all locked in the church. They… they killed everyone. They shot the men. They burnt down the church with the women and little ones inside. Sick old women. Mothers with babes in arms. Young children – they emptied the four schools in the town and murdered them all. The people you see are parents of those schoolchildren who live outside the town. They have come to look for their sons and daughters... but there is no one. They are all dead. That smell? It is the smell of their death. Go, look inside the burnt ruins of the church. The bodies of the angels are there. Some don't even look human anymore.' The man began to weep. 'This is my house. This was my home. I was away working. Someone came to find me. But it was too late. My family have all gone. My wife. My parents. My children. My neighbours. My friends. No one is left. No one. There were over six hundred people here. One or two escaped, three at most.'

As he told us this most terrible story I noticed a number of dogs walking around, some coming to us, sniffing around and howling.

'I know these dogs. They are from here. They are looking for their masters, but they are all gone,' said the man.

We walked over to the place where the church had stood just a day before, passing a huge number of empty ammunition cases by the entrance. The smell was unbearable, and the sight was nightmarish: twisted, burnt bodies of mothers who tried in vain to shield their babies, and young children piled together behind the altar. Only a few still had their faces, some looked peaceful – perhaps those were the lucky ones who had been shot dead before the fire took hold. The others had the tortured look of people dying in agony.

Georgette

Louveciennes
June 1944

Our routine at the new house was similar to that of the old house: Jacqueline helped us get dressed, served our food and washed our clothes. She took us to the Marly woods to play and helped us to put on shows and celebrate our birthdays. She had even started sleeping in our bedroom and comforting the girls who would wake from nightmares. Henriette and I shared a bed and always slept well, but we were the lucky ones; we had each other.

One change was that a German officer now came every day, rather than every week, to make sure no one had run away. One of the little girls, Karin Rozenbaum, had disappeared. One day, Karin's brother came to visit; he asked Karin to show him the garden and the next thing we knew, they had both run off! The grown-ups were terrified of what the German officer would say when he came by that day, but he just wrote it down on his list and left. I hoped Karin and her brother were alright.

****

We were playing in the garden at the front of the orphanage when the gate opened and a girl around the same age as Jacqueline walked in.

'Christina? Is that you?' said Jacqueline.

'Jacqueline!' They ran to each other and hugged.

'Children, come and meet an old friend of mine. This is Christina. We used to attend school together,' said Jacqueline.

'*Bonjour,* Christina,' we all chorused.

'*Bonjour, les enfants*,' she replied. Turning to her friend she said, 'Wow, you have a lot of children!' and they both laughed.

'They're not actually mine, although some of them think they are!' she explained, looking at Corinne in particular, who was always being told not to call her 'Maman'. 'I'm only looking after them while their parents are away. I'm sure I will be handing them all back soon,' she said, although she didn't sound too convincing.

'No, Maman, I want to stay with you!' cried Corinne, making Jacqueline and Christina giggle again.

'Christina, it's so good to see you,' said Jacqueline. 'How is your family?'

'Everyone is fine. I saw your grandmother and she told me you were here. I must say, it was a relief. When you first disappeared, I went to your apartment and it was locked up with a seal on the door. That was over a year ago. I thought I'd never see you again.'

'I'm so pleased you came, it's great to see an old friend. Now, tell me about school and what I've missed.'

'Nothing interesting. I can't understand what you like so much about school.'

'You'd think differently if you weren't allowed to go anymore,' Jacqueline said, and Christina looked a little ashamed.

'I asked my father if I could come to visit you. At first he said "no" because it would be too dangerous, but I pleaded with him and he eventually agreed. It's not safe to travel anywhere now, but I don't care; I told him I would leave early and be back well before dark. When he finally gave me permission, he said I should bring my camera. Would you like me to take some pictures of you?'

'Sure. Take one of me with the children so I can remember them when they've all gone back to their families. Come on, children, let's stand on the front steps so Christina can take our photograph.'

Henriette and I stood in the middle of the back row with two others, three on the middle step, the two smallest at the front and Jacqueline next to us. We all smiled for the camera and Christina took the photograph.

****

I love summer when I don't have to wear a coat and I can run around barefoot in the garden. That summer we often stayed out until late in Marly Park, such a wonderful place where the only things that mattered were the blue skies, green grass and trees. We weren't far from Paris, but Louveciennes could have been on the other side of the world.

One day there was great excitement in the orphanage. Jacqueline looked happier than I had seen her for a long time. She took us to a corner of the garden and tried to explain what was happening.

'Children, I have good news. The war will soon be ending. The British and American soldiers are coming, and the Germans will be leaving.'

We didn't really understand what this meant, but it was good to see the grown-ups and older children all smiling.

'Are we going home?' asked Irene.

'Not yet,' said Jacqueline. 'We have to stay here for the moment, but someone will come for us soon, I'm sure. The good soldiers will come, and the bad soldiers will have to leave.'

This sounded reason enough to put on a show to celebrate, even the monitors joined in; singing and dancing and looking forward to being free soon and going home to our families.

****

Weeks passed, but no news came of when we could return home. The German soldiers still came every day with their lists, and the Denis family continued to be mean, so we stayed out of their way as much as possible. We did get a bit more food for a few days after Jacqueline complained to the Jewish Agency about Monsieur Denis and his family dining on platefuls of meat in front of us when we always went hungry. An inspection was carried out and we suddenly found pieces of meat in our soup. I know Jacqueline was as scared of the director as the rest of us, so it was brave of her to complain knowing she could have been punished for it, but freedom was just around the corner... wasn't it? That's what we had thought when the news first arrived of the good soldiers coming but we hadn't seen any sign of them yet and, day by day, our happiness and excitement faded.

'Maybe they've forgotten about us?' suggested one.

'Maybe no one knows we are here,' said another.

If only that were true.

****

The sun was at its hottest in mid-July and there wasn't a cloud in the sky. Jacqueline promised us another picnic in Marly Park. We didn't have much to take in the way of food, but that wouldn't stop us from having fun. She told us to wait for her on the front steps as she got our picnic ready. The other children were jumping up and down with excitement, but I felt tired. I sat on the top step and watched them.

'Come on, Georgette,' shouted Henriette. 'We're having a race up and down the stairs.'

'I don't want to play,' I said.

'Oh, you lazy thing!'

'Leave me alone, I don't feel well.'

'What's the matter?'

'I don't know. I'm going inside,' I said, my voice shaking. I felt weepy and I didn't want the others to see me cry. The bright sunshine hurt my eyes. I had a headache and I felt hot and uncomfortable, so I sat down in the cool, dark hallway.

'Georgette, are you ready to go?' asked Jacqueline when she appeared from the kitchen.

'Yes. No. I don't know,' I replied and then I couldn't stop myself from crying, which is not something I did very often. Jacqueline could tell there was something wrong.

She felt my forehead. 'You do feel a bit warm. Have you been running around outside?'

'No.'

'It's a bit dark here. Come outside and let me look at you.'

Jacqueline took my hand and led me through the front door. When we got outside I shielded my eyes against the bright sunshine.

'Oh, my dear. Your eyes are quite red.'

'Yes, they are really sore,' I managed to say between sobs.

Jacqueline took me upstairs and put me to bed. She opened the window and brought me a glass of water.

'I need to take the other children out now, but Louisa will look after you until I get back,' she said.

Louisa was head supervisor now that Mademoiselle Furst had left. She was usually too busy to have much time for us, but she was kind when she came to see me that morning.

'Ah, it's little Georgette. How are you feeling?' she asked as she walked into the bedroom. I didn't know how long it was since Jacqueline and the other children left for their picnic because I had fallen asleep.

'I'm tired and my body hurts a bit,' I said.

Louisa came over and touched my forehead as Jacqueline had also done. I was rarely sick, so I couldn't remember anyone else doing that to me before. It felt nice.

'You're quite warm.'

'It's a hot day,' I said.

'Yes, it is,' laughed Louisa, 'and you are a clever girl!' She stroked my hair.

I didn't feel at all well but I enjoyed the attention.

'And who is this?' she pointed to the doll lying next to me.

'This is Bernadette,' I said. 'When my sister is not here Bernadette stays with me instead.'

'I can see she's doing a good job of looking after you,' said Louisa. 'Why don't you sleep a bit more and I'll come back and see you soon.'

Sleep didn't come so easily now and every time I drifted off I would wake myself up coughing. I felt uncomfortable. By the time Jacqueline and the others returned from the park I had been moved to a small room at the top of the house, which is where the sick children slept. There were two beds in the room and a small table with a basin and jug of water. There was a bedpan too, as it was quite a walk to the bathroom, especially for anyone not feeling well. Opposite the door was a window overlooking the street. The curtains were pulled shut so I could sleep, but the window was left open as it was stuffy at the top of the house. I knew a few children who had spent time here, but all had recovered and moved back downstairs so I wasn't scared. Until it was known whether I had a cold or something more serious, nobody was supposed to visit me, but when they returned from the park Jacqueline brought Henriette and Claude upstairs to say a quick hello.

'Are you coming back to our bedroom later?' asked Henriette.

'Not tonight,' said Jacqueline. 'Both of you will sleep better if Georgette stays up here. She's quite hot and fidgety.'

'Do you have Bernadette to keep you company?' said Henriette.

'Yes,' I said, as I pulled our doll out from under the covers.

'Now, Bernadette,' said Henriette sternly. 'Look after Georgette for me. This will be the first night we haven't slept together so it's going to be strange… for both of us.'

'Once Georgette is better you will share your bed again and, anyway, one day you will both have your own husband and family and live with them and not with each other, so this will be good practice.'

'Never!' said Henriette. 'I'm never getting married. Georgette and I will live together for ever!' Everyone laughed except me; I wanted them to leave me alone so I could sleep. I think Jacqueline could see that.

'Come on, children. Let's go downstairs and leave Georgette in peace. We can come back tomorrow.'

****

I didn't feel any better the next day. When Louisa came to see me, she checked inside my mouth and found some white spots. No one could come and see me, just in case. I didn't mind not having visitors; I wasn't in the mood to play. When the doctor came, he confirmed what Louisa had suspected: measles. He said I should be taken to the hospital at Saint-Germain-en-Laye. Louisa came to tell me the news.

'I don't want to go,' I said. 'I want to stay here. I'll be better soon.'

'Now, now, Georgette. The doctor knows best.'

'But they will cut me open at the hospital! That's what happened to Jacqueline!'

'Yes, but Jacqueline had appendicitis. You have measles and that is quite different. They won't "cut you open". They'll look after you until you feel well enough to come home. It will probably be for one week at the most. They have lovely, kind nurses who will take care of you.'

'Can Henriette and Claude and Jacqueline come and visit me?'

'No. Other people can catch measles easily, so no one is allowed to come and see you for a few days.'

'But what about you?'

'I had measles when I was young so I can't catch it again. Now, let's get you ready to go.'

Louisa helped me out of bed. As she got my clothes ready, I turned to look out of the window. At that moment my sister was in the garden and happened to look up. When she saw me at the window she smiled and waved, and I waved back. I guess she thought I was feeling better to have been out of bed and looking out of the window. She called something to me. I couldn't hear but it looked like she asked if I was coming outside to play with her, so I shook my head and waved goodbye. I looked around for Claude, but he was not outside.

When I first arrived at the hospital I was very tired and fell asleep as soon as I was put into a bed. Louisa had come with me, but she had to rush back to Louveciennes and she wasn't allowed on the ward. When I woke up for the first time in my hospital bed it took me a minute to realise where I was. I looked to either side and saw I was in the middle of a long row of beds, each one the same. White metal bed frames, white walls, white sheets, white curtains on the windows. There were a few nurses walking around and they were wearing white too. It was the cleanest-looking room I could ever remember seeing. There were girls and boys of different ages on the ward. The beds were far apart from each other, not like those in the orphanage, where everyone was squashed together. There was a little table between each bed and some even had screens around them, so you couldn't see who was in them.

A nurse came over. 'Hello. Who have we here?'

'I'm Georgette.'

'How do you do, Georgette? I am Nurse Emily. Let me look at your chart to see why you're here. Oh yes, measles. I see that the rash has only just started. Once it's cleared up and you're feeling better then you can go home.'

'Home?'

'Let me look again, where have you come from? Oh, I see, from the orphanage at Louveciennes. We will do our best to get you back as soon as we can.'

'Yes, Henriette and Claude will be missing me. We didn't say goodbye,' I said.

'Who are they?'

'Claude is my brother and Henriette is my twin sister. This is the first time Henriette and I have been apart. Well, I slept in a different room last night and Henriette was not allowed to come and see me much because I'm *congagious*.'

'*Congagious*? Oh, you mean contagious!' said the kind nurse, laughing gently. 'Yes, it is best if other people stay away. But we will look after you here.'

'Thank you.'

'You're a very polite girl. I can see we are going to get along just fine.'

When I got to know some of the other children on the ward, it turned out I was one of the lucky ones. Although I had a fever and a rash and felt horribly uncomfortable, some of the other children were much sicker than I was. I wasn't sure why I was even in the hospital, so I asked Nurse Emily when she next came to check on me.

'What is measles?'

'It's an illness which can sometimes make children very sick and that's why it is best to stay in hospital.'

'Am I very sick?'

'No, but we want to keep an eye on you just in case.'

There was a box in the children's ward with books, toys and puzzles in it. Almost all were broken or had pieces missing, pages ripped or scribbled on, but that box was like a treasure trove to me. I was only allowed to get out of bed to use the bathroom but every time I would make sure to visit the toy box and borrow something to take back to my bed. I couldn't read the books, but I could look at the pictures. No one had time to read to me, I had to imagine the stories they were telling. When I felt tired I wouldn't actually play with a toy, I would only hold it and make up an adventure for it in my head. There was no such toy box at the orphanage and I had never seen such wonderful things.

****

I had been at the hospital for a few days. The doctor was now satisfied that my measles had been a mild case and I wouldn't experience any of the nasty complications it can cause. The nurses told me I would soon be going back to Rue de la Paix. I was in bed playing with a puzzle from the toy box. It wasn't easy as many of the pieces were missing. Suddenly, someone rushed onto the ward and called the nurses over. They were obviously in a hurry and had something important to say. They were talking urgently but quietly. I couldn't hear anything that was said so I wasn't sure if it was my imagination, but it looked like they were all looking over at me. When they finished, Nurse Emily came over to my bed.

'Georgette, you have to leave the hospital now.' She started to pull off my bedclothes and help me to sit up.

'Am I going back to the orphanage now?' I said. I was surprised because I had been told I wouldn't be leaving for a few days yet.

'No. You will be going to stay with the bonne sœurs, the sisters.'

'The sisters? I only have one sister. You mean Henriette, my twin. I'm going back to my sister.'

'Not right now. The sisters are the kind ladies of the church who will look after you,' she explained.

'But—'

Nurse Emily's voice turned stern. 'No time for questions! We have to get you ready as quickly as possible.'

I couldn't understand what the hurry was. I thought I was here to rest, but I stayed quiet and within minutes we were walking out of the ward. I was the only one leaving. The other children were still in their beds, watching me.

I was taken to a small room in another part of the hospital and told to wait quietly. 'I have to leave you now, Georgette,' said Nurse Emily, sitting me down. She sounded upset, and there were tears in her eyes. 'Good luck, child,' she said before leaving me alone. In the next room I could hear a telephone ring and a muffled conversation. Then the door opened, and a man walked in.

'Hello, Georgette.'

I couldn't remember having seen this man before.

'Hello,' I replied.

The man walked around the small room. He was rubbing his chin, just like I had seen other people do when they had something important to say but weren't sure how to say it.

'How are you feeling?'

I didn't think that was the important thing he had to say. 'My head hurts but I feel better than before.'

'Good, good. Now, Georgette, you must leave the hospital. A man called François will take you to the bonne sœurs who will look after you.'

'Yes, sir. Nurse Emily told me.'

'Excellent, but you have to pretend you are someone else. Your name is Isabel and the man who you will be travelling with – François – is your father. That is if anyone stops you or talks to you. Do you understand?'

'No, sir.'

'Oh dear. Let's play a game. Are you good at playing games?'

'Um, I think so.' My head began to ache and I wanted this to end.

'The game is that your name is Isabel and you are travelling with your father François, although of course you call him Papa. You are going to travel by horse and cart. You can sleep in the back if you feel tired or unwell. If anyone stops you, then François will speak to them. You only need to speak if someone speaks to you. Your name is Isabel and you are travelling with your father. That is all you need to say.'

'Alright,' I said. This game didn't sound much fun.

'So, let's start now.' He walked around the small room again and then stopped in front of me. 'Hello, young lady. What is your name?'

'My name is Geor— My name is Isabel!' I realised just in time what I was supposed to answer. Thank goodness. If not, we probably would have had to go through the whole thing again and again until I got it right. The thought of lying down in the back of a cart began to feel inviting.

'Well done, *Isabel*,' said the man, winking at me. 'Ready to go?'

'Yes, sir.' I wasn't ready to go anywhere, but I was ready to go to sleep.

I was led through the back of the hospital and out a small door into the yard where a man was waiting with a horse and cart. He was introduced as François and I was introduced as Isabel. The cart was full of hay and I had been given a couple of blankets, one of which I lay on and the other I allowed François to cover me with despite it being a warm day; it felt safer that way. The only thing I had with me was my doll Bernadette. In a few moments François was driving the cart out of the hospital courtyard and we went on our way.

****

I slept for the first part of the journey. It was difficult to keep my eyes open; the rocking of the cart made me sleepy although I did wake a couple of times when we crossed a bumpy part of the road. We were travelling on narrow roads and lanes, stopping only for a toilet break in the long grass. We had a bottle of water each and some bread and cheese which we ate as we travelled. François spent most of the journey whistling or singing quietly and spoke more to the horse than he did to me, although he did ask me how I was feeling a few times. I was confused and pleased to be left in peace.

François stopped the horse and cart in front of a large stone building at the end of a village. I had no idea where we were. He got down and knocked on the huge wooden door which was opened by a woman dressed in a long grey tunic and a white veil. I had seen women dressed like that in

Louveciennes when walking to and from the park with Jacqueline and she had explained they were bonne sœurs from the Catholic Church who devoted their lives to serving God. François helped me off the cart, Bernadette clutched firmly under my arm. He handed me over to my next guardian then, bowing to me and the nun and wishing me well, he got back on the cart and left. I followed the nun inside and the door closed behind us. The hallway was dark and cool.

'Hello, Isabel. Welcome to our home. My name is Sister Marie.'

'I have a sister. Her name is Henriette.'

'No, Isabel does not have a sister or brothers. You must remember that. You are Isabel now.'

'But where is Henriette? I want Henriette!' I started to cry. I felt weak from the long day of travelling. I wanted to see my sister. Where was Jacqueline? Where was Claude?

'Everything we do is for your safety,' explained Sister Marie gently, kneeling down to my height. 'You must pretend now that your name is Isabel. It is very important. Your name is Isabel. You have no family. We are your family now. Remember that and everything will be fine.'

****

I shared a bedroom with other young girls at the convent. No one ever spoke of their families or where they came from. I thought about Henriette and Claude many times a day, and I wondered where they were, but I never mentioned them. I wished I was with them and I thought of running away and going back to the orphanage, but I wouldn't know how to get there. All I could do was wait for someone to come and find me: Maman or Papa, Pierre, Sam, Claude or Henriette, or maybe even Jacqueline. But was anyone even looking for me?

Our bedroom was simple but none of us were used to anything better. The only difference from the orphanage was the crucifix and picture of the Virgin Mary that hung above our beds. On the one table was a copy of the Holy Bible, but most of us were too young to read. Within days of arriving, I was baptised. This seemed to give the sisters much pleasure, so I was happy to go along with it. I had no idea about religion. I didn't know that not everyone had the same beliefs. Since my parents had been taken away I'd spent one year with a Catholic neighbour and one year in a Jewish orphanage where we weren't allowed to celebrate any of the Jewish customs. The nuns had no interest in playing with us or making sure we had fun like Jacqueline had. We prayed seven times a day. I soon picked up the psalms and hymns which were sung daily and I enjoyed joining in. We learnt Bible stories and memorised our prayers. We recited the Holy Rosary together. I was taught of Saint Isabel of France, my patron saint who had spent her life looking after the sick and poor. I was told I would celebrate her life on 26 February; birthdays were not acknowledged at the convent. There wasn't a lot of food to eat, even less than we had been given at the orphanage. The sisters believed this was the key to a good religious life, as eating too much took one's mind off prayer. 'Hunger is an excellent reminder of the sacrifices that Christ our Lord had undertaken for us.' Despite there being little to eat we still had to say prayers before and after each meal, to thank the Lord for providing the few scraps given to us.

On Sunday morning we would line up in the chapel and receive Holy Communion: a papery wafer and sip of wine 'to symbolise receiving the flesh and blood of Christ into our bodies'. Oh, how we prayed we could do that every day! In our hunger we considered the thin, bland host a feast. We learnt how to bless ourselves with holy water and the correct way to cross ourselves (forehead, tummy, left shoulder, right shoulder). I became a good Catholic and was rewarded with a safe place to live. In time I didn't think of who and when my family would come rescue me, I simply forgot.

After over a year at the convent, I was alarmed to one day be called to the office of the mère supérieure.

Pierre

'Brave Free French fighters! We move out tonight to assist in the liberation of our capital city. Victory is near!'

We cheered as the officer gave us our orders. We were a short distance outside Paris, having spent the last few weeks successfully sabotaging the movement of German troops travelling by road. The Allies were close and now almost all of Paris had joined the struggle to take back control from the invaders.

I wondered if I could go to Louveciennes to check on Claude and the girls, but as we approached the centre of Paris it was clear I wouldn't get away. The entire city was on strike, including the transport system. Our job was to defend the barricades which had been set up all over, and to prepare for a siege.

We were there for five days, battling against the last German troops until the Allies marched in and the Germans surrendered.

****

Once Paris had been liberated, I asked my officer for permission to travel to Louveciennes. I was told to wait while he tried to arrange transport for me – the city was still in a terrible mess. He came to find me later and said, 'Son, I've asked around about the orphanage. It's not good news, I'm afraid.'

Samuel

Pyrennes

August 1944

After the Allies had taken Italy and were advancing into France, Monsieur Fournier took all twenty Jewish boys from the school to his country estate near the Pyrenees. We stayed for three carefree months until liberation came in August. We would fish and swim in the lakes, hike in the hills and walk into the village to meet the local girls! Any Germans were long gone from the area, although there were plenty of locals who were Jew-haters, so we tried to keep a low profile to avoid discovery. Not everyone was unsympathetic though: it was rumoured some had helped Jews cross the Pyrenees into Spain.

The estate had a traditional two-storey stone farmhouse with small shuttered windows. The low ceilings were not a problem as none of us had grown particularly tall in the last few years. We divided ourselves between the rooms and each of us had our own sleeping space. The lucky ones were in a bed but most of us were on make-shift mattresses on the floor. It didn't matter though: we were young and free and there were no Catholic priests to rap our knuckles or

German soldiers to run from. The house had a stone patio around it and beyond that there was just grass and trees and lush countryside, mostly unspoilt by war.

Monsieur Fournier had arranged for a neighbour to help with the cooking and washing. He would come himself every second weekend to see us. When he did, he would bring newspapers and tell us what was happening outside of our idyllic little world. On 15 August the Allied forces landed in the south of France, and by the end of August southern France was liberated. The Germans in Paris were defeated on 25 August. I was so happy when I read that last piece of news! My younger brother and sisters would be allowed to leave the orphanage, and my parents would be let out of camp. But I was worried about Pierre. I'd written to him at the farm but I hadn't heard back for a long time.

****

The season passed, but with war always on our minds we barely took notice of rich greens transforming into stunning autumn colours. The lakes became too cold for swimming, so we spent our time fishing and laying crude, but occasionally successful, hunting traps for rabbits. On our return from one such hunting trip we were surprised to see Monsieur Fournier.

'Hello, boys!' he greeted us. 'Where have you been?'

'Hunting.'

'Did you catch anything?'

'Not today. Potato soup for dinner again!' We all groaned and laughed.

'Listen, boys, I have some news for you. The Jewish agencies are setting up homes for young people like yourselves who have been separated from their parents. They are going to begin the process of reuniting families now the Germans have been defeated. You are all to go to a place called Perreux. It's not too far, just north of Toulouse.'

'Why can't we stay here until our parents come back?' asked one.

'*If* they come back, you mean,' said another, which was what most of us were thinking even if we didn't care to admit it.

'Thousands upon thousands of people within France have been displaced by the war. It is going to be a long process, putting families back together again. Most of you will have brothers and sisters who are elsewhere so it would be to everyone's advantage if you go to Perreux. That way the Jewish agencies will know where you are. I have been told it is a nice place to be, although maybe not as nice as here!'

The thought of leaving the freedom of the Pyrenees for another children's home was grim, but the prospect of reuniting with our families was too good to pass up. We left to pack our few belongings right away.

Pierre

Paris

October 1944

As I approached Boulevard Saint-Germain, I noticed the lines of people outside the large corner building that was the Hôtel Grande. Even now, bearing the scars of war, you could see it had once been an upmarket establishment. At the beginning of the German occupation it had been used as a refuge for bohemians and intellectuals but then it was taken over by the German military intelligence as somewhere to wine, dine and entertain their officers. Now the German troops had fled, and the hotel was used as a repatriation centre.

I joined the queue. In front of me were people of all ages – some women with young children, a few teenagers around Samuel's age, but mostly older people looking for their own children and grandchildren. Almost everyone held precious photographs tightly in their hands. It was a warm day, but a few wore jackets and if you looked closely you could see where the yellow star had been only weeks before; on some it had been unpicked carefully so as to minimise damage to the garment, while on others it had been ripped off in a hurry.

I worried about what the commander had said. As the queue slowly worked its way forwards we moved from the street into the lobby of the hotel. I had been waiting for a few hours now and had got to know some of the people around me in the queue. Everyone had a story to tell, each one more heart-breaking than the last. Once inside it was a pleasure to have something else to focus on. The interior of the building was, without doubt, the most luxurious place I had ever been in, even in its current condition. I knew little of art at the time, but I admired the art nouveau decor and wondered if I might one day create something as beautiful.

To distract myself, I thought about my future during the long wait. I had left the Free French forces following the liberation of Paris. Now I needed to find work. I had become a decent farmworker but that was not something I wanted to do forever. I had no desire to return to Metz; our apartment, which I hadn't seen since war broke out, had been rented and I wasn't aware of any other family property that needed to be reclaimed. Should I stay in Paris? I had heard stories of Jews leaving for Palestine, London and New York. Who could blame them, not wanting to stay in this country that had turned its back on us in our time of need? But, first things first, I had to reunite with my family before deciding where to go next.

I reached the front of the queue, marked by a bank of desks with chairs on either side. Behind the desks was a hub of activity. Dozens of people answering ringing telephones, taking notes, typing lists, and hurrying in and out through doors to makeshift offices all over the hotel. There was a sense of urgency in everything they did; no one sat around idly chatting. Finally, it was my turn to be seen.

'How can I help you?' the lady behind the desk asked wearily when I sat down in front of her. In all the hours I had been waiting I hadn't seen any of the people behind the desks leave.

'I'm looking for my brothers and sisters and parents.'

'Tell me about your brothers and sisters first.'

'Our family name is Laskowski. I have five-year-old… no, wait, six-year-old twin sisters. It's been so long since I've seen them, they must be six now. Their names are Henriette and Georgette. Their date of birth is 9 April 1938. I also have a brother named Claude – oh my goodness, he is twelve now! His date of birth is 12 April 1932. All three were born in Metz. The last time I saw them was last year in the summer at the Jewish Agency orphanage in Louveciennes. I tried to get them released but the director, Monsieur Denis, assured me they would be safe and refused to hand them over. I couldn't get them out.' As I was saying these words, I realised how pathetic they sounded. Why had I left my siblings in that place? Would it really have been so difficult to get them out? After all, Samuel managed to escape from the trade school easily enough.

The lady behind the desk waited patiently for me to stop speaking and then she asked kindly, 'What is your name?'

'Pierre.'

'Pierre, I know this because others today have asked me about children who were in one of the Jewish Agency homes in Paris. I'm sorry to tell you that all of the children's homes were emptied on 22 July.'

'Yes, I was already told that,' I said. That was what my officer had found out after the liberation of Paris. 'Do you know where the children are now?'

'They were taken to Drancy.'

'That's where our parents were taken, so hopefully they're all together?'

'Many people were sent from Drancy to other camps, and the reports coming through are not positive,' said the woman gently. 'I hate having to tell you this but I don't want to get your hopes up.'

Her words filled me with dread. I realised that for some time now I had felt deep down that my parents were dead, but I had never allowed myself to believe it... until now. I felt sick with grief. But what of my brother and sisters?

'And the children from the homes? Where are they now? Surely they were freed as soon as Paris was liberated? That must have been a top priority – to save the children,' I said, my voice trembling while I held back tears.

'I'm so sorry but we don't know where they are. Some Jewish children were placed with other families or in convents or boarding schools. We have lists of some of those children and we are getting more information every day. Let me look on those lists now and see if I can find out anything. Here is a pen and paper. Write down the names and dates of birth for your brother and sisters.'

'I have another brother, Samuel. He is fifteen.' My heart was racing as the hopelessness of it all sunk in.

'Put his name down too,' said the lady. 'You said you're also looking for your parents?'

'Yes. They were both arrested in 1942. First my father, and then my mother. And also my aunt and uncle, my grandmother, my cousins...'

'Let's start with your immediate family. Write down the details of your parents and siblings please.'

My hand shook as I wrote down six names and dates of birth on the piece of paper. My entire family was missing. Were any of them looking for me in another repatriation centre somewhere else? Or maybe they had even come to this same centre on another day? The lady behind the desk took the list and told me to wait as she went off to check the documents.

'Pierre?' The voice calling my name rescued me from the dozens of possible scenarios I was working through in my head.

'Yes?'

'I'm sorry, Pierre. I can't find anything about your family. Our information is currently very limited and disorganised. We are learning more all the time; be patient and come back regularly to check again. It's still early in the process but it has been estimated there are many thousands of people missing. Many of the missing are immigrants from Poland and traditional Polish names are being misspelt which makes our job even more difficult, but I promise you we are making progress.'

My head was spinning as I finally accepted that I might never see any of my family again.

****

I decided to stay in Paris for the time being and was given a room in a small hotel arranged by the Jewish Agency. The entire building was filled with waifs and strays like me, all still reeling from the effects of war; as was the whole city. There were other repatriation centres apart from the one at the Hôtel Grande run by different Jewish and Red Cross aid agencies, but it was the same story at each one.

'Please be patient and come back regularly to check.'

'It is still early days.'

'The information is coming through, but slowly.'

The queues only seemed to get longer as more people came to Paris to search for news of their loved ones. I felt I was wasting my time, convinced that my family would never be found, but then news of a success story would circulate, someone would be reunited with their brother or sister and my resolve would be renewed.

And then one day, my cousin Georges Hofman contacted me. His father was one of my mother's brothers and he was considerably older than me. Georges had fought in the French army and been a prisoner of war in Germany. On his return to Paris he continued his career as an upholsterer and he offered to take me on as his apprentice, teaching me the trade. I was grateful for the opportunity. Georges was good company and helped the days pass quickly with stories of his experiences during the war. I had met other POWs who had returned broken men, but at least they had returned. Georges was a lucky one who came out intact. He told me that it was hope that got him through the terrible times, which made me realise hope was what I needed now – hope that I would reunite with my family.

****

Those of us who had survived the war told ourselves our missing loved ones would want us to enjoy life and make the most of every moment, but it was difficult to do so. On my days off, I would join the queue at the repatriation centre as usual. As I approached the desk on one particular day I allowed myself a renewed sense of optimism. Months had passed and there had been more and more stories of reunited families, so why shouldn't it be my turn now?

'Good morning. Who are you looking for?'

I passed over the piece of paper which I now carried with me all the time, with the names of my lost family members.

'Let's see what we can find...' And they went through the now-familiar routine of trawling through the lists. Over time they had become more organised and now information could be checked quickly from each desk.

'When were you last here?'

'I come every week, so exactly seven days ago,' I said.

'We've had a list of names through from the Jewish Scout Movement. Let me check. Wait a second, I think we have something...'

Samuel

The south of France was liberated by the Allies. All twenty of us travelled from Monsieur Fournier's country house in the Pyrenees to Perreux, north of Toulouse. Perreux had provided a safe home to over three hundred Jewish children during the war, and now the Jewish Scout Movement had taken over a small hotel. We were welcomed and given a home while the agencies worked to reunite families.

I was assigned a bedroom on the first floor, that I shared with one other boy. It was basic but, at the same time, it felt luxurious to have such privacy; the last few years had been spent sleeping in crowded dormitories. The second floor was for the girls of around my age, and the top floor was split, with the oldest boys on one side of the building and the oldest girls on the other side. The younger children slept in another building nearby.

My bedroom overlooked the river and from my window I could see the huge bridge, its wide arches stretching from one side of the riverbank to the other. It reminded me of the bridge in Metz, and I felt homesick for the first time in a while.

Once again we were offered a choice of trades to learn. Of everything I had learnt so far, I had progressed best with woodwork, so I chose cabinet-making. Rudy Kohn wanted to be a butcher so he became an apprentice with the local butcher and his brother Marcus fancied himself as a baker so he was given an apprenticeship in town too. Rudy brought bones back from work which we cooked over a bonfire on the river bank and ate the marrow with bread brought back by Marcus. It was quite a feast, especially as food was still rationed. There were doctors to look after us and even a dentist, who most of us visited for the first time in our lives.

All boys aged thirteen and over were called to the dinner hall one day. There were around fifty of us. One of the Scout leaders went around the room. 'You, you, you and you,' he said, tapping four boys at random on their heads. Those four went to the front of the room where an altar had been created from a table balanced on wooden crates and a Torah placed on top. While the rest of us watched, the four boys were helped to read from the Torah after which the Scout leader announced, 'Okay, you are *all* bar mitzvah!' The adults shouted, 'Mazel tov!' and went around the room shaking the hands of every one of us.

I thought back to when I turned thirteen, when my family had still been complete. I was thinking about my parents and siblings more and more these days. I was sad my parents were not with me at my makeshift bar mitzvah, but now the war was over, I felt renewed hope we would all be together again one day soon.

The next day I went for supper with my pals. As I had never received a letter, I didn't bother to check the mail which arrived and was left on a table to be collected.

'Hey, Sam!' called Paul.

'What?' I said.

'Look here! You've got a letter.'

Pierre

The repatriation centre had found Samuel's name on a list. I was overcome with joy when they told me the news. He was with the Jewish Scouts, in a centre near Toulouse. I cried with happiness when I realised I wasn't alone and that the system for reuniting families was working. The last time I saw Samuel was when I put him on a bus for Beaulieu-sur-Dordogne eighteen months before.

I wrote to him immediately and quickly received a letter back saying we would meet in Paris. I waited for him at the bus station. When he got off the bus and saw me waiting, he ran over to me and we hugged tightly. He was fifteen now, still small and skinny but he looked so much more grown up.

'I'm so happy to see you,' he said.

'Me too. Let me look at you. See how you've changed – you're almost a man.'

'I've had quite a few adventures along the way. I sure don't feel like a kid anymore.'

'Come, let's go eat and you can tell me all about it.'

As we walked to the cafe together it was a huge relief knowing that at least one of my siblings was still alive.

I had explained in my letter that there was no news so far of our parents or our brother and sisters. As we chatted, we discussed whether there was anything else we could be doing to look for them.

'It is likely that Maman and Papa were sent to one of the camps in Germany or Poland,' I told my brother. 'There are plenty of rumours about those places but no facts yet, so we shouldn't assume anything.'

'What of Claude and the girls?' asked Samuel. 'Where are they now?'

'We don't know. There are many children still missing and their names have not appeared on any lists yet. I go every week to ask them to check again,' I said.

'Can I come with you?'

'Yes, we can go tomorrow and see if there's any news. They found you so hopefully it won't be long now before they find the others too.'

Samuel

Perreux
February 1945

It was good to spend time with Pierre in Paris. Just knowing that we had each other was comforting, but it was also really hard to realise we might be the only two survivors from our family. He took me to the repatriation centre. We had a long wait before we were seen and then another long wait while they checked the lists for any mention of Maman, Papa, Claude, Henriette or Georgette – but there was none. I was devastated. Apart from us, our entire family had disappeared. I felt sorry for Pierre who had been through this scenario dozens of times now. The hope, the anticipation, the wait… and then the disappointment and despair.

My brother showed me where he was working with our cousin Georges. He was learning upholstery and I was learning cabinet-making. We thought that one day we could start a furniture business together. It felt good thinking about the future although I felt guilty for doing so when my siblings might not even have one.

Pierre asked if I wanted to stay with him, but there was nothing for me in Paris. He promised to go every week for news of the others and we agreed to write to each other regularly. The Scout leaders had told me that I would have plenty of time for a long visit in the summer so, after our short reunion, I returned to Perreux.

****

We were treated well at Perreux: fed, taught a trade and given plenty of freedom to enjoy ourselves. We were all waiting for news of loved ones but there were few reunions during those months. We heard about the first people returning from Germany and Poland although the names of our missing family members were still classified as 'not returned from a concentration camp'. Some children returning from the camps came to Perreux. It was easy to identify them – they were emaciated and in bad health, most had shaved heads and some had numbers tattooed on their arms.

****

Marcus, Rudy and I would swim in the river before dinner. For me it was a good way to wash off the wood dust and sweat after a long day in my cabinet-making class, while my friends washed off the smell of raw meat and flour from their days. The current was strong but we were accomplished swimmers and made it easily from one side of the river to the other. Sometimes we would float and allow the water to carry us downstream to the bridge where we would grab on to its arches and rest a while before swimming back upstream against the current. It gave us a good appetite for our evening meal, not that having an appetite was ever a problem. When we entered the dining room after our swim one evening, we noticed a crowd of the older children standing by the far wall. They were reading some papers stuck on the wall. The atmosphere in the room was unusually sombre.

'What's going on?' asked Marcus.

Someone said, 'We've received a list of the survivors liberated from the concentration camps. Take a look and see if anyone from your family is on it. They are the ones who will be coming back.'

We went over and waited patiently while the children in front of us studied the list. I was in no hurry to find out the fate of my family. If their names were on there, it would still be days or perhaps weeks before we would be reunited, and if they were not on the list – well, that didn't bear thinking about.

Name – Date of Birth – Place of Birth

Some names, especially the more traditional Polish spellings, had been corrected by hand which didn't make reading them any easier. I started on the left and found the names beginning with 'L'. I scanned the entire section, up and down each of the columns methodically... Landau. Lazar. Levy. Liberman. Lipmann... and then Mandel. Marcovitz... I realised there were no Laskowski in the list, and my spirit began to break. But did this mean they were dead or simply missing? I went through the list searching for Hofman, but again found nothing. For Marcus and Rudy Kohn it was the opposite – there were hundreds of 'Kohns', 'Kohnns' and 'Cohns' on the list and they had to check each one carefully to see if they were from their family. Even though they split the job between the two of them, they took a long time to check the list but in the end we all had the same result – not one single survivor from either of our families.

'This can't be right!' I shouted, angrily. 'Not one member of my family is on this list.'

'It's the same for most of us,' said a boy with tears in his eyes.

I resolved the only way to be sure I hadn't missed a name was to check the whole thing, line by line. By the time I'd finished, my head throbbed. There was not one single Laskowski or Hofman or anything remotely similar out of the thousands of names on the list. I was desolate. I slumped down on a chair, put my head in my hands and wept silently for my lost family.

****

They couldn't have been kinder to us at Perreux, but no amount of kindness could help us to get over the loss of our families. At the beginning of summer we were told we had two and a half months to go and do whatever we wanted, and we were each given a small amount of money to spend. First, I went to Paris and stayed with Pierre for a few days, where I told him what I had learnt about our family. Pierre said he had read the same list in the repatriation centre where he was told that because our parents had been taken so long ago it was unlikely they had survived the concentration camps. But the children might still have survived as they were taken only weeks before the end of the war. They said we shouldn't lose hope.

After I left Pierre in Paris, I met up with seven pals from Perreux and we went off for an adventure. We promised ourselves that the summer was our time: no worries, no feeling sad, just living life to the fullest. None of us had ever seen the ocean and we decided to go and get our feet wet in the Mediterranean. We hitch-hiked over two hundred kilometres down to the coast. When we arrived we were speechless at the beauty in front of us. The war was over. We were alive. The sun was shining, and the shimmering water was calling us. We took off our shoes and started walking towards the sea, the golden sand warm between our toes. Suddenly one of the boys stopped dead.

'Guys,' he said, almost whispering. Then, 'Guys. Stop!'

He called several times, until we finally took notice of him. He lifted his arm slowly and pointed to a sign. '*Achtung! Minen*!' We looked around. There were more of the same signs all around us. The entire beach was riddled with landmines.

'What do we do now?'

'Turn around and walk carefully back,' he said. 'Look out for anything sticking up in the sand and try to walk on the same spots as before.'

'We need to retrace our footsteps,' said another.

'That's what I just said, wise guy!'

We made it back to safety, furious that the Germans had denied us the pleasure of going into the sea for the first time in our lives. We resolved to not let this ruin our trip and we caught a train back north, but we got on the wrong one and ended up further down the coast. We didn't want to use up our meagre resources on train tickets – it had to last us the whole summer – so we walked up and down the carriages to avoid the ticket inspector. When he suspected foul play, we got off the train at the next station. We were in Perpignan.

The weather had turned nasty and it was nearly evening, so we decided to get a hotel room.

We were travelling light, but we all had our Scout uniforms. We went into an alleyway and changed into our uniforms so we all looked the same. We chipped in a few francs each and tossed a coin to decide who would go and get the room.

'When you get the key, come out and let us know the room number and then we'll all come in, one by one,' we said.

We were all similar in height and wearing the same clothes; the plan was to make the hotel staff believe there was only one of us. It worked! The room was tiny with one bed. We put the mattress on the floor and all eight of us had somewhere to sleep. It was tight, but at least we were sheltered from the rain. We left the following morning leaving the hotel staff none the wiser!

We hitch-hiked all over. We stopped at farms and asked if we could pick fruit; in return we got a place to sleep and ate the fruit that fell on the ground. It was a great summer full of distractions from the aftermath of the war.

By the start of the next school year we were ready to go back to Perreux and return to our apprenticeships. The day we arrived back, a letter from Pierre was waiting.

Pierre

Paris

September 1945

I was pleased when Samuel told me of his plans to travel around with his friends from Perreux. Why shouldn't he enjoy himself instead of sitting around feeling sad? One thing this war had taught us was to live life to the fullest when you had the chance. I chose to stay in Paris and continue working, as I was making good progress in learning a trade. Now that we knew for certain our family was not coming back, I needed to start thinking about my future.

I wasn't sure Samuel had made his peace with the loss of our parents yet, but I knew I could not dwell on my feelings – I had to take care of him now. I was still having difficulty coming to terms with losing the children though – how could they have murdered my innocent siblings? Maybe they had gotten out in time and hadn't been identified yet. I was determined to keep looking for them, and I continued asking the repatriation centre to check their lists.

As more people returned from the camps or hiding places, the Hôtel Grande was a fascinating place to be. Families sobbed with joy as they were reunited in one of its many rooms. Survivors were treated like royalty; identities and optimism for the future were returned through new papers and passports. But for the survivors with families who did not return, hope was smashed to pieces; families destroyed for ever and lives broken beyond repair. Each time I returned, I wondered if I would join one of those groups or remain in the purgatory of uncertainty.

One day in September, I waited patiently in line for my turn at the enquiry desk. I watched a man wait nervously on a chair in the lobby until he was called and taken upstairs. An hour later, when I was close to the front of the line, the same man came downstairs holding the hand of a young child. He was smiling nervously and talking constantly. The child was silent and looked confused. I wondered if it was a sign – would I one day walk out of here, not with one child holding my hand but with two little girls and a thirteen-year-old boy too? When would it be our turn?

'How can I help you?' asked the lady behind the desk. I had seen her several times before and despite having searched for my family on a number of occasions, I still needed to show her the list of names I always carried with me. The staff and volunteers dealt with thousands of people and I didn't blame them for not remembering me.

I handed over the piece of paper.

The lady scanned through the lists on her desk, then said, 'Please wait here,' and went into a back office. It seemed as if I waited longer than usual and I began to feel hopeful. Had they found someone?

'I'm sorry for the delay,' she said, sitting down opposite me. 'I think we may have some news for you.'

My heart started racing. After months and months of weekly visits and hours of waiting patiently in queues, there was finally some news. Please God let it be good news.

'There is a young girl we think may be your sister.'

'Just one? Are you sure there are not two – twins?'

'It says there is only one and I did telephone just now to confirm it before I told you. We don't want to give anyone false hope. Only one child was mentioned.'

My heart sank. This must be a mistake.

'I don't think this young girl can be my sister. There's no way my sisters would leave one another.'

'Shall we check her name? She is staying at a convent and the nuns call her Isabel.'

'I was right,' I said. 'Neither of my sisters are called Isabel. You've got the wrong person.' I got up to leave.

'Wait a minute. They call her Isabel for her own safety. She has been living with them for over a year and the sisters are so fond of her they would like her to continue with them, but we've insisted she be returned to her family if there are any left – too many people have lost their loved ones. Her real name is Georgette Laskowski.' She was reading from a file she had brought back to the desk. 'Born 9 April 1938 in Metz.'

I was in shock. I didn't know what to think or how to feel. I had just been told one of my sisters was alive. But what about Henriette? How was it possible they had been separated?

'Pierre? This is good news.'

'Yes, yes sorry. It is wonderful news that Georgette is well. Thank you. But please, please check again. There must be some mistake. Can you check again to see if Henriette

Laskowski is also on the list. Born 9 April 1938 in Metz. They are twins. They were together in the Jewish orphanage in Louveciennes. And my brother Claude, he was there too. Please check again. I beg you.'

'We already did,' came the gentle reply. 'Georgette was alone when she arrived at the end of July 1944. We specifically asked about her sister, but they don't know anything about Henriette. I'm so sorry.'

'When can I see her? She will know what happened to the others,' I said.

'Your sister is seven years old and probably suffered trauma. We don't know how she is or what she knows. Children can be very resilient or very delicate. Please be prepared for the fact she may not be able to tell you anything.'

How could I be so stupid? She was so young when she was taken. But she had been found. I should concentrate on the positive.

'Yes, of course,' I said. 'Where is she?'

'The sisters have asked that the location of the convent not be shared, but they will bring Georgette here tomorrow.'

'Why the secrecy? What have they got to hide?'

'Some people in the Church think the children they have been looking after should stay with them. Most of them have been baptised and have been living as Catholics for some years. You are fortunate that Georgette has been identified.'

I was told to return the next afternoon to be reunited with my sister.

Georgette

When I was called to the office of the mère supérieure, I wondered if I was in trouble. I had only been in that room once before, the day when I was welcomed to the convent. Sister Marie accompanied me, looking as nervous as I felt. We waited outside until we were invited to enter. The mère supérieure sat behind her desk and told us to sit down.

'Hello, Isabel. Hello, Sister Marie.'

'Good morning, Mère Supérieure,' said Sister Marie, speaking for us both.

'How are you, Isabel?'

'Well, thank you, Mère Supérieure. I have been learning my Bible stories,' I replied politely.

'Good girl. Now, Isabel, I have received a telephone call. Do you remember your brother Pierre?'

There was a moment of silence. Why was she asking me about Pierre? For as long as I had been living here I had been told to never mention my family and now I was being asked about my brother. I had thought of Henriette every day and every night, wondering where she and Claude were and if they were doing the same things I was, and I thought about the others too, but I had never spoken of them. I wasn't sure if I should talk about them now – maybe this was a test?

'It's alright, Isabel. Please answer the mère supérieure,' said Sister Marie.

'Yes, Mère Supérieure,' was all I could manage to say.

'That is good. The call I received was from Paris to say that your brother Pierre is looking for you.' The mère supérieure studied my face for my reaction.

'Are Henriette, Claude and Samuel there too?' I asked. It felt strange saying their names out loud after a year of silence. 'And Maman and Papa?'

'We only know about Pierre, but you will be taken to see him tomorrow.' She sounded like she was trying not to cry. 'It is almost time for prayers now. Off you go, Georgette. God bless you, child.'

I hurried out of her office and it wasn't until the door shut behind me that I realised she had called me Georgette.

****

I couldn't believe my eyes. This was the most beautiful place I had ever seen. It was like a palace. I was in a room with a lady called Lucille. She collected me early that morning and brought me to Paris. I ran my hands over the velvet chairs that, despite being very worn, felt like dancing fairies under my fingertips. The convent seemed a million miles away.

I wanted to stay forever but Lucille explained I was only here to reunite with Pierre. I was given lunch while we waited for him to arrive. It was delicious! There was only a small amount of food on my plate, but I couldn't eat it all anyway.

Lucille told me my stomach was now small – I thought that was strange because my tummy seemed quite fat – so I could only eat a little at a time. But she said that soon I would get used to more food, and then I could have proper meals. When someone came to take my lunch plate away, Lucille told them to leave it so I could eat some more when I got hungry again. What was this place? Was I in Heaven?

The strict modesty we lived by at the convent meant there were no mirrors, so it was a huge surprise when I first saw my own image. I went to use the bathroom and, while I washed my hands in the marble sink with the bar of soap which smelt of lavender, I looked up and saw a girl my age looking back at me.

'Henriette?' I cried with joy. 'Is that you? They didn't tell me you were coming.'

I went to touch the girl's face, but my hand stroked the glass instead. I touched my own face and watched as the girl in the mirror did the same.

'I miss you so much. Where are you?' Tears fell down my cheeks and I watched as the girl in front of me wept too.

'Georgette? Are you alright?' called Lucille from the other side of the door.

'Yes. Just washing my hands,' I said. I splashed some water on my face and dried it with the soft white towel. I looked in the mirror again. 'Come on, Henriette, we're going to see Pierre now!'

Pierre

Paris
September 1945
I didn't sleep the night before my reunion with Georgette. It had been two years since I last saw her. I worried that I wouldn't recognise her, that she wouldn't remember me, but mostly that I wouldn't be able to answer her questions about where the others had gone. I was concerned for her emotional state; everyone had suffered during the war but what must it have felt like to be separated from Henriette? They had never been apart before. I couldn't imagine what she had gone through and how it must have affected her. The people at the Jewish Agency had prepped me for the reunion, telling me what to expect and how best to speak to my sister. The main consolation was their assurance that children of that age were resilient.

I returned to the Hôtel Grande at the arranged time. I was told Georgette had arrived earlier and was looking forward to seeing me. At least I now knew she remembered me, which was one thing less to worry about. As we climbed the stairs, I chatted nervously with the Jewish Agency staff, asking about her well-being. 'She is suffering from malnutrition, but that is quite usual. It's important to not let her eat too much at one time, little and often is best, and nothing too rich. Her stomach is distended – bloated – due to protein deficiency. The doctor has seen her briefly and she's well apart from that.'

'I planned to take her to the pâtisserie,' I said. It was all I could think of doing with a seven-year-old girl.

'It's a good thing we are having this conversation then,' she laughed. 'It would be better to take her to eat some meat or fish and leave the *gateaux* for later!'

We stopped outside a room.

'Here we are,' I was told.

I took a deep breath as we knocked gently on the door and entered. Georgette was standing in the middle of the room. She wore a simple white dress and had a white bow in her short hair. She didn't look much taller than the last time I saw her but the main thing I noticed was her bloated stomach. I was pleased that I had been forewarned as I wouldn't have wanted her to see my shock.

'Pierre!' she screamed with delight and came running over to me. I crouched down to her height and we hugged tightly, as if we never wanted to let go of each other again.

Samuel

Dear Samuel,

I suppose you will read this letter when you return from your summer adventure. I have happy news. Georgette has been found and is staying with me for a few days in Paris. She is quite well. She has spent the past year in a convent, hidden by the nuns. She doesn't speak much about it and she doesn't know where Henriette and Claude are.

I have been told that Georgette was taken to the hospital in Saint-Germain-en-Laye from Louveciennes with measles and that is how the children were separated. This was in July 1944 and we know the children's homes were emptied on 22 July and the children taken to Drancy. Georgette was sent to the convent by the doctors and nurses when they were told the Gestapo were coming to the hospital to collect her. The nuns called her Isabel and told her to never speak of her family.

The people at the Hôtel Grande are very helpful. Everyone agrees it would be best for Georgette to come to Perreux and be with you.

She'll spend another few days here and then she will arrive. I need to return to work so I can't come with her, but you can both come and see me in Paris soon.

Your brother,
Pierre

****

My sister arrived shortly after I got back from my hitch-hiking holiday. It had been over two years since we last saw each other. The day I left for the trade school in Paris seemed a lifetime ago. So much had happened during those years, and Georgette was so young that it was a huge chunk of her life. But her youth was a blessing; she didn't ask me questions I couldn't answer, and she quickly settled into her new surroundings and made friends.

Georgette

My bedroom was in a separate building to Sam's, with other girls like me. I went to school for the first time and played with my new friends. Samuel carried on with his cabinet-making classes and hung around with the Kohn brothers, who always made me laugh. I saw my brother every day and spent Saturdays with him. A few of the children found their families, but most did not. When someone turned eighteen they were encouraged to go and find work and make lives for themselves elsewhere. We were given everything we needed and the days passed quickly in the company of kind friends.

I never stopped thinking about my family, and Henriette most of all. Every time I looked in the mirror I saw her; when I spoke I heard her voice; when I hurt myself and cried I felt her pain; and when I laughed with joy I shared her happiness.

I don't know if anyone was fooled by my silence, but inside I felt incomplete, as if half of me was missing. My new friends had similar experiences but none of us spoke about them. Some had nightmares, and others wet the bed when they were old enough to know better. Many struggled to concentrate in lessons or refused to join in with games. We were all looked after with tolerance and understanding. It was a period of calm before we were sent off, one by one, to family members we had never met in strange lands.

Now it was my turn. I was playing with the other children when the supervisor called me to her office. I was surprised to see Samuel as he was usually at his classes at this time of the day.

'*Bonjour*, Georgette. Come in, come in,' said the supervisor. 'Sit down next to your brother.'

I did as I was told. Samuel held my hand and winked at me.

The Jewish Agency had been searching for relatives of the orphaned children in their care in Britain, America and Canada. As the oldest sibling, Pierre had a clearer memory of aunts and uncles who had moved abroad before the war began, and contact had eventually been made with our mother's eldest sister Cloe in London and another sister, Alisa, in New York.

'Georgette, we have found your aunt in England and she would like you to go and live with her.' The supervisor spoke quickly. Looking back, I suppose she had learnt the hard way that when she started speaking of news and family having been found, some of the children would immediately think their parents had returned... only to be disappointed once again. Probably all of us there still dreamt of our parents coming back. After all, once that dream was gone, what was left?

I was to be sent to London to live with my Aunt Cloe. She was in her sixties by this time; her three children Joanne, Stan and Danielle were grown up and married. Part of me wanted to stay in France in case Henriette and Claude were discovered, hidden somewhere like I had been, but the other part of me was pleased to leave and start a new life somewhere completely different. Samuel and Pierre would stay in France for the time being, but they promised to visit me in England once I was settled. They said England wasn't far from France but I would need to get on a boat to cross the sea.

Weeks later I was taken to the north coast where I saw the ocean for the first time. There was no golden sandy beach like I had seen in some of the picture books at Perreux, just an ugly-looking port, screeching seagulls flying over our heads and choppy grey water slapping against the harbour wall. A label was hung around my neck with my name and the name of the person collecting me once I arrived in England. All I carried with me was a tiny suitcase containing my few belongings. These were mainly clothes but also some small toys which Samuel and Pierre had given me and the photograph of the family which Pierre had rescued from the house in Sarry. And, of course, I still had my precious Bernadette, who now felt like my only link to Henriette.

The crossing was mercifully short. The rough sea tossed the boat around and made me feel sick so I stayed below board but as we approached England I could see through the window a white line on the horizon which, as we got closer, turned out to be chalk cliffs. The sun came out for the first time that day, the water turned from dark grey to blue, and even the seagulls seemed less annoying on this side of the ocean.

When I got off the boat I was handed over to a woman who hugged me so tightly I could hardly breathe. She wouldn't let me go for ages and I couldn't even see her face until she loosened her grip. Then, when I was able to look at her properly, I saw she was crying and smiling at the same time. That seemed strange, but I think I understood why. She told me in broken French that she was my cousin Danielle and she introduced her husband Jacob, who stood nearby. He took off his hat and shook my hand which I thought was funny; I thought maybe he didn't kiss me because of the cigarette hanging out of his mouth.

Jacob drove us to Aunt Cloe's home in Canons Park, in the north-west of London. The house had a garden! It was a good start to my life in England. I was introduced to the rest of my new family. I spoke no English, but my cousins spoke a few words of French and some Yiddish. My first cousins, Stan, Joanne and Danielle were all much older than me; the only other child in the family was Joanne's son Robert, who was around my age.

Danielle and her husband Jacob didn't have any children of their own. They smothered me with love and attention which I gratefully accepted, and it was soon agreed they would adopt me. I was enrolled in a local school and went to a Jewish youth club. I was desperate to fit in and learnt to speak English quickly although my French accent stayed with me for a few years, so I became known as the 'little French girl'.

****

Pierre and Samuel came to visit. They brought me our mother's handbag which was one of the few items still in the house in Sarry. Apart from Bernadette and a family photograph in which Henriette and I were small babies, this bag was the only thing I had left to remember my mother. I wrapped the small leather handbag carefully and stored it away. It was too precious to use. My brothers made contact with our Aunt Alisa, who had moved from Metz to New York ten years before. She had been searching for any survivors from our family, and when she learnt the boys were alive she offered to make the arrangements for them to go to America. Samuel wanted to travel to Palestine but Pierre said he wouldn't go to America without his brother so Samuel agreed to follow him but only for as long as it took to make enough money to leave for Palestine. Meanwhile our family in London were busy trying to convince my brothers to stay in England. Cousin Sid took the boys to Petticoat Lane, where he knew all the market traders. He bought the boys a whole wardrobe each, and even offered to adopt Sam. Samuel was eighteen by then and had been making his own way in the world for long enough to not want to be adopted by anyone.

My adoption was not formalised until 18 October, 1950 when my cousin became my mother and my aunt became my grandmother. Pierre said my mother would have had a laugh trying to explain all these family relations, but I wasn't sure what he meant by it.

Georgette

Jacqueline took me to her favourite restaurant on the beach. The maître d' greeted her warmly and she introduced me as an old friend. She ordered champagne for us and we made small talk about the beauty of this town she had made her home. She asked me about Alan, who had gone for a walk to leave us time to catch up.

'When we married forty-eight years ago, he didn't know anything about my childhood. I never spoke about it. I remember little of what happened to me – I was very young. I just have a few static memories, like photographs. Probably my strongest memory is of taking Holy Communion when I was with the nuns,' I said.

'What about your brothers?' Jacqueline asked.

'They both settled in America. Pierre died some years ago, Samuel is well. We're as close as we can be considering the distance between us. We spend most of our holidays together. Pierre and Samuel found out what happened to our family once the records appeared. Everyone, including our parents, were sent to Auschwitz in 1942 and never returned. The only person in the family who was not sent to Auschwitz was my grandmother Bubbe. She was sent to an old people's home not far from Poitiers where she died from natural causes. And, of course, it was Sam's daughter Sharon who discovered your book and recognised me and Henriette in the photograph on the front cover.'

'Ah, yes. I remember when that was taken. My friend Christina had come to visit me at the orphanage in Louveciennes and brought her camera. After the war she gave me a copy of the photograph.'

'It was quite a shock for me to see it. It was the first time I had seen myself at that age. I must have been six years old then. And it was the last photograph of my dear sister,' I said.

'I'm so pleased that you contacted me. When the publisher said one of the children in the photograph wanted to speak to me I was very surprised!'

'Can you tell me what happened to my brother and sister?' I asked.

Jacqueline hesitated. I suspected she knew the question would be coming.

'I wasn't able to save them.' Tears came to Jacqueline's eyes and I held her hand.

'I know. It wasn't your fault. But I need you to tell me. It's time.'

Jacqueline

Juan les Pins
June 2006

'It was 6 a.m. on 22 July 1944. The streets of Louveciennes were usually empty this early but I heard a noise and looked out of the bedroom window. I saw some men walking quickly towards the house. There was at least one German officer but I couldn't tell if the others were German or French. I got dressed and ran to Monsieur Denis's office, but the German officer was already there. It was Alois Brunner, the SS officer in charge of Drancy. He was barking orders: the building was surrounded and we were all to be arrested. I was told to quickly wake the children, and get them ready to leave. The Germans wanted to make sure we were gone before the villagers woke and witnessed them taking us.

'Brunner called out our names from his list. You weren't there and he demanded to know where you were. Monsieur Denis told him you were in the hospital at Saint-Germain-en-Laye. It would have been easy for him to say you were somewhere else, but he was scared of reprisals and didn't dare. I was so worried about you; I knew Brunner would send someone to the hospital but there was nothing I could do. I was the only monitor and the only one on their list, the others were free to leave in the evenings and were at their homes sleeping, as were the kitchen staff. I prayed that when they arrived for work and saw we were all gone, someone would get word to the hospital and ask them to hide you before the Germans arrived. I guess this is what happened, but I have no idea who it was who saved your life.

'Within minutes, we were boarding a bus. The little ones didn't understand what was happening and I told them that we were going for an outing to the countryside. We all sang songs. I knew we were being taken to Drancy but I didn't despair: the Allies had landed in Normandy weeks earlier, the war was nearly over and soon we would be free. As we arrived at Drancy, I saw other buses filled with children, and I realised there had been a round-up from all ten UGIF centres in the Paris region.

'Monsieur Denis, his wife and daughter, Michèle, were released as they were not Jewish. Five others were identified as children of prisoners of war and sent to Bergen-Belsen, from where they would all later return. The other thirty-four children, including Henriette and Claude, and I were given purple tickets to indicate we were Category B, "deportable". The alternatives were a red ticket for Category A – spouses of Aryans, or a green ticket for Category C – assigned to work. But we didn't see any of those, only purple. Our only hope was that the Allies would arrive soon.

'On 31 July we were taken as part of a group of 1300 people to Bobigny, a small station near Drancy. I told the children they were going to join their parents. We were crammed into cattle wagons parked in the sidings and at midday the convoy rattled off on its journey. It was convoy no. 77, the last one to leave for Drancy. Three weeks later, Paris was liberated and the remaining prisoners at Drancy released. The conditions in the wagons were horrific. It was unbearably hot and there were only tiny openings to let in the smallest amount of fresh air. The stench of bodies and excrement soon became overpowering.

'There were sixty of us in one wagon. Fifty of them were children. I was the only monitor. The others were adults who complained about the children crying, which they did because they were hot and thirsty and couldn't breathe because of the stench, or when they were bumped into, which was unavoidable as there were so many of us in a small space. I wore an armband which allowed me to get off the train the few times it stopped at a station to fetch water, as much as I could carry in makeshift containers, and to empty the slop buckets which were always overflowing onto the floor of the wagon.

'By the third day we were desperate. That night the train stopped with a jolt. The wagon doors were thrown open and the children were woken to shouts of: '*RAUS! SCHNELL!*' 'OUT! QUICK!' Emaciated men with shaved heads and dressed in striped clothing pulled the terrorised children out of the wagon. They spoke in French but they didn't even look human. They wouldn't let the children take their belongings with them. One of the men looked at me with his big blue eyes, which made him look less sinister than the others. I asked him if he was French. He pulled me inside to the back of the wagon, out of sight, before he spoke.

'"We are in Auschwitz. This place is Hell. There is nowhere to sleep and maybe just enough food to keep you alive. Whatever you do, don't carry a kid in your arms," he told me.

'I said that I didn't understand, and he said I would understand soon enough. He pointed to the children and said, "They will be made into soap."

'I thought he must be mad to say such things. I asked him if he knew any Goldsteins at the camp and he almost laughed.

'"Do you know how many thousands of people are here? Listen to me. Don't ask about your family. Forget about them."

'I climbed off the wagon and spotted a little girl all alone. She was crying. I took her hand and she looked up at me, tears pouring down her face. The same Frenchman came quickly over.

'"Don't you understand? Do not hold the child's hand!" he shouted at me angrily. I was so confused I didn't know what to do. I dropped the child's hand and walked along the railway platform as we were ordered. I left that little girl by herself in the middle of the throng of people and I didn't even dare look back at her. It was night but the scene was illuminated by harsh floodlights. I think I saw Claude and Henriette ahead of me, walking together, holding hands and I was grateful that many of the children had siblings with them so they were not alone.

'Up ahead were five or six Nazi officers. One of them had a riding crop and he was using it to direct people, pointing to the left or right without saying a word. The children and older people were sent to the right and the others to the left. Families were being brutally separated. Husband and wife, mother and child, brother and sister, clinging to each other until the Germans came along and beat anyone who wouldn't comply. Those who still resisted were sent to the right. When it was my turn I was sent to the left. I turned to look to the right and saw Henriette with Claude and all my other little children from Louveciennes. I watched them walk away towards the gas chambers.'

Georgette

'Come on, Georgette. Come outside and play with me.'

'Is that you, Henriette?'

'Yes of course it is, silly. Are you coming to play now? I've been waiting for such a long time.'

****

'Mrs Barnes?'

'Yes?'

'Mrs Barnes. Did you hear what I said? I'm sure it must have come as quite a shock.'

'Yes. I heard you.'

'The results show there are malignant cells. You can beat this. We can operate to remove the cancer and then start a course of treatment. Take these leaflets home and think of any questions you might have, then I will see you here again in a few days.'

Alan took me home. I cried. We cried together. I was seventy-one years old. I had enjoyed a happy marriage and a loving family. I had travelled and made lots of wonderful friends. I had lived. I had done everything my twin sister had never had the chance to do. And all along I had carried the guilt. I had lived through the nightmares. I had suffered because I was the one who survived. And now I was almost free. I could go outside and play with Henriette. I wouldn't have to hear her calling me in vain anymore.

'I'm coming, my darling sister. I'm coming to play very soon.'

Acknowledgements

The first person I want to thank for inspiring me to write *The Young Survivors* is my mother, Paulette. I'm heart-broken that she won't get to read it, and yet it would never have occurred to me to write this book while she was alive. The Holocaust was not a subject we spoke about at home. I can't be sure that she would have even wanted to read it.

I don't remember when I first found out my mother was a Holocaust survivor. Mum spoke English without a trace of a French accent, so it came as a shock to many to learn that she was born in France and had endured such a traumatic childhood. Who could imagine the pain of losing a twin sister at age six, as well as your mother, father and brother? Yet Mum seemed happy and carefree. She had a dry sense of humour, a loving marriage and a large circle of friends. She chose to not share her pain.

Thank you to my family both in London and in the States for their support while I was writing this book. To my darling husband Adam, who not only is my better half but is also the talented photographer who took my author portraits and designed my website. To my exceptional daughters Cloe and Aimee, two strong independent women of whom I am so proud. To my sister Caron, I wrote this book for both of us, and our dad Maurice for his encouragement. And to my miniature schnauzer Pepper for making me leave my computer and take her for a walk from time to time.

In 2014 I travelled to the south of France to meet Denise Holstein, who had looked after my mother in the orphanages during the war. I was relieved when she told me that the children had been happy, not knowing what was going on around them and not crying for their parents. Thank you, Denise, both for looking after Mum and for sharing your experiences with me.

When I started to blog about my research, I was contacted by people who identified with the subject. André Convers is a French Jewish historian from Louveciennes who kindly took me to visit the orphanages in 2015 and introduced me to members of the Jewish community there. Laurence Fitoussi-Brust and I made contact when I read a blog post by her mother, Marthe Szwarcbart, about how she was smuggled out of the orphanage in Louveciennes by her brother André (Schwart-Bart), who would become a world-renowned novelist. Fred Katz emailed to tell me that, like my mother, he was born in Metz in 1938 and his family had moved to the same village near Poitiers where his six-year-old brother was run over and killed by German officers. Thank you to André, Laurence and Fred for their help with my research.

My decision to write a novel about the Holocaust was largely influenced by reading *The Lost Wife* by Alyson Richman. It made me want to write a story which people would enjoy reading while telling them about the fate of the Jews in wartime France, something which is not often mentioned. *The Young Survivors* is a tribute to the 76,000 French Jews who lost their lives in the Holocaust. Thank you, Alyson.

I want to thank Hazel Michaels, my mother-in-law and one of the most prolific readers I know, for her honest review of my first draft which spurred me on to a much-improved second draft. Thanks also to Tracy Fenton and the anonymous readers from THE Book Club on Facebook who kindly helped me decide whether to stick to writing in the first person or to change to the third person.

For the past ten years I have been a member of The Best Book Club Ever, a group of eight keen readers who have become so much more than just book buddies. We support each other through whatever life throws at us while reading the occasional book along the way. A huge thank-you to (in alphabetical order): Alisa, Corinne, Danielle, Jo, Karin, Marcia and Sharon. I hope you enjoy the little surprise I have left you in the book.

In early 2019, a chance meeting with a historical novelist in A&E led me to hire an editor to look through my manuscript before I self-published. This in turn led me to sign with Duckworth Books. So, thank you to Elizabeth Fremantle and Hugh Barker for helping me achieve my dream, and also to Louise Thornton and the Society of Authors for advising on contracts.

And finally, to the brilliant team at Duckworth Books. Matt Casbourne – going through his notes on my manuscript was akin to doing an 'ology' in creative writing. Matt has been an absolutely amazing publisher to work with and it's been a blast. Thanks also to Pete Duncan, Fanny Lewis for her great marketing and PR skills, and Nicky Jeanes for copy-editing and Abbie Rutherford for proofreading. It's my name on the front cover but having a book published is a team effort. Thank you to everyone.

Debra Barnes. London, March 2020

About the Author

Debra Barnes studied journalism and has been a regular contributor to the *Jewish News*. Since January 2017, she runs a project for The Association of Jewish Refugees (AJR) to produce individual life story books for Holocaust survivors and refugees. She has been interviewed by BBC Radio regarding her mother's story and has had a short documentary made about her research. This is her first novel, inspired by the true story of her mother's survival of the Holocaust.